Desert Eagle
Bears And Eagles Six
RP Wollbaum

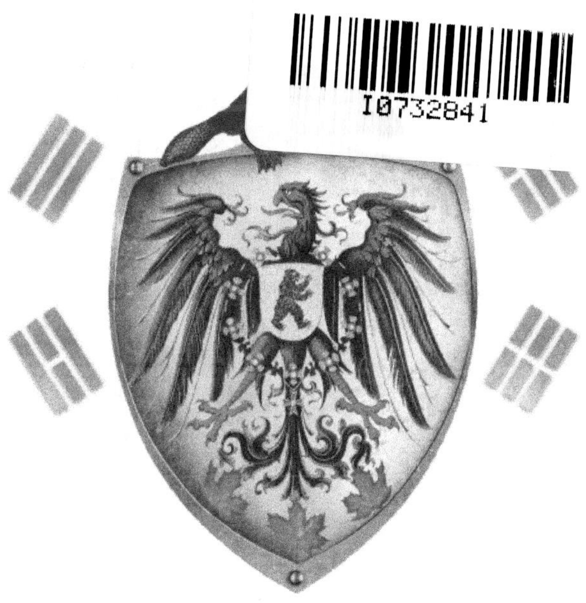

Determination Against All Odds

Chapter One

"I'm sorry George," said the voice on the phone. "I have already told you, our army is overextended already and the troops are worn out. We have committed two destroyers and a supply ship and half of our air force. That is all we can afford at this time."

"Look Brian," the American President said, "we appreciate the help you have committed, but we could use your ground troops as well. We understand you have some problems, but you have a compete battalion sitting doing nothing. They are highly trained and know the area well. They would be a great help to us."

"No, no," the Prime Minister said. "We need them here in case of a domestic issue. We are not like your country, we only have a small amount of qualified troops and they are all committed or are resting. We need this battalion here at home."

"Very well then," the President said. "We will have to find a battalion somewhere else. Once again, thank you for the commitments you have made to this point."

They conclude their talk with some personal matters and the president hung up the phone and looked to his Secretary of State.

"Just like you said," the president said. "He will not give us those troops."

"There is an election coming up and troops on the ground are usually an issue," the Secretary of State said. "Quebec is flirting with separation again and they don't want to risk it."

"Ok time to turn up the screws," the President said. "Call the Saudis and the Brits. Who have we got that the regiment will talk to?"

"Some people they do business with in Texas and California perhaps." The Secretary replied. "I'll give them a call."

"Look Faud," Paul said. "We understand your problem, but the government refuses to listen to us and in fact, the more we talk about this to them the more likely they will be to not send us. They are doing everything they can to stay in power and the only way they can do it is to keep Quebec happy and Ontario happier. That means nothing that can possibly credit Alberta or Western Canada will be allowed. Nor do they want to be seen cozying up to the Americans. Unless you can find a way to pressure them from some other direction, we are going to be staying here twiddling our thumbs."

"Yes Faud, I understand the danger the man poses," Paul said. "But if the Americans can't put pressure on the Prime Minister, I doubt anyone else can. There is a way around the problem, but if the Royal Family does not wish to get involved, it is out of my hands Faud."

"Well if you can make something happen, let us know, we can be there in a very short period of time as you know." Paul hung up the telephone and shrugged his shoulders.

"What's the matter with those people in Ottawa?" Paul said. "If I'm getting all of these calls surely they must be getting more."

"Oh you know, they are scared of the Ontario voters," Emily said. "If they even loose just a few seats, they will be out of power. Being friends with us and the Americans and the Saudis is a bad thing right now."

"London on the line sir," Paul's over worked aide said.

"Master Warrant Bekenbaum speaking," Paul said. "How may I direct your call sir?"

"We wish you would give yourself the rank you deserve Mr. Bekenbaum. In any of our other Armies you would be a general."

"The rank is irrelevant Your Majesty, but thank you for the thought." Paul said raising his eyebrows.

"How soon can you have Our regiment ready for Us to use?" the Queen asked.

"It will take two weeks to be combat ready for deployment mam," Paul said. "Mam, you do know that our charter does specify the Royal Family has precedence, but mam, we can refuse if the terms of the deployment are not conducive to a successful completion with minimal loss of personal and material. In addition, all costs must be provided after the initial investment as well as all transportation, food, fuel and material usage must be supplied. Finally, the matter must be brought before the host for approval."

"Yes Mr. Bekenbaum, We understand We will be funding the operation," the Queen said. "We ourselves are not in the position to be directly funding the operation, but a number of interested parties are willing to make it a joint venture. You can expect a call from Our Governor General shortly to covey Our orders to deploy and your plan for deployment at the first and fastest opportunity."

"Yes mam," Paul said, as the Queen hung up the phone.

"Ok," Paul said. "Captain call in the department heads right now. The faster they can get here the better. The boss has gone over the Prime Ministers head."

It was the first week of November and Elizabeth had received permission from her parents to take her 17-year-old brother out of school for two weeks to go out in the bush, supposedly to do some hunting. In reality, she needed some time away and to council her little brother who had been getting himself into some trouble at home lately. They had packed two pack horses and ridden three days to their favourite spot in the Forest Reserve west of their land. They could have just as easily driven the fifty or so miles with the horses in a trailer, but doing it this way was not only a link to their past, that Elizabeth wanted her brother to experience, but also time away from most things modern. They had set up their camp some miles up from where most of the hunters ventured and because this was a vehicle restricted area, not many people ventured the ten or so miles off of the last vehicle access trail to reach this spot. Even in the summer time, it was rarely visited. Which was a shame, because of the area's natural beauty and stillness. Brother and sister had cleared an area for their tent and erected the canvas walled structure together. Then while her brother gathered firewood, Elizabeth had put together the collapsible wood stove, found some large rocks to sit it up off the ground on and stuck the chimney up out of the asbestos ringed hole in the tent roof.

After that was complete, she took out the long lengths of rope they had stashed in one of the saddle packs and roped off an area using trees as fence posts, to use as a temporary corral. She then took off the four horses bridals and turned them loose into the make shift corral. After that, she took the foam mattresses and arctic sleeping bags from the backs of their saddles and arranged them in the tent. Next came the pack boxes which would serve as tables and chairs when required and finally, the saddles and other horse tack. By then, her brother had returned and started a fire in the small stove, placing a pot full of snow on it to melt for some coffee. Then taking an axe and a firewood saw, both of them cut up and split enough wood for a couple of days, placing it inside the tent to the rear of the stove. The next step was to take shovels and pile snow up along the bottom of the tent to keep out the wind and help hold it down from the inevitable Chinook winds that would hopefully be coming.

Hopefully was right, Elizabeth thought, it was thirty below zero without any wind during the day. Well it would be a good learning experience for her brother, when he pulled the trigger on his C7 only to find it frozen. She had warned him not to lubricate the bolt, but like any teenager, he had known better than she and oiled it any way. The sun was going down as brother and sister filled four nose bags full of oats for the horses and ducked under the rope to attach them to the horses. Elizabeth left her brother to tend to the animals and returned to the tent rummaging through a pack until she found two kerosene lanterns and the plastic jug of kerosene. Filled both of them and lit them. This provided light to the inside of the tent, as she hung one at the rear of the tent and the other at the front on the centre ridge pole they had run inside the tent.

The fire was crackling happily and the tent was warming nicely, so Elizabeth loaded the stove up with wood and turned down both dampers. After that, she found two potatoes, wrapped them in foil and tossed them into the fire box where they would bake for a half hour or so. Her little brother walked into the tent with an arm full of firewood and tossed it behind the stove, then stood in front of it holding his cold hands over the top.

"So what are you going to do about that Von Hoedel that's been eyeing you?" her brother asked.

"Probably the same thing you do with all the girls that eyeball you." Elizabeth said. "He can look all he wants but if he doesn't ask me out, it means nothing."

Elizabeth had first met Rudy on her summer training as a first-year cadet. While Olds and Didsbury combined to make up the whole regiment, they were two separate colonies, but governed by the same rules. Residence of both colonies began cadet training at thirteen years of age and had mandatory five-year military service terms for anyone that wanted the full colony residence status. As a Freshman in high school, she began to run into him more often. She played basketball and volleyball, he football and basketball. The two schools played against each other often and attended each others school dances. She would also see him on the odd family get together, as both families knew each other and in fact, were partners in many business concerns.

Then had come their three months of basic training. Both colonies contributed candidates. Rudy and Elizabeth had both qualified for advanced training and both had received the coveted eagles for their uniform collars that showed they were combat troopers.

They had formed a connection during that time and had gone out a few times, but on the quiet. Nobody suspected anything and they could not really do anything anyway. They both had to finish their five years first. In any case, Rudy had chosen the heavy armour route, which Olds favoured, while Elizabeth had followed the light armour route, which was the tradition of her people. While both units combined for joint training exercises, there was not much call for heavy armour for the types of peace keeping missions the regiment was normally engaged in.

Deployments generally lasted a year, so Elizabeth did not see him the year after she had graduated with her eagle. Then, he had been sent for advanced training in Germany for a year, learning how to best operate the German tanks the regiment used. At best, they only had two or three months when they were both at home at the same time and rarely when they were not both on duty.

But they made the best of it and she thought this might be it. Their five years was almost up, they could finally make it official. But now it would have to wait. Her brother needed her more right now.

Rick was four years younger than her and had been becoming difficult at home. Not that a teenaged boy having difficulties at home was ground breaking news, but for her family it was. He would be giving up a lot if he chose to keep on the path he was choosing. She wanted to make sure he was making the right choice for himself. This was something a parent had difficulty accomplishing and she hoped she could get through to him.

"Well, if you didn't spend all your time being tougher than most guys and playing army guy all the time, maybe you could attract a man," her brother said, in that matter of fact annoying manner teenagers had.

"I don't see why all of you people insist on being in the army anyway," Rick said. "None of my on line Canadian and American friends are forced into the army like we are. It isn't fair."

"Sometimes life is not fair Rick," Elizabeth said. "Sometimes life kicks you in the balls and you need to know how to handle it."

"Nobody is forcing you Rick, that is a big myth," she continued. "You don't have to join the military and if you did, nobody says you have to be in a combat role."

"Ya, but if I don't join," Rick said looking at his feet, "I can't be a part of the colony or inherit the legacy."

"Life is all about choice Rick," Elizabeth said. "We all make choices all the time. You can choose to be like your friends and live a good life. The same way you could have watched that bully beat up that little kid the other day and done nothing about it, like the rest of your friends."

"I want to show you something," Elizabeth said, rooting through her saddle bags until she found the package she was looking for.

She opened it up and slid Rick a few pictures that were inside. His breath did a hard up take as he saw the first one, then she saw him swallow repeatedly as he looked through the others.

"That was last summer in Chad Rick," Elizabeth said. "Those were school girls between the ages of ten and fifteen. The extremists attacked their school, raped them and then threw battery acid on them, finally killing them by cutting their throats. All because they were girls and they were going to school. This is why I serve Rick, someone has to stand up for these poor girls and their sisters around the world."

"In Sudan," she said handing him some more pictures. "You would have been stolen, our parents killed, I would be made a sex slave or worse and they would load you up with heroin and make you kill for them to get more once you were hooked. Eastern Europe is no better. Christians kill Muslims, Muslims kill Christians, Serbs kill anyone not Serbian. They wipe out whole villages and districts. They say it is about ethnic purity or religious freedom. But it is really about power and who has it or who keeps it."

"Here are some more," Elizabeth said. "Here we are rebuilding that school in Chad with the parents. In the next one, we have rebuilt the medical centre in Sudan and those are some of the boys we rescued after going through rehab. Now they are in trade school or higher learning centres, depending on their capabilities.

"That is the other side of what we do Rick, it's not just all killing and fighting. We spend a lot of time building school houses, medical centres, roads and wells. We teach locals how to run them and help set up simple things like bicycle repair shops, motorcycle and small engine repair shops. We are starting to supply and train people on running sun and wind powered generator stations. Our signals people are setting up cell phone services and internet access hubs, usually in the local library or post office. Things you take for granted, in a lot of cases they have never heard of Rick.

"You can walk to the sink and turn on a tap for clean clear water. They have to travel four or five miles just to get five gallons of muddy water. You walk to the fridge and get food for yourself that most of them would use in a week."

"But we send them food and money," Rick said. "Millions of dollars' worth of aide and supplies."

"Most of it goes to corrupt government officials or warlords," Elizabeth said. "Very little gets to the people. Look at Zimbabwe for example. Before, when it was Rhodesia, they had so much food they exported it. Anyone who wanted a job had one and made a fair living, able to support themselves and their families, sent their children to school and could afford health care. Now the white farmers and white people in general have been forced out or killed. One race of native people discriminates against all others, they have no exports, import all of their food and they have been shunned by the rest of the non-Communist world, most of the communist world and are barely tolerated by the Commonwealth countries.

"But the ruling class does not care Rick. They eat well, drive fancy cars and live in big houses. They take trips all over the world and their people starve. If they say anything or try to demonstrate for rights, they are shot or worse. Chavez will be doing the same in Venezuela, an oil and agriculturally rich country, much like ours. He is already destroying it and his people, all so he and his friends can have power."

"Here," she said handing him a letter. It was yellowed with age, the writing legible but barely.

"Your grandfather wrote this to our father. Dad was only four at that time and Oppa had only been home for three or four years after being away for close to ten. You read this and I will cook up some chops and beans."

She handed him the letter and found the large cast iron frying pan and dumped two large pork chops into it, before finding a large can of beans in molasses and opening it. She looked over at her brother and saw him trying to hold tears back as he read, then let his hand drop to his side and closing his eyes, he leaned his head back and took some deep breaths as a tear ran down a cheek.

"Paul my dear son," the letter began. *"I have known your mother for almost ten years now but only been home with her for four. That is because I am a soldier and I have been at war for most of my life. This is my job and is what I do and who I am.*

There are bad people in this world, who want to hurt and kill people so that they can be in power. They kill anyone that opposes them and will not allow anyone the freedom to move or to be whatever or whoever they wish to be. In Canada, you can do and be whatever you choose, can say whatever you want to say, belong or not to belong to any religion you choose. Other people in other countries are not so lucky and the leaders of those countries want to take those freedoms away from us whenever they can.

That is why I am here in Korea. Some very bad people are trying to take over a democratic country and take their freedoms away from them. The Regiment is here to try and stop them and I am the leader of the Regiment. We have been ordered to hold a position against superior numbers, something like ten against our one. I don't have much hope that many of us will survive.

We will stand our ground and sing our song of freedom and fight until we can fight no longer. Thinking all the time of our families and friends back home, knowing they know why we are here and why we are doing this.

It is my hope that you and your sons will not have to do what I have done, that our sacrifice has not been in vain. But I will always be on guard and fight to the last against tyranny and to protect the weak. Daily we in the field pray for peace but train for war. Willing to pay the price, so that you and your mother and other mothers and fathers and children, can sleep safe at night. Knowing the bad people will not be coming tonight.

I love you and miss you and your mother very much. Know that my thoughts are and always will be of you.

Your father

NAJ"

The chops were sizzling nicely in the pan and Elizabeth stirred in the can of beans before opening the door to the stove and using a log pair of tongs, pulled out the two foil wrapped potatoes placing them beside the pan of beans and chops. Then she found the two blue enamel plates and cups, placing them on the stove top face down to warm them up. The final act was to pour the melted snow water into a blue enamel coffee pot, adding some grounds to it and placing it on the hottest part of the stove to boil. By then the chops and beans were done and she split them evenly into the two plates and handing one to her brother, sat down and began to eat.

"It always amazes me how much better things taste out here," she said. "And how much we eat, must be the cold and the air."

Rick said nothing, barely eating with a faraway look in his eyes. He poked and prodded at the food and Elizabeth let the silence take hold. The only sounds were the odd thump or snort from a horse outside and the crackle of the wood in the stove, competing with the sound of the wind rustling through the trees. She let her mind drift and soon was picturing Rudy in her mind. Maybe it was time, she thought, he is a pretty nice guy. Tall, handsome, smart and it seemed he really did care for her. He often made the trip from Olds to the ranch in his old Ford 4 by 4 with some lame excuse or other, but usually it was to see her. Grandmother, being grandmother, embarrassed both Elizabeth and Rudy on his last visit by telling him to ask her out already. They would go out on a date this Saturday. Going for dinner and dance in Olds with a group of their friends.

"I like Rudy," Rick said breaking the silence. "He's nicer than the other guys you've gone out with, especially that lawyer asshole from Calgary."

"I thought the both of you got along well," Elizabeth said. "He did not like the military either."

"There is a difference Liz," Rick said. "I don't like the fact that people have to die and get hurt fighting far away from home. He naively thinks he and the other lawyers can talk their way out of war. It's actually guys like him that start the bloody things. Then he stays as far away from it as he can. Guys like him are never in the front lines.

"Reading grandfathers letter has helped make things clearer for me," Rick said in halting, badly accented Russian. "That was in Korea wasn't it? I didn't know we were there, I thought it was the PPCLI. He was badly frightened and thought he was about to die, but went anyway."

"Any person who gets in a situation like that and tells you he was not scared is lying, is a psychopath or was never there," Elizabeth said. "Your grandfather was a highly experienced and decorated veteran from WW2, yet he knew they were all probably going to die up on that hill that day. A large number of them did and many of them, Oppa included, were gravely wounded. But their sacrifice stopped the Chinese in their tracks and eventually led to the cessation of the fighting. The regiment does a lot of things that no one knows about or sees Rick and we like it like that."

"You and Oppa are officers," Rick said. "Why is Pappa not? Why, he doesn't even have an eagle either. Grandmother even has an eagle and she's a major."

"Pride I think," Elizabeth said. "I don't really know why Dad never wore an eagle or became an official officer. He is more than qualified to wear the eagle and he is in fact the commanding officer of the Regiment. You will have to ask him about it yourself Rick. I never felt it was important. You both have a lot in common you know. He is always tinkering out in his workshop with electronic gismos. When we get back home, go out there and talk with him like you used to when you were a kid."

"Well you do the dishes brother, I'm going to sleep, it was a long day," Elizabeth said finishing her coffee and she rolled into her semi warm sleeping bag, rolling away from the lamp, light with thoughts of her own future on her mind as she fell asleep.

Elizabeth gathered the split kindling they had left in front of the stove, opened the front of the stove and tossed it in on top of several pages of crumpled up newspaper. Then she lit the newspaper and left the door to the stove open a crack and waited a second until she heard the wood start to crackle. Then she dove back into the warm sleeping bag. The fire had gone out overnight and the tent was almost as cold as it was outside. Hearing the fire catch fully, she summoned up her courage, reached over for her jacket and quickly jumped out of her warm sleeping bag, jammed her feet into her insulated boots, grabbed a roll of toilet paper and dashed outside into the bush outside the tent and as fast as she could, did her morning business.

She heard Rick muter how cold it was as he dashed to the nearest tree and as Elizabeth was walking back to the tent, her jacket now semi warm, Rick jacket less, dove back into the tent.

"Goddamn," Rick said, the sleeping bag back up to his nose, "it's bloody cold out here."

Elizabeth pondered jumping back into her sleeping bag, but holding a hand out, found it was becoming warm already and changed her mind. She tossed enough wood into the stove to fill it, then shut the door tight, gabbed the bag of horse feed and filled the four nose bags. Buttoning her jacket up and pulling the flaps of her warm fur hat down over her ears, she took the nose bags outside and trudged through the snow to the rope corral and fastened the nose bags around the waiting animals heads. It had snowed lightly overnight and the animals backs were covered in a light dusting of it. They would brush the horses down after both the animals and themselves had eaten breakfast. The full moon was providing enough light to see, as it was still an hour away from daylight, but the tent would still be dark and she walked back in prepared to light the lamps. Rick had already done that and was tossing some bacon into the frying pan.

He tossed the coffee pot at her and gestured to the axe by the front of the tent.

"The ice shouldn't be that thick," he said. "Try not to fall in."

"Smart ass," Elizabeth replied.

"Hey you left," Rick said smiling. "That means I'm doing breakfast by this nice warm stove and you're going to chop a hole in the ice to get us and the horses some water. If you would have filled the bucket last night in the daylight you wouldn't have to do it now"

"Smart ass," Elizabeth said again. "Nobody likes a smart ass, especially when they are right."

She took the lamp from the back of the tent, gabbed the axe and the coffee pot and trudged the twenty yards to the river bank. She gingerly walked out past the edge a bit and cut a hole in the ice. The ice was not thick and she was through in no time, filling the coffee pot with cold water and walking back to the tent. Once back inside, she put the pot on the stove and tossed the axe back in a corner, before grabbing the collapsible five gallon pail and heading back to the hole in the ice. She filled the bucket and brought it back inside, her nose picking up the smell of the bacon as it started to fry. Hanging the lamp back up on the ridge pole, she stripped off her jacket and fur hat, tossing them onto her sleeping bag and found the plates and cups from the night before, placing them by the stove to warm up. The area around the stove was already warm and Rick had cut down the air flow into the stove by closing the dampers.

"You're going to make some lucky girl a good husband one day," Elizabeth said, as Rick scooped out the fried bacon and eggs onto the two plates and poured the steaming coffee into the waiting cups.

"Ya our mother taught me well," he said with a laugh. Today they were talking in German, which Rick had a little better grasp of.

"Do you know why we speak Russian anyway?" Rick asked.

"I think it is just tradition," Elizabeth answered. "We came here from Russia, not Germany and many of the original Cossack families could not speak German."

"Cossacks?" Rick asked. "You mean the Ukrainians?"

"Oh my," Elizabeth said. "The teachers are not teaching you guys the same things they taught us."

"You have much to discuss with our parents I think," Elizabeth said. "It's too bad great grandmother died while you were so young. She was never shy of speaking her mind or sharing stories of the old days. There is more going on in the family than they tell us Rick."

Chapter Two

The sun was up fully and they had cleaned the breakfast dishes when they walked out into the cold clear air. If a person was not used to it, the silence would be very painful, not even a branch was stirring in the breezeless air and being this high up and this cold, you could hear the horses breathing ten feet away from them. Both of the Bekenbaum's picked up a horse brush and walked into the corral, picking one animal each to brush off the snow and groom. They had finished the first horse when the sound of a distant helicopter could be heard approaching.

"Probably practicing for a search and rescue," Elizabeth said. Every year during hunting season at least one hunter would get hurt or find themselves lost. The Regiment used their own helicopters to assist the RCMP to look for people, it was good training for them.

As the helicopter came to the clearing they had camped in, it slowed and circled, then landed a hundred yards downstream from them and as the rotor blades slowed down, two troopers in uniform got out of it and walked their way. Rick looked at Elizabeth who shrugged her shoulders and with a last quick sweep of the brush, grabbed her two nose feed bags and ducked under the corral rope, walking toward the approaching troopers.

"'Morning mam," the sergeant said. "Captain you have been recalled to duty. The whole Regiment has. We are to deploy ASAP and I am to escort you back to base. This trooper here will escort your brother back home mam."

Elizabeth walked quickly to the tent and grabbed her personal saddle bags, her hunting rifle and walked back out.

"What's going on sergeant?" she asked.

"Iraq has invaded Kuwait and the Queen has activated the Regiment mam," the sergeant said.

"Right," she said briskly. "Rick saddle up and head back home, this trooper will help you. I have to go. Be quick but don't be foolish."

She followed the sergeant and climbed into the idling helicopter which took off moments after she had buckled herself in. This must be serious she thought, for them to send a chopper after me. Minutes later they were landing at the barracks complex, which was alive with activity. Three helicopters were in the process of landing or taking off, personnel in both civilian and military dress were rushing around and vehicles were coming up the road from all directions. It was indeed a full call up.

"You are to report to HQ as soon as possible mam," the sergeant said as they exited the helicopter, to be replaced by a lieutenant and the helicopter took off once again.

"I will just let them know you have arrived and will be reporting shortly mam," the sergeant said, which meant she needed to be in uniform.

Elizabeth walked quickly to the barracks she was assigned to, found her locker, unlocked it and changed into her forest green cammo fatigue uniform, stashed her rifle and relocked it. Quickly braiding her long blond hair, she pinned it up and around her head, before jamming her cap down to come just over her plucked eyebrows and taking one last look in the mirror, she marched over to the headquarters office.

She was surprised and pleased to see Rudy in his captain's uniform there, as well as a lieutenant from the artillery section of the Regiment.

"Hey Rudy," she said. "Who let the iron slow pokes in here?"

"Ha, ha," Rudy replied. "Funny joke. I don't know, they called us all up and I am to report here that's all I know. How about you?"

"Something about Iraq invading Kuwait," Elizabeth said. "I was out in the bush with Rick and they pulled me in with a chopper so I guess it's big all right."

"A little brother sister bonding time?" Rudy asked. "I heard he was becoming a handful."

"This new crop of teachers is becoming a problem," Elizabeth said. "I thought they would. It was a mistake to let the provincial government dictate who we could hire. They are calling us Ukrainians now."

"Oh it's worse than that," Rudy said. "They are trying to eliminate our culture altogether and there is a definite anti-military agenda in place. Most of these teachers are very socialist leaning. Perhaps some of the old timers should enlighten the teachers on what the 'socialists' did to our people."

"I'll have a chat with mother about this," Elizabeth said. "She is still the head of the board. Do you have to go home right away after this? Maybe we could go for dinner together?"

Rudy turned a wonderful colour of red and looked down for a minute before replying.

"Sure, if they let us," Rudy said pointing at the closed door.

"Well if Rudy doesn't I will," the artillery lieutenant said.

"Oh that is very nice of you Junior," Elizabeth said. "But your sister told me hands off, she has someone else in mind for you. Besides I'm two years older than you. No, I'm afraid Rudy is stuck with me."

The door to the main office opened and a harried looking Master Corporal motioned them to enter. Being the senior member of the group, Elizabeth marched in first, dragging her hat off her head and stuffing it under her left elbow. The group came to a crashing halt, lifting right legs high and stomping them into the floor, Rudy on her right and Junior on her left.

"Captains Bekenbaum and Von Hoaedle, Lieutenant Horshe, reporting as ordered sir," she barked out, all three at attention facing the senior officers seated around a board table.

"At ease!" her grandfather growled and the trio shot a right leg out ward and placed their arms in the pits of their backs.

"Her Majesty has exercised her prerogative and ordered us to active duty," the General said, his voice raspy. "The Regiment and its supporting formations will deploy to Saudi Arabia on Friday morning. Major Bekenbaum, you and your troop, will report to Penhold Airport Friday morning, fully equipped and ready for immediate operations against hostile forces. Your immediate task is to secure the Regiments bivouac area. Once that has been completed, you are to gain intelligence into what the enemy is doing and what we, the Regiment will be tasked to do once we arrive.

"You will not, I repeat will not, engage in any hostile actions unless to defend your selves or our allies in the base. Is that clear?

"Any orders to the contrary are to be ignored unless they come directly from an Eagle with higher rank.

"Alberta Tanks will be supplying a number of Leopard tanks, which is why Captain Von Hoaedle and his Cougar will be accompanying you and Lieutenant Horshe and his Cougar will be your artillery spotters.

"At Penhold will be two Star Lifter's from the US, two Ilusian's from Ukraine and two 747's from Saudi Arabia. You will load your Cougars, Lavs and personnel. Your support vehicles will be coming the next day. The Regiment, along with Alberta Tanks and Artillery, will be arriving six weeks later by ship. We expect to be ready for operations two days after that.

"You will be on your own until then Major. Expect the Americans to try and push you around and the Saudis to ignore you. If the Saudis become a problem, you are to request a meeting with this colonel. Make sure your Regimental badges and especially your Eagle are clearly visible when you meet him. That should put an end to them not talking to our female troopers."

"We plan a full parade at 13:00 Thursday, you will be handed your colours at that time. All of you will be there and in dress uniform, clear?

"Now get out of here, we have a lot more planning to do" the General continued. "Make sure you have the proper insignia Major and congratulations, dismissed."

The three officers brought their feet together with a crash, smartly about faced, marched out the door being held open by the Master Corporal, out past the next three officers and into the street, where they tugged back on their caps.

"Do all your troops have dress uniforms?" Elizabeth asked.

"We're going to have to scramble to make it by Thursday," Rudy said looking at the ground. "I don't think we have ever worn them since the first war anyway. We'll manage Liz."

"A lot of my guys are not from the colony," Junior said. "We have Canadian Forces dress though."

"It will have to do," Elizabeth said. "Everybody in the same uniform though Junior, not some in Blue and some in Green. It will probably be better if you were all in green. Is your Cougar fully equipped?"

"Some of our electronics are not as good as yours Liz," Junior said. "We are not on the Regiments list and are classed as a Regular Reserve unit, so we don't have the best equipment."

"As of right now, your section is placed on active duty and attached to my company," Elizabeth said firmly. "Tell your section to show up here tomorrow morning in their civies but to have their dress uniforms with them. We will kit you out here with your personal gear and one of our \Cougars. I will have one of my Cougar crews take you out and familiarize you after that."

"What about you Rudy?" she asked.

"Our stuff is ok Liz," Rudy said. "My guys and I could use a refresher though."

"Ok, you and your guys run through with Junior and his guys," Elizabeth said. "Anything else?"

"OK, get your people mobilized and meet back here tomorrow morning," Elizabeth said. "Except for you Captain, you will report to me at six for extra duty. I think dancing at the Flame?"

"Isn't there some kind of regulation about senior officers throwing their weight around?" Rudy asked.

"You make sure you are in front of my house by six you bum," Elizabeth said punching Rudy's right arm, then kissing him quickly on the cheek.

She accepted and returned their salutes, then headed for her own barracks, which to her surprise was already manned. Her sergeant and master corporal already manning the phones.

"The call out has already gone out mam," her sergeant said. "Congratulations on the promotion mam."

"Thank you sergeant," Elizabeth said. "If our machines are not ready by Thursday afternoon, I'm going to be extremely pissed sergeant. An artillery Lieutenant and his section will be showing up here tomorrow morning, sergeant. They will need full kit including a Cougar and I want them given training on our systems. There will also be a section form the Alberta's coming, they have their own gear, but want some training as well.

"As of now we are on active duty, I want a parade tomorrow at ten, officers at nine, clear?"

"Yes mam," the sergeant said as more of the office staff walked in along with a lieutenant.

"We can handle all this mam," the sergeant said. "The lieutenant there is the OOD, officer of the day, and has been informed about the call up. I'll let her know about your orders mam. You have meetings the rest of the day mam, here is the schedule."

"Get your ass home right now!" was written in her mother's hand writing.

"Is she pissed?" Elizabeth said.

"Not yet, but it sounded like she and your grandmother were well on their way," the master corporal said laughing.

"It's about time!" Emily said as Elizabeth walked into the kitchen. "I was just about to call and give those guys shit for keeping you."

Her mother poured her a tall glass of clear liquid which Elizabeth knew was not water and made her sit down. Then she and Katherine came one on each side of her, unpinned her captain's insignia and then pinned on the major's ones.

"Those are mine," Katherine said. "These are Tatiana's." She handed Elizabeth a dark blue box with her great grandmothers rank insignia inside.

"Pin those on your dress uniform," Emily said.

"To the new Major Bekenbaum" her grandmother said, raising her glass and the three of them drained the fiery vodka down in one shot, slamming the glasses onto the table top. Emily poured each another shot.

"I have a date with Rudy tonight mom, I have to take it easy," Elizabeth said.

"He finally asked you out?" her mother said.

"No, I asked him out," Elizabeth said with a shy grin.

"Just like your name sakes," Katherine said. "Tatiana would have asked what took you so long."

"You going to let him into your pants tonight?" Emily asked.

"Mom!" Elizabeth burst out. "Probably, if it's any of your business."

"It's about time for that too," Katherine said. "You've been too bitchy lately."

"Well thank you for all of your concern," Elizabeth said. "Most mothers and grandmothers would be worried about those kinds of things."

"Most mothers are hypocrites," Emily said. "I was jumping your dad way before we were married."

"And I wanted to but Nicolas wouldn't" Katherine piped in.

"Be that as it may," Elizabeth said. "I had some time with Rick at last and it made me aware of something. He tried talking Russian, but it was really bad and his German is not all that good either. His French is ok, better than his German or Russian. He was not planning on joining the regiment and asked me why it was so important. He was changing his mind, but I am afraid the sentiment is wide spread and if we don't get on this right away we are going to lose a generation or maybe two. Rudy says it's as bad or worse in Olds and Junior has mostly non regiment people in his batteries.

"Rick tells me that the teachers are calling our people Ukrainians, which I guess technically might be true. They are learning nothing about Cossacks or their culture and spend more time on America and Eastern Canada than anything else. With Britain and France running third and fourth. Not much about Western Canada, Russia or Germany."

"It's as bad as that?" Emily asked. "We had heard rumours, but nothing substantial. I knew if we let that AUPE take over classes like the minister wanted, we would get here. How many of the old teachers are still around and willing to teach and do we have anymore graduating?"

"We'll have a meeting and get the word out Liz," Katherine said. "I have even heard some of the high school teachers are talking about Marx and Lenin. Maybe some of the old timers should have a chat with them."

"Maybe we should set them up," Elizabeth said. "Have a couple of the old timers attend those teacher's classes and tell them the truth of what the Bolsheviks did to us."

"The parade will evoke some interest," Katherine said. "All of us will be there in our uniforms. Maybe it's time parents started talking to their kids about this, we haven't had a full parade for ten years or so. Can your company ride?"

"We all can ride grandmother, but I'm not sure about formation riding, why?" Elizabeth asked.

"We need to show them our roots," Katherine said. "We are a cavalry regiment after all. Ok the horses pretty much know what they are doing, you take your whole company and spend a couple of days at it."

"Rudy has a section attached to us grandmother," Elizabeth said. "More importantly, so does Junior and he is the only one in his section from the colony."

"He's easy," Emily said. "He knows how to ride, so does his sergeant, they can ride the trace horses and the other three the ammo cart. It will make a good show. I'll have a talk with Rudy's mother, but they are a cavalry regiment as well and I know they have a show company. Shit that reminds me, we'll have to contact the Strathcona's and the Mounties, they have been part of the Regiment in the past, the Pixlies and the Calgary's too."

"Yes," Katherine said. "I have a feeling the Colonel in Chief or her designate will be here."

"I think Ann is taking over for her," Emily said. "Margaret's hard living is getting the best of her lately."

"When is hunky Rudy coming?" Emily asked.

"I told him if he is not in front by six I would kick his ass," Elizabeth said.

"Now you sound like a Bekenbaum woman," Emily said. "Now go get all prettied up so he thinks it's his idea."

Elizabeth had the shortest skirt she thought she could get away with on, her long powerful legs without stockings or pantyhose. Her long blond hair was lying free down her back and her stylish tight winter jacket, covered a low cut sweater that would have all the men and most of the women staring at her. Luckily Rudy's old Ford truck had a bench seat and she was sitting almost on top of him while he drove trying to concentrate on the road with her perfume in his nose and her hand on his right thigh.

"Are you going to be alright in that getup?" he asked. "It's fifteen below you know."

"If your heater or your truck breaks, you are going to be one cold SOB," Elizabeth said. "Because you're going to have to give me your pants and jacket. Being as you are taking me out, you are responsible for my safety. Oh and you're buying too."

"Oh man," Rudy said. "Good thing I got paid today."

"We won't be needing much money for a while love," Elizabeth said, shifting her hand from his thigh to the back of his neck.

"If you keep that up, we won't make it to town," he said.

"Promise?" Elizabeth asked. "If I remember right, there's an old farmstead just up there with a lot of trees around it."

"Are you sure about this?" Rudy asked. "I mean we haven't even been on a real date yet."

"I can't help it if you were too scared to ask," Elizabeth said, letting her left hand drop to his crotch and with her right hand unbuttoned her jacket.

Rudy reached down, pulling the lever to engage the four wheel drive and skidded the truck into the old farm stead as Elizabeth moved over to the passenger door. By the time he put the truck in park and looked over at her, she had her jacket pulled wide open, her skirt hiked up and was undoing his fly.

"I thought you two were going to be here an hour ago," Junior said. Most of their class was there, some on the dance floor already, but most just getting their meals.

"Well you know that old truck of Rudy's," Elizabeth said shrugging her shoulders. "You'd think he would at least make sure the tires were full of air before he picked his girl up."

"Oh you're his girl now then?" Junior said elbowing his girl Heidi. "Looks like Liz finally got her hooks into him."

"It's about time," Heidi said. "You two have been making eyes at each other since first year of high school."

"Enough already," Elizabeth said. "Is that anyway to talk to your commanding officer? Now where is my rum and coke?"

"Holy shit it's cold!" Elizabeth said several hours and drinks later. "This truck better have a good heater."

"What did you expect wearing that short skirt?" Rudy asked. "It's not summer in California here you know."

"You weren't complaining about the short skirt when you picked me up," Elizabeth said, sliding next to him on the bench seat as he started the truck.

"Ya well it was warmer then," Rudy said putting his right hand on the inside of her left thigh.

"Yie!!" Elizabeth yelled as she pulled his hand away. "Your hand is colder than the stupid truck is."

They pulled out of the parking lot and headed south. Soon enough they were on the two lane highway that linked Olds with Didsbury heading south. Fifteen minutes later they were pulling into the Bekenbaum complex and Rudy slowed the truck down.

"Drive to the end of the lane and turn left," Elizabeth said. "I don't live in the main house, I'm in the last guest house."

Rudy did as he was instructed and pulled up to a stop in front of the last of four guest houses. It was the smallest one at just under seven hundred square feet and it had a front porch that ran all along the front with an extended roof covering it. He put the transmission lever in park, turned off the headlights and turned to Elizabeth expecting a good night kiss.

"My bed is a lot softer and has more room," Elizabeth said, turning the engine off and taking his keys out of the ignition, then sliding to the passenger side of the truck. "It's also a lot warmer in there. Come on then."

The sun had been up for an hour and Elizabeth was frying up some bacon wearing a large Calgary Flames hockey jersey and nothing else, when Rudy came out of the bedroom shirtless and bare foot. He came up behind her, put his arms around her middle and kissed her neck tenderly.

"No time for another round love," Elizabeth said. "I only have this bacon and I don't want it ruined, maybe after breakfast."

"Jeez, you think I'm a machine?" Rudy asked. "Even a machine needs some fuel and rest now and then."

"Really?" Elizabeth said turning around and kissing him. "We'll see about that after we eat. Now the dishes are in that cupboard over there, the utensils in the drawer under it."

"Oh shit I almost forgot," Elizabeth said, as they were cleaning up the dishes after breakfast. "How many of your troopers can ride good enough for the parade Thursday? My company will be mounted and they want your platoon mounted as well."

"Troop dear," Rudy said. "We are called a troop in the cavalry, not a platoon. All of us have some training and we should have enough trained horses. We have our traditions as well remember?"

"I just had to ask," Elizabeth said. "I think they want a couple of Leopards too, but that is not my department. They want the initial group made special and that would be us. So traditional uniform and weapons I suppose, not the rifles though. I'll split my company into two troops, one in the lead and one in the rear, your platoon to escort the gun and the crew in the middle."

"Column of four?" Rudy asked.

"Yes I suppose that would be best," Elizabeth said.

"OK," Rudy said. "So, it will take just under two hours for us to get there. I don't feel like trucking the horses and then unloading. We'll ride there and it will make a good show for the locals."

"That sounds like an excellent idea," Elizabeth said. "I am going to suggest we join you. It may be a good PR move. It's not often people get to see massed cavalry moving in formation, especially around here. I'll take it up with command and see what happens."

Both of their cell phones signalled an incoming text message within seconds of each other and sure enough they were from Regiment ordering them to a lunch meeting.

"Did you leave a uniform in the barracks?" Elizabeth asked. "I hope so, because you are going to have to leave right now to get home and change and get back in time."

"Ya, I've got a spare uniform in my locker over there," Rudy replied.

"Good, we can have a shower together then," Elizabeth said. "You might as well bring all of your gear over here, you'll most likely be spending all your nights here."

"Well my roommate is definitely nicer on the eyes over here," Rudy said lifting her up off her feet and walking to the shower.

"Yes and the benefits she provides are also better," Elizabeth replied, as he put her down and lifted the sweater over her shoulders. "We only have an hour love and my hair takes longer to dry than yours."

"Oh, somehow I think we'll make it," he said and they did, just.

Chapter Three

"Well major I have it on good authority that the captain is being afforded every possible hospitality here at base?" the general, her grandfather said smirking.

"Sir, yes sir!" Elizabeth said. "The captain has proven very enthusiastic about his accommodations sir. However his vehicle is rather shabby sir, but I suppose it will do for now."

Her father snorted the cup of coffee he was drinking all over his shoes and her grandmother laughed out loud. Rudy was turning a wonderful shade of deep red, being the brunt of the jokes.

"Oh, I am afraid we have embarrassed the poor captain," Emily said. "Perhaps the Colonel should enquire of the Captain's mother if it is ok for him to spend his nights with my daughter?"

"I believe I will do just that Lieutenant Colonel," Katherine said. "It would not do if the Captain's mother did not approve of her son cohabiting with my granddaughter."

"Ok ladies enough," Nicolas said. "We have had our fun with the youngsters. Now to business. You will be ready for Friday departure captain?"

"Yes sir," Rudy said. "I don't believe the transition will be all that difficult, we have been training on LAV's for a couple of years now. I have my electronics guys working with the Majors people right now and the drivers are out in the forest reserve as we speak."

"That should be pleasing the hunting crowd to no end," Paul said sarcastically. "I can just see it, a city yahoo playing at being an outdoorsman, riding his quad at full speed down a cutline, going around a blind corner and confronting a ten ton Cougar head on."

"Ya and then when he and his two buddies start to whine and snivel," Nicolas continued, "the boys in the back come out with body armour and automatic weapons. I bet that shut's 'em up in a hurry."

"I am sure we will be hearing from Fish and Wildlife shortly," Paul said as they all laughed.

"The Major spoke to you about the parade?" Paul asked.

"Yes sir," Rudy replied. "I think it best that we ride down escorting the gun. It should only take a little over an hour."

"You know that is a heck of a good idea," Emily said. "I'll let the local news media know what we are planning and the route we will be taking and coordinate with the Mounties and the Sheriffs for road and crowd control."

"Liz," Emily said snapping her fingers, "you could pull out of here by nine, ride to Olds and escort the troop back here by one couldn't you?"

"It would be better if we left by eight," Elizabeth said, "but yes, it is possible."

"The Strathconna's say no problem with staging out of Olds," Paul said. "Rudy's commander has already made arrangements with the collage for putting the animals up."

"Ok," Nicolas said, also reading an email. "The Mounties are in and the 'package' will be diverted to Olds in time for the trip. The Ride is already en route and will be diverted to Olds as well."

"The 'Package' says she is delighted," Katherine said. "She wants one of Paul's purebreds and two others. She will need trappings for her standard. Yes I warned her how cold it is. She's a lot like her Aunt."

"Ok fine it's her body," Nicolas said. "Ok Em, let the media know the time and the route, but not about the 'Package' that will be a surprise. One carriage then, for the GG and LG?"

"No, we will be needing two," Katherine said. "HRH and sons will be attending as well. The sons are to be riders. The Premier will be here, but he says he will ride with the Lieutenant Governor."

"I didn't think he would miss it," Nicolas said. "His family is from the Odessa area too, they came later than we did though.

"The Strathconas to escort the 'Package' then," Paul said. "The Mounties escort the carriage. Captain, your people we will place between the two carriages, ten troopers before the gun, ten behind, five on each side. Major, forty of your people in front and behind, ten flankers each side, just like a field deployment. Everyone's firearms loaded and ready. We aren't expecting trouble, but it may come looking for us and we might need a little more than sharp steel."

"There hasn't been that much sharp steel on that road since we first arrived here," Nicolas said.

"What a fabulous idea," Emily blurted out. "It's a hundred and thirty years since we came to this country, we can play that up."

"My daughter in law could market an ice cutting competition in Iceland and make it sound like you just have to be there," Nicolas said. "Good thing too, with all the antiwar and anti-American sentiments flying around right now."

"Protocol conflict perhaps?" Elizabeth asked.

"The Princess is Colonel in Chief to everyone but the Mounties," Katherine said. "The Regiment and that includes Rudy's as well as the artillery, are senior, but we generally don't let it be known we are involved, we usually attach ourselves to other units. Rudy's unit was designated 'Alberta Tanks,' in WW2 and is now a reserve unit, so that means the Strathconas are the senior unit and Rudy and we are attached to it. The Princess can wear their uniform and they can escort her."

"We're going to need a baby sitter for the youngsters," Paul said. "I know we have tame horses for them."

"Not a problem," Elizabeth said. "Rick just got placed on active duty as my aide, he can handle that duty."

"He's not old enough," Emily said.

"It's only a few months early," Elizabeth replied. "He's old enough to be enrolled as a cadet, the rest of his class is."

"Alright Liz, it's your call," Paul said. "The last time I talked to him he was dead set against anything to do with the Regiment."

"He's a teenager," Elizabeth said. "I'm sure I gave mom fits at that age."

"As I gave mine dear," Emily said. "As we still are at times, especially with my mom."

"I think it has a lot to do with the new teachers," Elizabeth said. "The Colonels and I have already discussed it."

"Alright," Paul said. "Get him some cold weather gear and uniform. Inform him of the protocol when dealing with the monarchy. His horse should be alright. He doesn't get a sword, get him a decent sling for his rifle and a pistol and show him how to dress and arm. Mom do you think you could help with him, I'm a little busy and I suspect Emm is going to be as well."

"Crash course, but it should be ok," Katherine said. "I'll handle it all Liz, you have other things to worry about. I'll have him report to you a couple of hours before you leave."

"I want the Regiment to ride to Olds," Elizabeth said. "It will be easier that way. We'll go up the west side and hit the Cow Palace from the west. If we leave here by seven, we'll be there by nine and the horses can have an hour or so of rest."

"What time are the flights Saturday?" Elizabeth asked.

"You need to be loaded by six hundred," Nicolas said. "So pull out of here by two hundred. Most of the country will still be sleeping and it will be too dark to notice the sand cammo instead of white UN colouring."

"We will be loading at eight hundred," Paul said. "Hopefully we will be done by eighteen hundred. We have to be in Galveston by the following Friday. So we will see you in about six weeks after you leave here."

"Ok that should about do it for now," Nicolas said. "This will be the first mass deployment since WW2, Korea wasn't even this big."

"Even in WW2 we didn't operate all together," Paul said. "This might be the first time since Afghanistan."

"Well let's pray for the same results," Nicolas said.

"Rudy, you look like you have something to say," Katherine said.

"It's personal business mam," Rudy responded, "nothing to do with the Regiment."

"Ok spit it out Rudy," Paul said. "Regiment business time is over."

"Sir," Rudy began after some hesitation. "I have spoken with my parents and family and they have given me their blessing and now I am asking yours. I am asking permission of your family to marry Elizabeth."

"Ahm," Paul gulped, "That's a little sudden is it not?"

"No sir," Rudy said. "Liz and I have known each other for four years sir. I have loved her for that long and if she will have me, I will make her a good husband sir."

Paul looked at Elizabeth, then to Emily. Elizabeth had lowered her head, her bangs covering her eyes, but he could see her right leg bouncing under the table and a tear slowly running down her right cheek. Emily had that mischievous look in her eyes and the faint smile that brooded ill for the star crossed couple.

"You promise to love my daughter, to cherish her the rest of her and your life?" Emily asked.

"Yes mam!" Rudy replied.

"You promise to look after her old and decrepit mother for the rest of her life?" Emily asked hardly able to keep from laughing.

"The Bekenbaum's have no objection Von Hoaidle." Paul said.

Rudy stood and walked to Elizabeth standing at attention in front of her.

"Elizabeth Susan Bekenbaum, would you be my wife?" he asked.

Elizabeth looked up at him and smiled. She stood and grasped both his hands with both of hers.

"I am Elizabeth, daughter of Emily, daughter of Katherine, daughter of Tatiana, daughter of Elizabeth," she began. "This is Rudy my husband, what is done to he and his, is done to me and mine. So say I in front of God and man."

"I am Rudy, son of George, son of Peter, son of Rudolf, house of Hoaidle," Rudy said. "This is Elizabeth, my wife. What is done to her and hers is done to me and mine. So say I in front of God and man."

The room was silent as all of them made the sign of the cross, blessing the union.

"Since the very beginning," Nicolas said. "Our two families have been linked. As far back as Germany, the Von Hoaidles and the Von Bekenbaums fought together. Andreas and Rudolf were fast friends and both made the same deals to come to this great land of ours, pledging solidarity to each other. We have been close all these long years, but never related."

"Liz, Rudy," he continued. "I would be lying if I said your parents and indeed Tatiana herself, had not hoped for this union."

"Liza my dear," Emily said. "My heart is overflowing. No matter my comments on why you should buy the cow when you are getting the milk for free. I, in my heart of hearts, hoped this would be the outcome. I knew Rudy was lost, but you Bekenbaum's hold your feelings so dear, I did not know how you felt."

"It is good that this is coming at just this time," Paul said. "There are other things besides your love for each other at play here."

"I know daddy," Elizabeth said. "All sides of the Regiment are here this week, the first time they have been together for a hundred and thirty some years. We will be having a gala regardless, making it a wedding gala will just put icing on the cake."

"No dear, there is more," Katherine said softly. "Rudy is heir to his father's Earldom and you are heir to your mother's barony. In addition to the oaths from both families, there will be a private one between the two families after."

"I will inform Her Majesty," Katherine said. "The Prince of Wales and the Princess Royal will have to be informed as soon as possible."

"Alright Liz, you and Rudy leave the details to us hmm?" Paul said. "All I want you telling Richard is that you and Rudy are being married, Thursday after the parade. Nothing more, is that clear?"

"I would like him to be my groomsman," Rudy said.

"Yes," Elizabeth agreed, "just as I would like Rudy's sister Mia to be my bridesmaid."

"That should not be a problem," Emily said. "They are both first year cadets, but they both will not be allowed to participate in the private ceremony. Nor will your best man and maid of honour. It is purely a family affair."

"All will be made clear in time," Nicolas said. "Nothing to fret about. Just more family hocus pock-us from the old days. But we must keep the traditions alive. Now off you two go, there is much to plan and little time to do it in."

"Liz, send Rick to see me after you talk to him," Nicolas concluded.

"I wonder what that last bit was all about," Elizabeth asked Rudy, as they walked down the lane toward the Regimental offices

"I think it has to do with the uniting of two Baronial families," Rudy said. "Your father and grandfather are not the Earls, at least in name, but your mother inherits her title when her father dies. It really does not matter much anymore these days, but we must keep the old folks happy."

"Well I am happy they are happy," Elizabeth said stopping and pulling Rudy close to her.

"Now before I have to become the 'Ice Princess' once again," she said. "I love you with every fibre of my body Rudy Hoaidle. I loved you from our basic training together."

"Ah Geeze, get a room already!" Rick said walking up to them, they were kissing against the hallway wall. Mia was standing beside him, grinning from ear to ear.

"Well dear brother," Elizabeth said. "Be careful or your future brother in law may get angry with you."

Mia squealed and grabbed Elizabeth in a big hug, both of them jumping up and down in glee.

"What the hell?" Rick asked looking at Rudy.

"Your sister and I are getting married after the parade Thursday Rick," Rudy said.

"Oh," Rick said. "Well congratulations, I guess."

"The proper response is to shake the man's hand Rick and to give your big sister a hug and a peck on the cheek," Elizabeth said, as Mia broke free of Elizabeth and grabbed her older brother, doing just that.

"Oh Rudy, you are so lucky!" Mia cried out, beginning to cry with joy. She then turned to Rick intending on hugging and kissing him. Rick backed away hastily and stuck out his right hand instead.

"Mia, I would be honoured if you would be my bridesmaid," Elizabeth said. "Rick, you WILL, be Rudy's groomsman."

"Javohl mine commandant!" Rick said, clicking his heels together and bowing his head.

"Ah, out of the mouths of babes," Elizabeth said smiling her wicked smile.

"Rick, Mia, you are hereby placed on active duty," Rudy said. "Mia, you shall be my aide while we are deploying and Rick, you are to be the Major's aide."

"Shit!" Rick said. "Which Major? How come Mia gets to be your aide and I have to be some cranky old major's aide?"

"Well, if you don't get your ass down to the QM's and get kitted out and report back within the hour, this cranky Major is going to kick your sorry ass all over the parade ground," Elizabeth said, pointing to her majors insignia.

"Oh Great!" Rick said, this time grabbing his sister in a big bear hug. "It's about time the old man saw how good you are."

"Speaking of the old man," Elizabeth said. "Grandfather wants to talk to you Rick, right now. Mia, would you be a dear and contact Heidi for me? I have something to ask her. And keep your mouth shut, understand?"

"Yes mam," Mia said saluting and then scampered away to the offices.

"Any hope for those two?" Rudy asked.

"No, I don't think so," Elizabeth said. "Mia is a romantic and Rick, well Rick is not. I don't know what he will end up being, but romantic it will not be."

"You wanted to see me Oppa?" Rick asked from the doorway to his grandfather's office.

"Yes come in Richard and close the door," Nicolas said rising from his seat behind his desk and walking over to his small liquor cabinet.

This must be serious, Rick thought, Oppa never ever calls me Richard when we are alone.

"A coke?" Nicolas asked holding up a can.

"Yes sir, thank you sir," Rick said taking his cue from his grandfather.

"Elizabeth let you read your fathers letter?" Nicolas asked.

"Yes sir," Rick said accepting the can of coke.

"I wrote that the day before I got this," he said, lifting his shirt and showing Rick the ugly scarring on his chest and stomach.

"Being a soldier is not all glory, Richard," Nicolas said. "I lost a lot of good people that day and almost died myself. I would do it all again in a heartbeat. That's what I am Richard. It is what I trained to be my whole life. I am a soldier Richard. I kill people for a living and I am damn good at it."

"I am also a life giver and a life bringer," Nicolas continued. "I kill only when I must, when I have no other option and I do it in the most efficient way I can to save as many of my people and the people I'm fighting's lives. My job as an officer is to train my people as well as I can, provide them with the best equipment and supplies as I can and plan operations as best I can, to protect my people.

"When we came to this country, we pledged to protect her and her people. In return, we are given certain rights and freedoms others in this country do not have. But they come at a cost Richard, a cost that some of our people cannot make themselves pay. That too is their right as citizens of this great nation. While none of us will stop them from leaving, or stop them from their inheritance, they have to leave and renounce claim to the colony.

"Some have tried to take us to court, one went to the Supreme Court of Canada. The colony does not belong to one family, it belongs to us all. In order to benefit from the colony you have to abide by the original Charter. So far the Bekenbaum family has done so. Stephan Bekenbaum's sons chose not to pursue the military and thus left the colony proper, to pursue the financial sector and that branch of the family has done well and has done us well. They manage the original family businesses which we all have a share in. As the heirs, they keep the title of Earle, but have no power over the colony.

"John Bekenbaum, stayed true to the traditions and leadership of the Horde was passed to him and down to us as time went by. Leadership of the Horde is not hereditary Richard. It is given by the members of the Horde and must be earned."

"But father is not an eagle, nor is he an officer," Rick said. "Yet he is the Ataman."

"Nowhere does it say the Ataman has to be an eagle Richard," Nicolas said. "And your father is an officer, just not a commissioned officer. Truth be known, your father qualifies for both and has since he was your age."

"I don't understand then," Rick said.

"There are only so many positions for eagles and officers Rick," Nicolas said. "An eagle comes with a lot more land than a bear does. Many of our people have been living on the same farms for generations and need to be an eagle to keep it. Also, the pay is better as an officer. We have enough wealth that we have purchased the land this ranch sits on and we lease it to the Regiment. We don't need the money or the prestige and up until now, we didn't need to be flag officers. I was able to handle those duties, but soon I will not be able to. So your sister is an officer. If you choose to be you can, or you can take your father's route. Or you can take your own and not be a part of any of it. I, nor anyone else in the family will think less of you."

"No. sir," Rick said shaking his head. "Liz told me of some of the stuff she witnessed in Africa and from what I hear, this Sudan Hussein fellow is almost as bad as Stalin was. As a family, we have a sacred duty to help those who need our help. Count me in Ataman Bekenbaum."

"Thank you Rick," Nicolas said proffering his right hand. "Now remember, always do the best you can. Nobody can ask more of you. Your duty for the rest of the week will be to prepare to escort the Princes William and Harry. Basically, you are a glorified babysitter, with a gun.

"We are not expecting any trouble, but if there is, your job is to get those two kids out of harm's way as fast as you can. If you have to use your weapon you have to use your weapon. And while all of us love you more than life itself, you will do everything possible, including being a human shield, to ensure those two boys survive. Clear?"

"Yes sir, you can count on me sir," Rick said.

"Ok, get out of here and draw your equipment," Nicolas said. "It's going to be cold Thursday and you are riding both ways, plus you will be ponying one of the princes mounts. Mia will be ponying the other one."

"Ah, is she going to be all gaga over the princes?' Rick asked. "I can't stand it when teeny boppers do that."

"She better not," Nicolas said. "She will be in uniform and working, not a spectator. Your grandmother will clue her in. Now get, I'm a busy man."

"Hey Rick," Paul said as Rick walked into the kitchen from his grandfather's office. "Grandpa didn't read the riot act did he?"

"No, he just clued me into a few more things that Liz had brought up," Rick said. "Look dad, I don't think I can measure up to what you and grandpa did."

"Nobody is asking you to," Paul said putting his arm around Rick's shoulders. "I am not my father and he was not his. We are all different people Rick, from a different era and life experience. You will find your niche and you will do well."

"Pop, please don't get angry, but I want an eagle," Rick said solemnly. "I think I owe it to my ancestors. I don't care to be even a warrant officer, but I want an eagle."

"I understand Rick," Paul said turning his son and placing his hands on his shoulders, looking him in his sky blue eyes.

"I cannot, nor can anyone else in the family, give you an eagle," Paul said. "It must be earned and so must the officers rank. If anything, it will be harder for you because of your name. Do your best, you are starting late, most of your class mates have a head start on you."

"None of my classmates are Bekenbaums," Rick said smiling. "I can fail every exam but the last one and still get my eagle. I have the best horses and a year to train."

"Now you sound like your great grandmother," Paul said laughing and patting Rick on the back. "There is hope for you yet."

"Yup," Rick agreed. "Now before you can say it, I'm getting, you are a busy man."

He had been in the barn since five. Elizabeth's horse was saddled as was the one he would be riding and three others. He would be riding Prince Harry's mount to Olds and his own on the way back. The horse Mia was saddling now would be Williams on the way back. It would settle the two horses down if they were ridden on the way up to Olds. Mia would be trailing her horse and Rick at least one. He was hoping someone else would take the other, but was prepared to trail both spare mounts if he had to.

The barn was busy with all the troopers grooming and saddling their mounts. Everyone was in their blue dress uniforms, only the full size medals missing. They would be putting those on only for the parade. Rifles, swords and lances were propped against the horse stalls and one by one, the troopers placed sword belts and rifles across their backs, picked up their lances and led their mounts out of the barn to join the others filling the yard.

Elizabeth and her command group were the last to arrive in the barn and the other officer's aides handed the reins of their horses to them as Rick and Mia did for Elizabeth and Rudy.

"Lorali," Elizabeth said to her captain, "have your aide take one of those horses off of Cadet Bekenbaums hands would you? Here Cadet, hang on to this for me for a minute."

Rick took Elizabeth's lance from her as she checked her horse tack and stirrup length. Her sword and rifle were already across her back and like the other troopers, two spare rifle clips and a spare pistol clip were attached to the pistol belt wrapped around her waist.

"OK Cadet good job," she said. "Your position on this formation is behind me, but in front of the colour party, the Master Sergeant will be beside you. On the way back, Harry will be on the right side of his father's coach and you will be on his right side. You wait for him to dismount at the reviewing stand and then you and Mia will take the horses and yourselves back to the barn. For this trip out, just follow my and the sergeants lead."

The yard was filled with troopers and their mounts, loosely grouped in their sections and troops and when Elizabeth nodded at the sergeant, he called them all to order and to prepare to mount. The yard went silent and the troopers moved into their lines and tightened cinches in preparation to mount. It was seven in the morning and still dark, the yard lit by a few scattered street lights and the full moon, but spectators lined both sides of the yard and the road leading out of the barracks and to the highway. It was rare to see the Regiment mounted on patrol and rarer yet, for them to be armed, in full uniform and with a whole company of over one hundred troopers and horses.

The four scout troopers would be a hundred yards ahead of the main body, then would come Elizabeth and Rudy, with Rick and the sergeant close behind, followed by the four colour party members. After that would come twenty rows of four horses each, split into two groups of ten rows. Unlike other cavalry troopers, the only pennants on lance tips were on the troop leader's lances. The order to mount was given and smoothly, all one hundred troopers mounted. Lances were placed in the scabbards mounted for them on the saddles behind the trooper's right leg.

After a few seconds to let everyone settle down, Elizabeth nodded and the advance guard moved out in a wide formation of four at a quick walk. Elizabeth nodded to Rudy and they walked slowly out into the road followed by Rick and the Sergeant, then the colour party and then in succession, groups of four troopers swung abreast into the road. When the last column reached the road, they let out a whistle and Elizabeth broke into a trot. The yard rang to the sound of thundering hooves and jangling equipment as the whole company broke into the trot behind her.

Before anyone in the company could start, the spectators started singing the Regimental song and starting with Elizabeth, as each column passed the ranch house, they turned and saluted the four uniformed people on the porch, who stood at attention and returned the salutes until the last column had passed.

Trotting for ten minutes and walking for five, the company reached the southern outskirts of Olds in an hour and swung to the east, heading for the complex that housed the fair grounds and exhibition buildings. The sun had come up by then and small crowds of spectators lined the road as the Regiment, proceeded by RCMP cruisers, lights flashing, rode down the centre of the street. Four blocks from the arena, Elizabeth raised her right hand over her head and made a twirling motion, the master sergeant followed her gesture with his own and Rick looked back to see it being duplicated by all the sergeants back through the column.

Elizabeth brought her arm down sharply and the company broke into a trot and began to sing the Regiments song all at the same time. The song matching the tempo of the beating hooves and if anyone in the town of Olds did not know they were coming, they knew it now, as a hundred sets of loud voices and a hundred sets of thundering hooves echoed through the streets and lanes of the town. Elizabeth raised her arm once more and as she brought it down, they broke into a canter, the beat of the song matching the speed of the horses.

The police cruisers had to speed up as they were in danger of being ridden over and as the company reached the fairground gates they swung in, still at the canter and formed up in two lines of fifty coming to a halt in front of the exhibition hall just as the last verse of the song ended.

"Company!" the Sergeant Major yelled after receiving a nod from Elizabeth. "Prepare to dismount!"

Then looking to his left and his right as he removed his lance from its scabbard and seeing the rest of the company had done the same. "Dismount!" he yelled and the company dismounted and loosened cinches. Every fourth trooper handed his reins to a partner and took a section of rope from his saddle bag and joining up with other troopers, soon had rope lines strung and troopers were hitching horses to them. They would be leaving in two hours and there was no sense to unsaddle just to saddle back up again.

Elizabeth stripped off her rifle from her back and handed it to Rick. Rudy doing the same but giving his to Mia and they disappeared into the arena along with all the other officers and senior noncoms, leaving the junior NCO's and troopers to stand in groups among the horses, trying to stay warm and out of the wind. Soon the senior NCO's were back and issuing orders to their sections.

"Every fourth trooper to stand guard," they were told. "You'll be changed at the half hour starting now."

"That includes you two," the master sergeant said to Mia and Rick. "Trade off with the colour party guards."

"I'll take the first watch," Rick volunteered, the other three smiling their thanks as they rushed into the warmth of the arena. Rick gave Mia Elizabeth's rifle, pulled his hat down so that it just left his eyes open and pulled up his collar to cover his nose. Unlike the other guards, he kept his rifle in the crook of his left arm and under his right armpit, his right hand not far from the trigger guard. The others had slung their rifles over a shoulder and had stuffed their hands into their pockets.

Rick kept moving up and down his section of horses, looking for loose ropes or a skittish horse that might cause a wreck. Besides, it kept his circulation going and his feet from freezing. Soon enough, his half hour was up and he was hurrying into the arena, looking for a washroom and then Mia.

He found her with Rudy and Elizabeth standing alone to one side of the milling troopers and dignitaries.

"That was awful nice of you to volunteer for the first watch," Mia said. "I was sure I was about to freeze."

"Oh there was nothing nice about that Mia," Elizabeth said laughing. "Rick's mom didn't raise any dummies. Now he gets three quarters of an hour to stay warm. Which shift did you take?"

"The last one," Mia said. "I get three quarters of an hour warm break too."

"Followed by an extra half hour of being in the cold when we go home," Rudy said laughing.

"That's not fair!" Mia said giving Rick a dirty look.

"Sure it is," Rick said keeping his face neutral. "I had to stay outside a half hour extra while all you folks were getting nice and warm. Nobody stopped you from being the first on watch."

"I thought you were never supposed to volunteer for anything," Mia said looking accusingly at Rudy.

"There are rules and then there are rules," Rudy said. "It is obvious why the Bekenbaums always have the advantage over the rest of us. They know when to follow them and when to bend them."

"And don't you ever forget that my dear husband," Elizabeth said as she grabbed him and kissed him.

"Oh get a room already," a British voice said behind them. "Just like your mother, breaking all the rules all the time."

"Officer on Deck!" Rick yelled out as he spotted the scarlet sash and the Colonels rank markings.

The four of them sprang to attention, Rudy and Elizabeth bowing their heads quickly at the neck.

"Forgive me Your Highness I did not see you there," Elizabeth said quickly.

"We have learned the art of disappearing," the Princess said. "It comes in handy at times."

"I am Anne, the Princes Royal," she said sticking out her hand. "You must be Elizabeth my escort commander?"

The Princess was dressed in a Full Dress Canadian military uniform. Dark Green with white belt and a cavalry sword scabbarded at her side. She had Colonels insignia on her epaulets and collars and her decorations and awards pinned to her scarlet sash which was draped across her chest and over a shoulder. Her uniform was a twin except for the sash and the insignia of the Lord Strathcona Horse Captain accompanying her.

"No mam," Elizabeth said. "I am Major Elizabeth Bekenbaum, commander of the Regiment assigned as protection detail man. I believe the good Captain there is your escort commander."

"Oh semantics," the Princess said. "Congratulations on your marriage my dear, this is the lucky man?"

"Yes mam," Elizabeth said proudly. "With your permission mam, this is my husband Rudy Von Hoaidle, Fourth Baron of Olds."

"Your Highness," Rudy said clicking his heels together and bowing his head once again as he shook her hand.

"Oh my, but you do know how to pick them my dear," Anne said to Elizabeth. "What is your function in today's parade Baron?"

"My platoon is accompanying the Regiment's company to Saudi Arabia mam," Rudy said. "Along with a battery of artillery. I am to set up logistics for our brigade of medium tanks and provide artillery and air support spotting for the Major's company mam."

"And these two?" Anne asked pointing to the two, still at rigid attention cadets, one in dark blue and one in light blue uniform.

"May it please you mam," Elizabeth said. "This is the Barons aide Mia and my aide Richard. Mia will be escorting William and Richard will be escorting Harry today mam."

Mia did a small curtsy and Rick mimicked Rudy, clicking his heels together and bobbing his head.

"And fine escorts they will be I am sure," Anne said.

"Mother said to tell you congratulations Liza and she wished she could be here for the formal ceremony," Anne said to Elizabeth. "She is insisting that you visit her on your way home from this unpleasantness."

"What, the queen wants to see me?" Elizabeth asked shocked.

"Why not?" Anne asked. "Your family has been close to my family for over a hundred years. Your mother I call one of my closest friends and your grandfather and grandmother are my parent's closest friends. Your father trained my aunt and tried to train my brother, lost cause that one. It is only fitting you visit her home on your way back to yours. Just as it is fitting for the new generation to get to know one another."

"Oh, I have been discovered," Anne said, pointing at the three scarlet clad men walking toward them accompanied by some civilians dressed in formal suits complete with tailed jackets and top hats.

"I will catch up with you after the formal ceremony Liza," Anne said. "Come along Captain, it's back to work for us."

Two of the red coated officers kept approaching Elizabeth's group while the third, an RCMP Inspector, introduced the civilians to the Princess Royal and the group of them moved off.

"Major, I am Major Black of the Welsh Dragoons and this is Captain White of the Royal Horse Guards," the Major said. "We will be accompanying you as the Prices Royal's personal escorts."

"Well Major Black and Captain White," Elizabeth said smiling. "I am Baroness Blue and this is Baron Grey of the Regiment and we are just here for show. How may we help the SAS today? Don't worry, your horses and the Princesses are very tame, for Cossack horses."

"How did you know?" the Major asked.

"Oh come on Sergeant, do you think the SAS has a patent on good intelligence," Elizabeth said. "Cadet Bekenbaum there spotted you the moment we rode into the yard. 'Sis' he said 'isn't that that SAS sergeant you trained last year?' Why yes it is, I replied, Sergeant Black I think he said his name was. Of course I was wrong Major Black, I am sorry about that."

"You know how that works mam," the major said smiling. "My partner here has not had the pleasure of an Alberta spring, yet. He will be getting a brief exposure to it today. We are both experienced cavalry troops mam and we have watch caps to put under our helmets and insulated gloves to put on under the dress gauntlets, we should be alright."

"Once we actually get moving, it won't be so bad" Elizabeth said. "It's only ten miles. Then we will off load and the main parade will be indoors."

"I must compliment you on this young lad here," the British Captain said pointing at Rick. "He was the only one on guard patrol that actually had his weapon ready for use."

"Well there really is very little chance of anything actually happening," Elizabeth said. "But bad habits are bad habits. Thank you for pointing that out."

"The Prince of Wales is doing some local things with the boys," the captain continued. "They should be done in ten minutes or so. Then we can begin the next phase."

Slightly behind schedule, the Prince of Wales and his two sons arrived, the Prince dressed in a Naval Aviators uniform and his sons in red army uniforms. The Princess Royal intercepted them and escorted them over to Elizabeth's small group.

"Charles, this is Paul's daughter Elizabeth and her husband Rudy," Anne said. "Elizabeth is in command of the Regiment's company today. This is Mia who will be Williams escort, and Richard, who will be Harry's escort."

The introductions done, Charles made a little polite small talk with the group before he was whisked away by his handlers leaving the boys and Anne with the Regiments people.

"Well one last pee brake then?" Anne said. "It's over an hour from here boys and stopping a single horse when the group is still moving is almost impossible. We meet back here in ten minutes? Then you will introduce us to our horses and hopefully we'll be off."

"Ok up you go Your Highness," Rick said as he cupped his hands for Prince Harry to step into. Rick boosted him up on the gelding's back and waited for him to find the stirrups, which were of course to long for him. After a few trial and error adjustments, Rick had them set up properly and Harry was adjusting himself on the saddle.

"The stirrups are a little longer than you are used to," Rick said. "But these are work horses not show horses and we like the stirrups long. You will also notice the reins are longer than you are used to and they are not tied together. That is for a reason as well. Keep the reins loose or you will most likely find yourself on your back. These horses are well trained and keeping a tight rein will make them think you want them to back up or stop. Neck rein or use your knees."

Rick made sure the cinch was tight, then took his mount from a waiting trooper, tightened the cinch and mounted in a single easy movement that betrayed hundreds of hours on horseback. Rick settled his rifle on his back, tightening the sling to keep it from bouncing too much and turned to face Mia and William. Mia was having a bit of a problem with the cinch on Williams saddle and Rick rode up and leaning over, pulled it tight and looped it in place.

"Can you stand up for me please Your Highness?" Rick asked and saw that what he had expected was true. The stirrups were adjusted to high. Dismounting, he handed his reins to Mia who had mounted her horse and in two quick movements had adjusted Williams stirrups properly.

"Like I just told your brother sir," Rick said. "These are work horses and we have a long way to go today. Riding with short stirrups like you are used to will be hard on the horse and hard on you."

"Keep the reins loose unless she gets away from you," Rick said pulling the reins so they made a small loop along both sides of the mare's neck. "We neck rein or use our knees. A tight rein will only upset her."

An angry whinny, followed by a colourful curse in Welsh accented English drew their attention a few yards over, where Captain White was picking himself off the ground and Princess Anne was grabbing hold of his prancing horse.

"So now you see why," Rick said, joining the laughter at the Captains expense.

"Mam," Rick said as the Princess rode up to them. "Would it be possible to take a photo of you and your nephews together? It will only be for our use mam."

"Yes you may," she replied. "After that, I want one with you and Mia with us please."

Rick pulled out his small camera and snapped the photo of the three royals together on the horses and then found a trooper who took the next photo of Rick and Mia on the outside of the three. Mia grinning ear to ear with pride beside William and Rick and Harry with their arms around each other and making rabbits ears behind each others head.

"Richard!" Emily said walking up to them with her own more powerful camera. "Behave, that is not a proper picture."

"Why?" both he and Harry said almost at the same time. "It's my picture."

Emily snapped a fast series of pictures that did not have Harry and Rick making funny faces or gestures.

"You are not the only ones in this picture," Emily said. "I am sure Mia wants a nice photo. Not one of your foolish ones."

"I thought you were staying at home today," Rick said.

"Her Majesty asked me to take pictures for her and the family," Emily said. "I'll be riding with the Premier and the Lieutenant Governor and freezing my ass off in that carriage."

"I have it on good authority that a propane heater has been installed in both carriages Emm," Anne said laughing. "So we are the stupid ones."

A preliminary bugle order from the Strathcona's bugler called everyone to attention that they were about to leave.

"Well places everyone," Anne said and the group walked their horses to where the carriages were. The red coated Mounties, with fur hats on instead of the traditional Stetsons, were forming up around the Crown Princes carriage, their steel tipped lances sparkling in the sunlight and held in the small scabbards attached to their stirrups with one hand, keeping them tight on their right legs.

The Princess Royal joined the Lord Strathcona Horse honour guard, their lances similarly housed, red and white pennants flapping in the slight breeze atop the lances, but below the spiked heads. The Strathconas chromed helmets were reflecting the suns light brightly, keeping the eyes from seeing the warm toques underneath.

The one hundred troopers of the Regiment were arranged in four lines of twenty five on each side of the single gun and its carriage and four horses. Three troopers were sitting on the ammunition carriage attached to the gun and two were seated on the left hand horse of the two pairs hitched to the gun. Rudy's troopers were in two lines of five troopers, one to each side of the gun. The blacks and dark brown horses of the RCMP, Strathcona Horse and Alberta Tanks contrasting with the rich reddish browns of the Regiments mounts. The Prince of Wales standard was flying on the wing of his carriage and the Princess Royals pennant was being carried by the Strancona standard bearer.

At a nod from Emily in the second carriage, the Strathcona's bugler played the prepare for movement signal and the Police Cruisers started off down the road, lights flashing, taking position abreast on the centre of the road heading to the highway. Four of the Regiments troopers followed them out and Elizabeth waited until they were a hundred yards down the road before she motioned her fifty troopers into motion, the national and Regimental colours uncased, but held furled by cords to keep them from flying in the wind. Then came the ten Mounted Policemen, five in front and five to the rear of the Princes carriage, with the Governor General of Canada and the Minister of Foreign Affairs and the Minister of Defence with the Prince, followed by Rudy's group arranged the same way in front and behind the gun. Next came the carriage carrying the Premier of Alberta, the Lieutenant Governor of Alberta and Emily, their carriage escorted by the Lord Strathcona Horse, led by Princess Anne and ten yards behind, the fifty Regimental troopers making up the rear guard.

The schools for miles around had bussed their students in to witness the spectacle. News vans from all the Canadian and two American, as well as the BBC television crews, were placed on both sides of the route, as well as a large number of members from print and magazine publications. Children were waving small Union Jacks and Maple Leaf flags and here and there among the crowd, miniatures of the Regiments flag could be spotted waving along with them.

Harry and Rick were keeping up with no problem to the Price of Wales's carriage as were Mia and William on the other side. They were positioned slightly behind the carriage to afford all the spectators a good look at the Prince and soon, the young teenage girls were calling out Williams name and the odd one Harry's. Both the young Princes smiled and waved, and the parade broke into a trot, preventing any onlookers from rushing the procession. The column swung north on the 2A highway and as they came abreast of the Olds Collage, an even larger crowd of students, young and old, were on both sides of the road, cheering and waving their flags enthusiastically and there were still more regimental flags seen in the crowd and more than a few blue uniforms could be seen, the members saluting as the procession went by. And then they were on the open road. At every intersection, there were spectators honking car horns and cheering as they went by.

"Oh this is fun," Harry called over to Rick as they slowed to the first walk to cool off the horses . "I wonder if you could answer some questions for me?"

"Ask away," Rick said. "If I can answer them, I will."

"Your people have their lances mounted in scabbards behind their right legs." Harry observed. "Not like the other lancers I have seen, is there a reason for that?"

"Yes sir," Rick said. "It is really simple. What happens if you leave your hand up in the air for a long time? Especially when it is this cold out. Those Mounties and Strathconas are going to be hating life by the end of the trip."

"Oh it is that simple," Harry laughed. "The difference between show and reality. What about those blue, yellow and red flags I am seeing what are they?"

"Those are miniatures of our regimental flag sir," Rick answered. "A large number of people in this area are retired members or family members of members."

"This is really uncomfortable having someone older than me calling me sir," Harry said. "I know it's protocol, but when we are alone like this can you just call me Harry?"

"Sure Harry," Rick said. "We are both just kids really."

"What's with all the girls screaming at me and Willy?" Harry asked.

"I don't know," Rick said. "Girls do some weird things. Mia was jumping up and down and screaming when she found out she would be escorting your party. I don't get it myself. Look at her, she can't take her eyes off your brother."

"You jealous?" Harry asked.

"You kidding me," Rick said. "I don't have time for girls and their weird ways."

"Auntie tells me you are a Cadet?" Harry asked. "What's that like? My dad was in the navy as a helicopter pilot for a while."

"I don't know for sure," Rick said, "I just started. It's going to be hard work though I think."

"Your dad and granddad are the leaders aren't they? Harry asked. "That should make it easier."

"No, if anything it will make it harder," Rick said. "Everyone has expectations of me, family traditions and the like. It doesn't help that my family is always at the top of their classes. But all I can do is my best."

"I overheard my dad's bodyguard tell the other one, it was the hardest training he ever did," Harry said, "and he is SAS and tough already."

"Really?" Rick replied. "I thought the Americans were way better than anyone else."

Princess Anne had dropped back and spent a few moments talking with William and Mia, now she came across to Harry and Rick's side.

"You two seem to be getting on together," she said. "Not too cold Harry?"

"Rick showed me a few tricks for my gloves and boots," Harry said. "I am quite warm actually."

"Willy's toes are getting cold and so are Mia's," Anne said, looking a little concerned. "Their fingers seem to be ok for now."

"Well Mia is a town girl," Rick said. "She is usually more concerned about how she looks than if she is going to be warm or not."

"I thought all you Canadians were smart about the cold," Anne asked.

"Are you kidding me?" Rick said. "Town people are in the cold for maybe ten minutes. They have heated cars, heated garages, heated houses. Maybe for something to do, they might go snowmobiling for an hour, but even the snowmobiles have heated seats now."

"I noticed that with my brother's carriage," the Princess said. "He actually has his jacket open."

"It's only about another fifteen minutes mam," Rick said. "You can see the water tower already. We should be turning right in a few minutes."

They chatted happily for a few more minutes and after they had turned the corner taking them off the highway onto the secondary highway that led to town, the Princess moved back to the carriage and began chatting with the occupants.

"She seems nice," Rick said, as the group in the carriage laughed at some joke Rick's mother had made.

"The newspapers make her look to be such a bitch," Harry said. "But she has a good heart and has always been nice to us."

"It must be hard to be followed around all the time," Rick said. "That's something I don't have to worry about. Nobody is interested in us."

"They will be," Harry said pointing at the top of the hill where a large group of print journalists were stationed to watch the Regiment wind through the river valley before hitting town. The whole Regiment would be in view at that point.

"Quick, look to your right!" Rick said pointing. Six mule deer, spooked by all the noise of the riders, were jumping through the snow towards the safety of the Birch trees lining the hillside.

"They are so big!" Harry said. "They are bigger than our deer back home. Are those the moose we hear about?"

"No." Rick said laughing. "A moose is about twice that size. Those are Mule deer. They have mule sized ears and they jump like that instead of run when they are scared."

Princess Anne moved back up to join her group and Rick and Harry became quiet as they reached the group of journalists who were taking pictures. The Regiment broke back into a trot as some of the journalists made to run into the street and get closer. Some were yelling questions at the Royals as they trotted by in a thunder of hoofs and made to run alongside the column, but were soon tripped, up or elbowed out of the way, by the locals who were trying to catch a glimpse of the Royals. The riders turned left as soon as they crossed the railway tracks and rode down main street with crowds of flag waving towns people lining both sides of the street.

Rick looking left as they passed the train station, saw a large number of flat deck, large box cars and passenger coaches, coupled together with several engines hooked up and ready to go. These would be the cars that the rest of the Regiment would be loading onto the next morning. The train crews were standing on the engines waving as they trotted by and Rick waved back as did Harry to the delight of the crowd, as one of the engineers let a long blast out of the trains horn.

They turned left again and now the Regiment started preening up, pulling down tunics, brushing frost from horses necks and coming into a tighter formation, almost touching knees. The standard bearers loosed the cords holding the flags and let them fly free, the red and white Maple Leaf beside the blue, yellow and red of the regiments. Elizabeth took her half of the Eagles, passed the lane entrance and stopped. The carriages and their escorts turned right into the lane leading to the barracks and barn complex where the ceremony was to be held.

The carriages came to a stop in front of a large reviewing stand, the rest of the regiment formed up on the east side of the lane at attention, rifles at the salute in front of them. The command group was also lined up on the podium all at attention and saluting, the Regimental standard lowered in salute by the bearer.

The second Prince Charles feet hit the ground his standard was hoisted on the main flag standard in the yard, an eighteen gun salute broke out from the massed battery and the band played God Save the Queen. Rick collected Harry's horse as he dismounted and then collected the Princess Royals from her body guard and then he and Mia, trailing the spare horses walked off the parade ground headed for the barns. They would miss the next part, but the horses came first and had to be unsaddled and groomed before the two teenagers could rejoin the festivities.

One of the Mounties stuck his head out of his cruiser and swirled his right hand over his head, signifying they were ready for the Regiment to make their entrance. Elizabeth looked at the Regimental Sergeant Major and nodded her head. The sergeant rode a few paces forward, turning his horse to face Rudy's people.

"The Tank platoon will prepare to march in review!" he hollered, and then after a few seconds said, "Tank platoon, March!"

Rudy's platoon, five riders abreast in front of the gun and five abreast after it, walked their horses off of the main road and into the laneway leading to the reviewing stand.

Elizabeth waited until they were a hundred yards down the lane and then she started her horse and without a word, the Regiment formed in behind her. The only sounds the horse's hooves on the road and the jangle of equipment. Not a single horse snorted or whinnied, as they sensed the importance of what was happening. Rudy stopped his platoon just to the left of the review stand centre and a few yards away from it. The gun was still in the centre and Rudy's two sections were still on each side of it.

The crowds anticipation was rising, people were whispering to each other and looking down the lane way. Then suddenly, without a word or a noise, the Regiment was there, turning the last corner into the yard. Elizabeth and the Sergeant Major were in the lead, followed by the colour party, they quietly rode to centre stage, Elizabeth drawing and presenting her sword and the Regimental colour bearer dipping the colour until it almost touched the ground. The Prince of Wales and the Royals, returned the salute and Elizabeth laid her sword on her right shoulder and she, the Sergeant and the colour party executed a flawless about face on horseback, just in time to greet the rest of the company as it rode into view in a tight column of four, the riders knees touching each other. As each column rode by the review stand, every head snapped to the right in unison and stayed that way until they reached the end of the platform, then snapped back forward. The company rode to their designated turning spot and deftly reversed direction and as they did so, Elizabeth and the colour party executed another about face, so that they were now facing the review stand. The company once again broke into two groups, one on each side of Rudy's platoon, but behind it and turned their horses so the columns were facing the podium. This whole time, not a word had been spoken, or a gesture given.

Now Elizabeth rode forward to within a few feet of the standing dignitaries, took the sword off of her shoulder, brought it up to her face, point up and then slashed it down and to the right.

"Company all present and accounted for, SIR!" she said, then without any apparent visible signals, her horse backed up to where it had started from.

"For the first time in fifty years," the Prince of Wales began, "this fine regiment will soon be going into harm's way together. I know they will do their best as they always do and shall return victorious."

Princess Anne then strode forward.

"For one hundred and fifty years this regiment and it's people has served our nations faithfully," she said. "From the very beginning, they were requested by my forefathers to come to our aide in

Afghanistan and then formed this regiment to do that and served us well."

She was holding the first honour ribbon as she said those words, then she went through them all, one by one naming the names of the engagements.

"There are more, much more than these ribbons, countless peace keeping missions, to places that the news media never covers. Assisting my nation in the Falkland Islands, the Americans in Grenada. No one ever hears about them or their great deeds, but like their great country, they come when they are asked, do their jobs and go home again."

"Once again the world needs your help. Once again a tyrant threatens the world's peace. Once again you have been called and once again you send your sons and daughters into harm's way.

"My country thanks you, the Kuwaiti people thank you, Her Majesty thanks you and I thank you. God keep you safe."

The whole regiment was called to attention and company by company they marched in front of both Elizabeth's company and the reviewing stand, the dark blue and light blue uniforms, together for the first time since Afghanistan.

Once the battalions had marched through, the mounted portion moved out, just as silently as they had moved in. There would be plenty of time to celebrate tonight. Now they just wanted to get off the saddles and warm.

After everyone had removed their tack, groomed their horses and turned them loose and then cleaned and put away the horse gear, Elizabeth called the company to order amidst the barn stalls. With some help, she climbed one of the stalls so everyone could see her.

"Good job people," Elizabeth said. "No wrecks or damage other than to our asses. Have a good time tonight, but remember, 05:00 be at the vehicle park, we have to load and be out of here by 08:00."

"Good thing my hubby is coming along then," Heidi said. "Otherwise I might not make it."

"From what I hear Liz and Rudy might have a hard time making it themselves," a trooper in light blue yelled to the laughter of the rest of the group.

"Ha ha, funny guy," Rudy said. "You just make sure you're there on time. Now everyone get out of here and get some food."

Rudy looked around to help Elizabeth down, but all he saw was her back, as she and Heidi walked toward the barn exit, grabbing Mia along with them as they went.

Rudy took his lance and started walking out of the barn toward the armoury along with the rest of the company. As he approached the door to the barn, he came across Rick struggling with four rifles and three lances.

"Private," Rudy said to a passing trooper in dark blue. "Do you think you could assist the poor cadet here? Maybe take those lances off of him with the help of some of your buddies."

"Cadet, give me the Majors and the lieutenants rifles," Rudy continued. "You keep the other two. We have to load these on the LAVs tomorrow anyway. You and Mia won't need yours for a while."

Rudy slung one rifle over each shoulder. As a hussar officer, he did not have his own rifle, this was not how hussar officers were armed historically. His rifle was already aboard his Cougar vehicle. He would drop his lance off and then go to the vehicle park to drop the other rifles off with the proper vehicle commanders.

"You can help me with these rifles after you drop yours off," Rudy said to Rick. "How did it go with you and the Prince?"

"Oh he's ok for a kid," Rick said. "He seems to be interested in a military career, but he is still just a kid. Things will change I am sure."

"So what happens now?" Rick asked.

"You hang around with me," Rudy said. "They have arranged some kind of ceremony for your sister and I. They never tell the groom anything, just to show up. Have you seen Junior anywhere?"

"Ya, he's right over there," Rick responded, pointing at the other end of the armoury where a bunch of troopers were gathered around a large coffee pot.

Rudy put the fingers of his right hand into his mouth and let go with a loud whistle which drew everyone's attention. Then he pointed at Junior and waved him over.

"Tell me you have your light blues and officers sword in your barracks," Rudy said to Junior as he walked up.

"Ya, it's there," Junior replied. "Is it that time then?"

"Well the girls disappeared into the main house and something hush hush is about," Rudy said. "We should probably be prepared."

"Right then," Junior said. "I'll meet you in the All Ranks in fifteen."

Rudy took Rick by the elbow and steered him toward the door of the armoury and as they walked out of the door he did not notice Junior grabbing several officers from both battalions and swiftly talking to them.

"Ok Rick," Rudy said. "Get your ass home and ask your dad for a sword, you're going to need it, then meet me in the All Ranks Mess ASAP. And I mean ASAP."

"Um, I don't think I'm allowed in there sir," Rick said. "I don't think I'm old enough."

"You're wearing the uniform and under arms," Rudy said. "If you get any static you tell them to see me and I'll kick their asses for them."

As Rick jogged towards home, Rudy, head down, slowly walked over to the All Ranks Mess and walking up to the bar, ordered himself a vodka shooter and two bottles of beer. He shot the vodka back in one gulp and then swallowed a mouthful of beer to cool off his throat before walking to a table and sitting down, right hand on the bottle before him, eyes on the bottle and deep in thought.

Rick burst into his father's office, catching his father and grandfather in the midst of pouring a glass of Canadian rye whiskey each.

"Pop, Rudy says I need a sword and am to report back to him at the All Ranks ASAP!" Rick blurted out before either man could say anything.

"A cadet with a sword?" Nicolas asked. "Why we must be in serious trouble don't you think Paul?"

"Rudy must be in major trouble indeed," Paul agreed. "Maybe us old coots should tag along then, just in case."

"Well it will just have to wait until we finish our morning drink," Nicolas said. "Dealing with politicians always leaves a foul taste in the mouth."

"Even with the Premier being a Black Sea German like us and not a bad guy, he's still a politician in public," Paul agreed.

"What are you three still doing here!" Emily said in exasperation at seeing the three Bekenbaum men in the office. "You know what's going on! We can't afford to be late! Where's Rudy, Richard? You are supposed to be making sure he stays out of trouble!"

"He is staying out of trouble," Rick answered. "He's at the All Ranks waiting for me and Junior. What's all the fuss about?"

"He's at the All Ranks? By himself?" Emily demanded. "You three get down there right now and make sure he stays sober!"

"And you two be back here in two hours to escort the ladies," Emily ordered pointing her finger at Nicolas and Paul. "You will behave and you will be sober!"

"Javohle mine Commandant!" both elder men yelled, jumping to attention and saluting.

"You, you!!" Emily exclaimed in frustration before swirling out of the room, her long black hair flying behind her.

"Right then," Nicolas said, laughing after she had left.

"Paul, give him your sword and show him how to hang it," Nicolas continued as he walked toward the door. "I will be right back."

Paul put his glass down and walked to the wardrobe in the back corner, opening it up and pulling down a well-worn sword scabbard and belt from the top shelf.

"This was given to me by my father," Paul said handing the scabbard to Rick to hold.

"It was given to him by his father, John and was made for him in the Old Country by his father, before his first deployment," Paul said, as Rick pulled the slightly curved Cossack blade from the scabbard.

"It is a functional blade," Paul continued, "not a ceremonial sword, like the one I will be wearing today."

Rick put it back into the scabbard and Paul helped him put it around his shoulder so that it hung across his back the hilt up over his left shoulder, adjusting the straps so that they fit his younger figure.

Nicolas walked back into the room with two items in his hands. One was an ornate sword in a jewel encrusted scabbard, the other a bottle of very old Scotch. He had a similar sword, the jewelled hilt poking up over his left shoulder on his back.

He handed the scabbard to Paul and found another glass, pouring three generous glasses full of Scotch.

"That my son is the sword Andreas was awarded for his work in Afghanistan by the Czar," Nicolas said. "It is to go to the current family leader of the Regiment. That would be you Paul."

"The one I am wearing is the one John received from the King after rescuing Tatiana from the Bolsheviks," Nicolas continued. "You will inherit it after I am gone."

He passed a glass to Rick and another to Paul after he had buckled on the sword and taking one with his right hand lifted it in the air, the other two men making the same gesture.

"The family!" he said, each man touching glasses and shooting back the Scotch.

Ricks eyes glazed over and he started to choke, unprepared for the fire the Scotch made in his throat and belly as it went down. His father and grandfather smiling as he coughed and choked, but with pride as he held it down.

"God Damn!" Rick exclaimed when he could talk. "How can you guys drink this shit!"

Now both the elder Bekenbaums laughed.

"It's an acquired taste," Nicolas said patting him on the back.

"What are you doing?" Emily demanded as she swept back into the room. "You know he's to young to drink!"

She grabbed the glass out of Ricks hand and spying the bottle on the table, filled it to the brim, before raising it to the men in salute and downing it in one gulp, slamming the glass back onto the table top.

"Damn, that's good shit!" she exclaimed, her eyes tearing.

"Now will you three quit pissing around and go rescue Rudy?" she demanded, pecking Paul on the cheek, spinning away from Paul's grasp as he tried to encircle her waist.

"No time for that," she said laughing. "Maybe later if you're a good boy." And she flounced out of the room once again.

"We better get out of here before Kat shows up or we'll all be in big shit," Nicolas said.

"To late you reprobate," Katherine said walking into the room. Unlike Emily, she pushed him down on a chair and sat on his lap as she also poured herself a generous drink, gasping as it hit the back of her throat.

"I thought you were keeping the good stuff to yourselves," she said, kissing Nicolas full on the lips. "Now get out of here for a couple of hours and let us do our female things eh?"

"Yes dear," Nicolas said returning the kiss, reluctantly letting her stand, their hands keeping touch until out of reach as she too left once again.

"Ok, let's get out of here before Rick gets into shit for being AWOL," Nicolas said rising.

The three men adjusted their tunics and swords, then together, Nicolas in the middle, Rick on the right, Paul on the left, the three Bekenbaum's walked down the middle of the lane toward the All Ranks Mess drawing a crowd of blue uniformed officers and troopers along the way. By the time they reached the mess, there was well above a hundred men following them into the mess, where another hundred blue uniformed troopers were already having refreshment, most of them from Elizabeth's company. There were also ample light blue uniforms in the mess to make the representation form both battalions about equal. Both groups were mixing freely, as men with eagles on their collars were among both groups, many having completed training with each other.

"Kurt it's been a while!" Nicolas said grabbing an older man by the shoulders and hugging him.

"It's too bad the old man kicked the bucket before he could see this day," Nicolas said.

"Ya well," Kurt said. "That's what happens when your only son gets married late in life like I did."

"Is that Rudy sitting there with is head down?" Nicolas asked. "What the hell is wrong with him?"

Rudy was indeed sitting at a table with Junior and several other light blue uniformed men, head down, still looking at the same beer bottle, now with the label pulled off.

"You too old to remember your wedding day?" Kurt asked.

"I was so scared I was almost pissing myself," Paul said.

"Naw that was because of all the vodka you drank before the wedding," Kurt said. "I know, was pouring them."

"Why so you were," Paul said laughing. "Come on let's go cheer your son up."

The older men grabbed a handful of beer from the bar each and dragged Rick along with them as they made their way through the throng of celebrating troopers to the table where Rudy was sitting.

"Is this the way you behave before you get married?" Nicolas asked Rudy handing him a fresh beer. "You dishonour my granddaughter by thinking of running away?"

"No," Rudy said quietly. "No sir, that's not it at all. I am truly blessed that a girl like Liz wants me instead of all the other guys."

"Oh it's the old, 'I'm not god enough for her' syndrome pop," Paul said.

"Ah," Nicolas responded. "I remember that well. I had that myself back when I asked your mother to marry me."

"Kat was so beautiful and had her own hotel and restaurant." Nicolas said, going quiet himself. "What did I have to offer? I was only a soldier and the only other job I had ever had was on the end of a shovel on a pipe line crew. But my sister slapped me hard and made me see the truth of things. Am I going to have to slap you?"

"Christ Rudy," Paul said. "You have two sections of land and a trucking company. You don't look so bad, for a guy and you're almost as tough as one of us. If you don't marry my daughter, I don't know what she will do."

"Excuse me sirs," Rick said. "May I say something?"

"Junior officers input is always appreciated, within reason," Nicolas said.

"My sister has been mooning over you for year's sir," Rick said. "When we were out in the bush last week together, she said she was going to get you drunk, then make you propose to her, sir. She is really, really in love with you I think. Whatever that means."

Rudy said nothing, just looked at Rick for a long minute. Finally a large grin broke across his face and he handed a beer to Rick.

"Out of the mouths of babes, parties on!" he said, chugging his beer down and calling for another. To the cheers of the group of men around him.

An hour and a half later, a worried looking captain with aide de camp insignia, threaded his way through the crowds of celebrating men to the table holding the older men.

"Sirs," he said. "The Colonels sent me to retrieve you sirs."

"Well, that's it then," Nicolas said standing, Paul rising and whistling loudly to get every ones attention.

"It's time gentlemen," he said loudly. "Finish your drinks and head to the drill hall."

"We will see you shortly," Paul said holding his hand out to Rudy. "You three had best head out right now."

Junior motioned to his companions as the elder Bekenbaums left the mess and they lifted Rudy bodily onto the table.

"To the groom!!" Junior shouted and the whole room full of men shouted Rudy's name and raised their glasses or bottles in his honour and drank a toast, before hauling him off the table and trundling him out the door toward the drill hall. They were followed by two hundred tipsy troopers, singing a bawdy marching song until they reached the drill hall and the door was flung open to reveal the gathered Regiment, past and present, male and female, the regimental and national colours at the front and British Red coats in the front row.

The grooms party pulled down their tunics and pulled their caps off, putting them under left arms. Rudy, flanked by Junior and Rick, marched up the isle way left open for them to the front of the hall where the flags were located and a priest was waiting.

Three older troopers in sky blue came forward, took their caps and they were left alone at the front of the hall for what seemed like an eternity.

Then the door at the back banged open once again and Nicolas, with Katherine on one arm and Emily on the other walked in, followed by Kurt and Ilene, Rudy's parents.

The Bekenbaum's turned to the right and stood beside the red coats and the dark blue uniformed troopers.

Kurt and Ilene, turned to the left and the sky blue uniformed troops, turned to the left and stood in their row, both groups sang in their languages together until the song was finished.

Mia slowly walked into the hall.

Heidi came next, walking slowly.

Both women were dressed in long white cotton dresses, red boots covering the showing ankles. Hair coiled around their heads with a crown of flowers holding it together and the blue, yellow and red of the Regiment in long coloured ribbons flowing around their shoulders and down their backs.

Now Elizabeth came down the aisle way.

Now as they reached the front and turned left, Mia and Heidi stood facing the priest.

Elizabeth was also dressed in a white cotton dress long to her ankles, where a pair of shiny red boots was showing. Her apron was of dark, almost black, blue with gold trim and flowers embroidered all through it. Her long unbound blond hair was cascading down to the middle of her back, a long white veil was draped over her head, covering her face and shoulders.

Paul came from her side to stand in front of her and with the help of Heidi, pulled the veil from her face, peeling it back to hang down the back of her head, revealing a tall diamond tiara on top of her curls. Paul looked into her eyes and smiled, his pride beaming, kissed her on the forehead and taking her right hand in both of his, handed it to Rudy and then nodding at the priest, walked back to his wife and parents. Emily, put her arm around his waist and held him close putting her head on his shoulder.

"Brothers and Sisters," the priest began. "These two warriors are, with their fellows, about to leave our sides as once again the Regiment sallies forth to protect those who cannot protect themselves. For a moment, let us ask our Lord to protect them if it is His Will and to see all of our brave men and women safe back home."

Not even a squeak in the floor or a sniffle in the crowd could be heard as all those present, silently prayed or contemplated the coming deployment and what it would mean. For some, they prayed for courage, not to falter when the time came, some for forgiveness of past wrongs and for the hurt they were about to do to their fellow human beings. Others prayed for their loved ones, to have the courage to do what they had to do and for help to let them come from harm, physical and mental. This was no civilian gathering. Everyone present had served or had friends and relatives that had served. They all knew what this was about and had no illusions that people were going to get hurt and possibly die, very soon.

"These two standing before us, in the traditions of their clans and families, have already pledged themselves to each other in front of their elders," the priest continued. "Now they have chosen to pledge themselves in front of you, their brothers and sisters in arms."

"I Elizabeth, daughter of Emily, daughter of Katherine, daughter of Tatiana, daughter of Elizabeth, name Rudy, my husband, in front of God and man," Elizabeth said

"I Rudy, son of Kurt, son of Conrad, son of Randolph, son of Rudolf, take Elizabeth to be my wife in front of God and man," Rudy said, taking both of Elizabeth's hands in his and looking into her sky blue eyes.

The priest put his left hand on top of both of theirs and made the sign of the cross, blessing the union and then Kurt came forward and placed his hands on Elizabeth's shoulders, turning her to face the assembly, he standing behind her.

"This is Elizabeth, my daughter, what is done to she and hers, is done to me and mine," he said, then turned her to face him and kissed her on both cheeks.

Paul stood next, gently pushing Emily away, tears streaming down her cheeks, he turned Rudy toward the assembly, standing behind him, hands on his shoulders.

"This is my son Rudy, what is done to he and his is done to me and mine, so say I," Paul said loudly, making the sign of the cross.

"So say all of us!" the massed dark blue uniforms belted out in unison, the members all making the sign of the cross.

Paul also kissed Rudy on both cheeks and then released him to Elizabeth, stepping back to Emily who grabbed his left arm with both hands, clearly getting control of her emotions.

"The families will now withdraw for a few moments to attend to the legal paperwork, while the rest of us prepare for the celebration," the priest said.

Rudy's mother and father stepped forward, as did Paul, Emily, Katherine and Nicolas. The women hugged and kissed the newlyweds and each other, the men shook hands solemnly and the Princess Royal, still in her Canadian Forces Dress Uniform, rose as did the Price of Wales. The two Royals congratulated the newlyweds and then the priest led the way for the party to exit into an anteroom at the edge of the parade floor, closing the door from the outside behind them.

The priest put his hand on Rick's chest as he closed the door, barring him from entry.

"I am sorry young Richard," he said. "It is only for the elders this time. You and Mia are to escort the princes."

"You look nice Mia," Rick said as he approached her.

"Thank you Rick," she replied. "It is nice of you to notice that I am a girl."

"Hey, I always knew you were a girl," Rick said. "But my grandfather told me it is always a good thing to compliment a girl when they look nice and I have."

"And so you have," Mia agreed, taking his preferred left arm, both of them mimicking what the adults had just done.

"I hope William noticed too!" she whispered into Rick's ear excitedly as they approached the princes.

"Oh jazus," Rick said. "Does this stuff never end?"

"If she is gushing about my brother," Harry said, "No it doesn't."

"My lady," William said, a mischievous twinkle in his eye. "Don't mind those two, they are only jealous the girls are not paying attention to them."

Mia took Williams arm and looking at Rick, stuck her tongue out at him.

"I wonder if my Lord Bekenbaum could spare a word with me before the night is over?" William asked.

"I can't promise anything sir," Rick said honestly. "I am the low man on the totem pole, but I will mention it to my superiors sir."

"As will I," William said smiling and taking Mia by the hand, walked toward the refreshments.

"Well My Lord, you seem to have made an impression on my brother," Harry said.

"What's all this My Lord shit?" Rick asked. "My grandfather is not here. I'm just a kid, Your Highness."

"Oh and I am just a kid too," Harry nodded. "Once in a while I even get to act like one. Poor William though. Things are different for him."

"When do you guys go home?" Rick asked.

"I am not sure," Harry answered. "Father has to leave tomorrow, but Aunty says she wants to stay for a week or so. Maybe I can con her into letting me stay. Would that be alright?"

"Anything that keeps me out of school is fine by me," Rick answered.

"Just what I was thinking," Harry said, holding his hand up for a high five, both youngsters laughing.

Nicolas stood in front of the newlyweds, the Royals on either side of him.

"It is time for both of you to receive your birthrights," Nicolas said. "This is never to be revealed to anyone not in this room right now, besides Her Majesty and members of the immediate Royal Family, is that clear?"

Kurt strode forward, withdrawing his sword from his side as he came and indicated for Rudy to Kneel.

"I Kurt von and zu Hoaiedle Earl of Olds, name you Rudy, my heir and successor, commander of Her Majesty's Loyal German Hussars," Kurt said, dropping his sword on Rudy's left shoulder.

The Prince of Wales stepped forward with his sister slightly behind and to one side.

"I dub you Sir Rudy, Knight of the realm, protector of the people of Our realm and of our Earldom of Olds," he said, tapping his sword on first one, then the other of Rudy's shoulders.

Nicolas motioned Elizabeth to kneel beside the still kneeling Rudy.

"I dub you Dame Elizabeth," The Princes Royal said, placing her sword on first one then the other of Elizabeth's shoulders. "Defender of Our people and of Our Earldom of Olds."

"So my granddaughter," Nicolas said smiling, as the Royals stepped back two paces so they were behind him. "You now have two Baronies, one in Germany and one here in Canada. Congratulations and to you as well Rudy.

"I cannot grant you leadership of the Host Granddaughter, that is not mine to grant, nor is it your fathers. But I can provide you with your birthright which must be held secret from all but close family members from this time forward. This is for all of our safety.

"Elizabeth, I Nicolas, Tsar of the Russias, son of Tatiana, Tsarina of the Russias, daughter of Nicolas, Tsar of the Russias, name you Grand Duchess Elizabeth Susan, third in line of succession to the Imperial Russian Throne."

He had spoken all of this in Russian and now raised her up so she was standing and kissed her on both cheeks, then stood back as Katherine placed a dark red sash so that it fell from her left shoulder to her right hip.

He then pinned a large jewelled and diamond studded broach to the sash and Paul, a similar sash now on his uniform, came forward and placed a gold Russian Imperial eagle on it. Then Emily came forward and pinned a duplicate of the Regiments crest, all in gold, beneath the eagle.

Then to Elizabeth's astonishment, the Prince of Wales bowed and the Princess Royal curtsied.

"Your Highness," they both said.

"Rudy rise," Nicolas said.

"We name you to the Order of St. George," Nicolas said, pinning a large medal to a white sash that Katherine had draped across his shoulder. "We also name you Rudy, Grand Duke and consort to Elizabeth."

"Welcome to the aristocracy, Rudy." Paul said shaking Rudy's hand. "Our families have been close ever since the days of Napoleon. Ours from Cologne and German, yours from Saxony and aligned with the British. Now we are united by marriage and soon by blood, as we are united with the House of Windsor."

"You both were sworn to allegiance to the Canadian Crown at birth and when you entered the armed forces. Now you are sworn to Our Crown by birth and marriage and we have sworn Our allegiance to the British Crown and They to Ours."

Chapter Four

Elizabeth placed her duffle bag of personal uniforms and items in the rack outside the turret, securing it with ratchet straps. The Coyote was running at high idle, pure white diesel exhaust blowing straight up in the windless morning. Climbing in the open commander's hatch, she secured her C7 rifle in the rack provided for it and dragged out a can of 7.62 ammo for the C6 mounted outside her hatch hanging it on the side of the weapon and making sure the can was full and the belt inside free and ready to feed.

Sliding back inside, she flipped a number of switches turning on radios and monitors and then ducked down.

"Everything firing up?" she asked her coms and crew chief.

"Damn cold, but ya," the Crew chief said. "It'll take a bit for the monitors to come clear, but now that we're running I've turned the electric heaters up full. You might want to put your earphones under your jacket for a bit though."

"Way ahead of you sergeant," Elizabeth said. "I had them at home with me last night. They are nice and toasty."

"How's my favourite Master Corporal this morning?"

"She's a little grumpy, but the driver's compartment has a good heater and it's smaller, she's probably getting warm already," the crew chief said.

"Speak for yourself Sarg," the driver said. "If I had a set of balls, I would have froze 'em off this morning getting this pig started. Good thing we had new batteries, it was close Liz."

"Ya well it's good for the hangovers. Another hour and we'll be loaded in the planes and then we can sleep for sixteen hours.

"Do I have comms yet lieutenant?"

"Yes mam," her comms officer said. "Visuals are going to take a while, but voice is ok."

"*Tango Force, Tango Force, Tango One, report by the numbers,*" Elizabeth said into the boom mic just in front of her mouth.

She climbed up through her open hatch in the turret and gave a quick look as the other armoured vehicles reported in, all of them running, all systems fine, so far.

"*Tang Force, Tango One is on the move. Eagle Base, Tango One. Tango Force is Mobile.*"

"Kick it in the ass Heidi, I want to be on the ramp before day-break," Elizabeth said on the intercom frequency.

"*Tango One, Eagle Four. Good luck and God speed Tango Force, we'll see you in six weeks.*"

"*Roger Eagle Four, keep the shiny side up,*" Elizabeth said, rocking back as Heidi put the Coyote into motion, pulling out of the bar-racks and onto the access road.

Once they hit the secondary highway and Elizabeth saw the ve-hicle behind her pull onto it, she slid down inside the vehicle, slam-ming the hatch shut behind her and dogging it shut. She pulled her gloves off, stuffed them in one of the oversized cargo pockets on her trousers and rolled the balaclava up over her forehead.

"Damn, what was the temp Sarge?" she said.

"Minus twenty five Liz," he said. "Supposed to be snowin' from Bowden all the way in."

"Can you see ok Heidi?" Elizabeth said.

"Ya, I'm ok until we merge on highway 2, then I'm gonna need some eyes."

"*Tango One, Tango Twelve, Tango Force on the highway.*"

"*Roger Tango Twelve, thank you.*" Elizabeth said.

"Hey Twelve, good thing you got lucky last night. I just had a look at mine and it about disappeared in this cold," another voice on the radio said.

"Ah cut Rudy some slack guys, he's only been married one day. He probly doesn't even know what it's for yet," a female voice said.

Elizabeth felt a big hand clamp on her boot as she was about to reply to the remarks. Looking down, she saw the crew chief shaking his head and putting a single finger to his lips.

"Not yet Liz," he said. "Let them have their fun."

"Infrared is up Liz," her coms Lieutenant said. "There looks like there's a fair bit of traffic on the main highway. Mostly semis."

"Ok, patch me into the CB radio net. I'll warn them once we are on the road. Heidi overpass in a klick."

"Roger Liz," Heidi said.

Two minutes later, she was accelerating onto the four lane highway. Liz looking out her turret view ports to make sure she had a clear path.

"Holy Shit!," Elizabeth heard on her earphones. *"There's a damn Tank on the Highway, shit, there's more of em.'"*

"What are you talking about? Canucks don't have no damn tanks! Woa shit, ur right!"

"North Bound traffic," Elizabeth said into her mic. *"We are a column of armoured vehicles traveling northbound. Be advised we are a column of armoured vehicles heading northbound. We will be traveling at one hundred kilometres per hour, for approximately the next hour."*

"They ain't no tanks you dummies, them there are LAV25's. We got all kinds of em in the Marines."

"Look some different than the LAV I served in. They look to be loaded for bear. Hell, five of 'em are haulin' 105's"

"I seen them markins before someplace. Shit, that's them EBB's! They go places Force Recon don't go!"

"Yo, Charley, we better find a landline and check in ASAP. If these guys are goin' someplace, chances are we're gonna get called up."

"Way ahead of ya Bubba. Drop your load in Edmonton and leave the rig there. We just been federalized. They got tickets waiting for us at Edmonton International back to Dallas."

"Good luck Marine," Elizabeth said.

"Semper FI Jany Canuck, we'll probly see ya in Reyad."

"If the yanks are calling in the National Guard, this is going to be a big deal," the crew chief said, as Elizabeth switched off the CB frequency.

"It was a big deal before they called us up Sarge, otherwise they wouldn't have called."

"There's our transport," the electronics officer said pointing at the two large AN124's sitting on the loading pads.

"Got em'" Heidi said slowing down as she approached. "Lieutenant, can you and the Sarge pull down the antennaes and swing my mirrors in for me?"

Elizabeth unplugged herself from her console, leaving the earphone combo on and pulled the balaclava back down over her mouth and nose. Pulling her thick gloves out of her pants pockets, she slid them on and then opened the top turret hatch as Heidi came to a stop, opening her turret up fully as well.

The other two crew members came out of the back of the vehicle. Each man pulling down one of the two large antennae on the rear bumpers and fastening them down to the front fenders. Then they swung the road mirrors inward so they were no longer protruding outside of the vehicle body.

Elizabeth climbed down to the ground, pushing the hatch shut before she did so and looking around, saw a group of four bundled up figures approaching from a parked G Wagon.

"Which one is ours?" Elizabeth asked the aircraft loadmaster as he came up and saluted.

"This one here mam. The Arty goes in the other one. The Pavs are already loaded on it. You'll have to split personnel between the two planes, we only have room for ninety tops on each one."

"Thanks Warrant, ok load em up,' she said.

"Good morning sirs," she said, saluting as an American Air force General, a Canadian Air Force and Saudi Army Colonel, with an American Air force Captain lagging behind, came up.

"Major Elizabeth Bekenbaum, Tango Force reporting sirs."

"A woman? I will not serve beside a woman! The Holy Koran forbids it!"

Elizabeth held her salute until the American General returned it.

"General sir, I apologize for my gender sir. It would appear that a grave mistake has been made and I will remedy it immediately sir."

"Colonel, if you would be so kind as to unload our HH60's?" she said to the Canadian Colonel. Then placing two fingers in her mouth, she blew a loud whistle.

"Unload 'em all! Back to base!"

"Gentlemen, I am sorry we have wasted your time," she said, saluting again and not waiting for a response she marched back to her now unloading vehicles.

"What the hell?" Rudy said as he and the rest of her staff officers ran up.

"Saudi Colonel doesn't want to serve with women," she said. "So I guess we go home to fight another day."

"Hold on there Major," The General said. "Let's not be so hasty."

"General, I am in command of this task force. The Saudis don't want us, no problem, we stay home. The whole damn Regiment stays home. We have women serving in all branches of the Regiment. It's no skin off our asses if we go or not. That assholes King asked for us by name. He and my father are personal friends and they have served together, with women, before."

"Listen, maybe a small compromise, just until we get this sorted out?" the general said.

"Look Liz, none of my people are female," Rudy said. "How about if the Saudi loads with us on the second plane and the rest of you load up as planned on this one?"

All activity on the ramp had stopped while the confrontation was going on and from all the hostile looks the Saudi Colonel was receiving, he knew something was not right.

Elizabeth dug a book out of her right pants leg cargo pocket and marched up to the Saudi.

"You look this Holy Koran over closely on the flight Colonel," she said tossing the book at the man. "Maybe I have a bad translation. You be sure and show me when we land, where in that book it says a woman cannot fight in or lead a troop of soldiers!"

"Alright! What are you all looking at? Get these machines loaded! You think we have all day!"

"Thank you Major," the general said. "I will smooth things over once we are airborne. I am sure the Master Warrant would not have been pleased had you gone back home. I was in his training class, he is one tough sob."

"Her mom trained me," the Canadian said. "Thanks Major. I think it was just a shock to the colonel that a woman was the commander. He was prepared to see women, just not one as the commander."

"Will you or some of your comrades be joining us colonel?" Elizabeth asked.

"You know better than that Major," the colonel said, his eyes twinkling.

"Jimmy, I want a full dossier on that major ASAP and a secure line to the pentagon once we are airborne," the general said to his aide as the two Canadians were talking.

"Liz, there is a lot of high level radio traffic going on," her electronics officer said. "I am going to put it through debugging and we should know pretty quick what is going on. I can tell you that Saudi Colonel got his ass handed to him by his bosses. Oh ya, your brother gave this to me to give to you once we were airborne."

Elizabeth took the sealed white envelope from him and exited the vehicle through the top hatch, siting half in and half out as she read.

'Liz,

Dad and I have been playing around with this toy for most of the summer and we think we have most of the bugs worked out of it. We want you to give them a try once you get in country.

They will fly about a thousand feet up and will fly for about eight hours on a tank of fuel. The electronics will work for about a hundred miles we think, best not to push it to that limit, keep it around eighty. They are not as fancy as the one the yanks have, but they work just as well. We have infrared and colour high sensitivity cameras installed as well as two high def black and white cameras.

Your electronics officer knows how to fly them and he knows who the other guys are that know how to as well. They will have to be hand tossed to take off, but should be able to land ok. I loaded both of them onto your turret last night while you guys were partying.

Good luck sis, love ya

Rick'

Taking a good look for the first time at all the gear strapped to the rear of the turret, Elizabeth saw two large hard plastic cases underneath some of the soft gear strapped there.

"They don't weigh much Liz," the Lieutenant said climbing up beside her. "Once they get up about two hundred feet, you can hardly see them or hear them. They will enhance or intelligence gathering a lot."

"Ya, I have a feeling we are going to be wayyy down on the intelligence reporting list," Elizabeth said.

"A word major?" the general asked.

"The Joint Chiefs, the Sec Def and the President have expressed grave concerns over the granddaughter of the Senator for California not only being in a war zone, but actually serving in a front line unit."

"Well general, when and if, I ever become an American citizen, I am sure that may impress me. As it is, I am not and until I receive word from my chain of command otherwise, I am in command of this task force. I will tell you the same thing I told that Saudi. It is no skin off of our ass if we go back home or not. You asked for us, we didn't ask for you."

"Message from Washington Major," the electronics officer said handing her a paper.

'Liz,

Kick Sadamm's ass hard for me. They refuse to let me go so it's up to you granddaughter.

Love

Oppa'

"That answer your questions about what my grandfather might say, general?"

"Bloody marines," the general said. "He was in Korea about the same time as your other grandfather wasn't he?"

"Not sure, but I think so. They go off together and have a few drinks by themselves when we have a gathering. My husband's grandfather was there on a battery too."

"Your uncle saved my ass in Vietnam Liz," the general said, his eyes suddenly very far away. "You need anything, you call me hear?"

"The pentagon has just been told to back off Liz, maybe we can get some sleep now," the electronics officer said as the general walked away.

"Thanks Hank," she said. She found a spot to curl up in underneath the Coyote and piling her duffle and jackets around her, laid down and was soon fast asleep.

"Wakey, wakey Bridezilla," Heidi said, kicking Elizabeth on the bottoms of what she thought were her feet. "We're on final for Frankfurt."

"Oh Jeez, just let me die here will ya," Elizabeth said.

"No can do leader mam, your legions of fans are clamouring for your attention."

"Ok, ok, don't push me and leave all my shit where it is, I just got it all comfy like."

"Call a department head meeting Hank and get me an itinerary ASAP," Elizabeth said, poking her head in the nearest hatch.

"Ok boys and girls," Elizabeth said. "We have two hours on the ground, that's it. Just enough time to fuel up, empty the toilets, grease some bearings and load some more God awful airport grub on board. So if you want to disembark and kiss the ground of *Das Fatterland*, do it quick. Myself, I find that if you've seen one airport you've seen them all. I plan on answering the multitudes of messages I am sure I have received, then falling back asleep as soon as we're air born. Questions?"

"That Saudi Colonel wants to come over and suck up Liz," Hank said waving a message over his head. "He's kind of been ordered to make nice and spend the next leg with us."

"I suppose we'll have to," Elizabeth said. "Everybody speaks German around him unless it has nothing to do with the mission.

"Ok final checks for landing and then everyone to their seats and strap in."

"Hey love, I missed you," Rudy said.

He was waiting at the bottom of the open loading ramp and they both embraced.

"Nice honeymoon I'm giving you," he said. "An all-expenses paid trip to the desserts of Arabia, flying in separate planes in fourth class."

"Well at least we don't have chickens, cows and kids along like our ancestors," she said kissing him again.

"No, we have big guns, diesel engines and big kids with big toys," Rudy said. "Even your great grandparents had a couple of months together before they went off to get killed."

"Different times, slower pace, things move faster now. At least it won't be forty or forty five degrees."

"Yet. Your mom says it gets right nasty come June."

"I don't see this lasting much more than a couple of months. The Iraqis talk big, but I don't think they have much depth. At least we will see how we match up against modern Russian equipment, even if it's not Russians manning them."

"Ah Colonel, welcome to the honeymoon suite," Rudy said, both he and Elizabeth saluting.

"Major Bekenbaum I would like to apologize for my behaviour earlier," the Colonel said returning the salute. "My uncle says I am to place myself under your command mam."

"Well actually colonel, your uncle said you are to come crawling on your hands and knees begging my forgiveness, but that bottle of Rum you have in your hand will do," Elizabeth said. "I think I will banish my new husband from my sight for the next eight hours as punishment for telling you how to bribe me. And yes I would like to see the new colts."

"How did you...You have broken our codes?"

"My electronics people are very good colonel, some of them speak your language better than you do. I myself do not. So can I have my Koran back now?"

"Yes I am sorry," the colonel said, handing it back to her. "It is a very good translation.

"My uncle said your father and your mother were both well-schooled in the Holy Koran. I should have listened."

"Ok enough of this. We will be leaving soon and I want some time with Rudy before we leave. Hand that bottle to that corporal with the red hair over there and find a place to sit. She's my driver and one of my body guards so be nice."

"Good afternoon corporal, I am to give you this bottle of rum for safe keeping and to find a place to sit for the next leg."

"There should be a few empty seats upstairs Colonel," Heidi said. "I think the General probably has some room around him."

"I am to stay close to you people."

"Well then, I have the back, behind the turret. I think the electronics wiz will be inside playing with his gizmos all flight and the crew chief likes to relax up in the turret. Liz has grabbed a nice spot underneath between the drive wheels, there might be some room down there, or between the vehicles there is some room."

"How many body guards does your commander have?"

"She doesn't need any Colonel, she's tougher than most all of us. But if I had to say, I'd say on this plane, there are almost a hundred of us. We all watch out for her."

"Maybe I could impose on you to explain why your regiment is so different than the rest of the North Americans?"

"We are not unlike you. We have a strong tribal influence and because there are not many of us, we all have to produce. Not just the males. Not all females are like me Colonel. A lot of them just want to stay home and be moms and when it is time for me to be a mom, I most likely will stay home too..."

"Liz the general wants to talk with you," the electronics officer said, tapping her foot under the Coyote.

"Argh, how much time?" Elizabeth said.

"Three hours until we land."

Elizabeth crawled out from under the vehicle, dragging her sleeping bag and the duffle bag she was using for a pillow out with her. Heidi was asleep on the top of the Coyote and Elizabeth tossed her gear to the lieutenant to store for her and made her way to the stairwell leading up to the passenger section of the huge transport plane.

She stopped at the small washroom and freshened up a bit on her way. Not much a body can do, she thought. We've been on this thing for almost sixteen hours now.

"You wanted to see me sir?" she said.

"Have a seat Major," the general said. "The rest of your battalion has already embarked and they will only be stopping for train crew changes and have number one priority all the way. They should be embarking in Texas in four days and should be joining you in no more than five weeks from then. Impressive, I wish our government moved that fast."

"I think it has more to do with being majority shareholders in the rail line and the shipping line general. Between what the family and various family members own individually, we control about thirty percent of the shares."

"Wow, that helps! Anyway, I have received your preliminary movement orders once we are in country. You will be barracked about 15 kilometres south of an oil storage and shipping town on the coast. It should be in range of your artillery pieces and after a few days of acclimatization and getting a feel of the lay of the land, you will be taking over two observation posts along the Saudi-Kuwait border. I think some of the Special Forces people want to grab some of your people and make use of your helicopters, but mostly we are in a quiet sector and I don't think Saddam wants to start anything. Once the rest of your forces arrive, things will most likely change."

"Ok, thank you sir, will there be anything else?' Elizabeth said as she caught her second in commands eye, signalling him with hand signals to assemble her officers for a meeting down stairs.

"No, we will be met once we land and further instructions will be given at that time."

After thanking the general for his time, Elizabeth, followed by her officers, walked back down to the main body of the airplane and found a spot where they could all be heard.

"Ok, we land in two hours, get your crews to check the vehicles. My electronics guy will send you the coordinates of our bivouac area and a defensive perimeter plan. I am not expecting anything for now, but we should be ready, we are less than twenty kilometres from the bad guys.

"We will be put in a couple of OPs in a few days and I want a rotation plan worked out. Also, noises are being made about behind the lines maneuvers and using our choppers. That won't be happening just yet. I want more intel than what we have right now on the situation at hand. Questions?

"Ok, go get your people and secure your vehicles, you can brief them while you're doing that.

"Hank, how long will it take you to put one of my brother's toy planes together and get it operational?"

"He gave you one of those? Outstanding. A couple of hours probably, then we will have eyes in the air for about three hours at a crack," Hank said.

"Actually we have two and he tells me they can stay air born for ten hours."

"Hot shit! That's the latest version from your daddy then. I can have one air born in two hours and the other one two hours after that. Tango Two and Three know how to operate them as well."

"Ok, get the first one up and testing, bring it back in and then number two. If everything checks out, I want one up all the time. We'll check the maps and set up patrol sectors and patch them into the Coyotes. I assume the toys have GPS capability?"

"Ya, it will take a couple of days to get the hang of flying them and the lay of the land, but it will increase our range of observation by a lot."

"OK, get your gear squared away and secured then get a seat upstairs."

Elizabeth crawled under the machine and grabbed her sleeping bag and duffle storing them back in the rack behind the turret. By the time she was finished, the cargo hold was bustling with crews making sure the vehicles and equipment were still stowed properly, within a short time the troopers were back up in the passenger area of the huge aircraft buckling in for the landing.

"All squared away Major?" the general said as she sat beside him. "Ready for departure, flags waving, bands playing?"

"No sir, we prefer the low key approach. I don't think you noticed, but we don't even have vehicle or unit numbers painted," she said. "We're just here to do a job, we'll let you people have all the glory.

"I understand you will be our liaison and we will be attached to a Saudi regiment Colonel?"

"Yes, an American Marine regiment is in overall charge, but you will be attached to one of our formations," The Saudi colonel said. "My uncle has invited you and Major Von Hoaeld to dinner and a reception tomorrow."

"I hope it's nothing fancy," Elizabeth said smiling and batting her eyes. "I left my party dress at home."

"Oh, I had not thought of that. But I am sure it will all be fine."

"Do try to leave the weapons in camp though major," the general said smiling.

"Good afternoon passengers, this is the captain speaking," came over the intercom. "We are on final approach and will be landing in ten minutes. Make sure your seats are in the upright position and the champaign and caviar are stowed away. It is 14:00 local time, the temperature is a cool 28 degrees Celsius and sunny. Make sure to put sunscreen on before you hit the beach. Thank you for flying with Bears Holiday Excursions and we hope you enjoy your time away from the snow and ice."

"Just what we needed," Elizabeth said, as she walked out the back ramp onto the tarmac placing her cap low on her forehead to block some of the bright sun. Engines were already being started and tie downs removed from the vehicles.

"I think they are here to welcome the general," the Saudi colonel said, as the band broke out with an American marching tune and the colour party and escort came to attention.

The band was drowned out by the next large transport plane taxing into position, with the third right on its tail.

"Have the lads park on the edge of the off ramp, but off the grass Hank," Elizabeth said as Hank was walking backwards in front of the Coyote slowly edging its way down onto the tarmac.

As the vehicles were coming out and deploying, Rudy came out of his aircraft and walked over to where Elizabeth was watching.

"Ah and here I thought the band and the flags were for us," he said nodding to the formation of American Marines greeting the general.

"Ya right," she said. "Hank is going to form you up on the edge of the ramp alongside us. Put your arty in the middle of the formation. We'll probably be sitting out here for a while if this is anything typical."

"Normal hurry up and wait. Hank has already radioed us about where to park. I suppose we don't know where our barracks are?"

"Not yet, come on I'll buy you a coke," she said, walking toward her Coyote.

"Major, your troopers know this is an Islamic country and that alcohol is forbidden?" the colonel said.

"Yes sir, the troops have been briefed. It should not be a problem."

"Yo Heidi!" Elizabeth yelled as she approached her Coyote. "Break open the cooler, we need three cokes out here."

"Thank you major, but I must decline," the colonel said. "I have to report in. I will check back with you shortly."

"OK if we shut down and relax a bit?" Heidi said, sticking her head out of the turret and tossing three cokes down to Elizabeth.

"Ya, tell everyone to shut down, no sense wasting fuel, we might as well relax some more. It's going to be a long afternoon once we find out where we are going," Elizabeth said, handing a coke to Rudy and climbing up to sit on a fender.

"How long will it take to get the Pavs running?" Rudy said, as the last of the three helicopters was wheeled out of its airplane and backed to the edge of the off ramp.

"Probably an hour or so. They've got enough guys with them by the looks of it."

Troopers were clambering all over the three machines, pulling blades into position and going over systems. Pilots were already in cockpits putting the electronics through diagnostics.

Rudy plunked himself beside her, opened his coke, took a swig and then kissed her, putting his arm around her and giving her a squeeze.

"Not the honeymoon I had planned," he said.

"No, you would probably have taken me out in the bush with your old beat up ford to camp in a tent for two weeks," she said squeezing him back.

"Hey, what's wrong with that?" he said, receiving a punch on the arm. "We'll make up for it once this is over. At least it's warm."

"I'm going to have to get out of this winter underwear, I'm already starting to cook," she said opening the top button of her tunic.

"Oh my, more please," Rudy said, raising his eye brows and receiving another punch for his efforts.

"All in good time love." She said kissing the shoulder she had just punched.

"We need those Pavs up and running ASAP with two troops of deep recon personal," a voice said behind them. "And we need those Coyotes on the line right now. Send your snipers over to our base, the Seals need them for a mission this afternoon."

Rudy and Elizabeth kept drinking their cokes not paying any attention to the person talking behind them.

"Do you people not speak English?" an American Marine Captain said, coming around to face them. He repeated the orders in French addressing Rudy and ignoring Elizabeth.

"Someone is speaking really horrible French, commander," Rudy said in the same language. "I think he is saying something about recon."

"Recon?" Elizabeth said also in French. "I have heard nothing. Is someone doing recon around here? Perhaps when someone from the official reception party deems it appropriate to tell us what is going on we will find out."

"Look Major Bekenbaum, this is important," the captain said still in French. "We need these troops in the line immediately."

"Heidi!" Elizabeth said, still in French. "There is an annoying man here, would you tell the crew chief to come out and deal with him. My Rudy and I are busy enjoying the sun and our cokes."

"But of course my commander," Heidi said also in French and the crew chief popped out of the turret hatch, swung the C6 on its mount to cover the captain and jacked a round into the breach.

"Officer on deck!" the Gunnery Sergeant with the captain said, coming to attention and saluting.

"So nice to see that the American enlisted men have manners," Elizabeth said still in French, returning the sergeants salute. "What can I do for you Gunnery Sergeant?"

"Mam, the captain meant no disrespect mam," the sergeant said.

"Very well if you say so. You were with us two years ago, no sergeant?"

"Yes mam, you trashed us good mam."

"Well you had the misfortune of having a marine training you instead of us," Elizabeth said. "I trust we rectified that for you?"

"Yes mam, toughest course I was ever on."

The captain finally got the picture and came to attention, saluting.

"Captain Millhouse, United States Marine Corp, National Guard mam," the captain said.

"Nice to meet you Captain Millhouse, this is Major Von Hoadle, my second in command and that is my crew chief, Warrant Eichmann on the C6 there. You may stand down now Warrant," Elizabeth said, returning the captains salute.

"Now Captain I know you are just the messenger, but my people will not be going anywhere except our barracks today. If your commander wants us for some missions, he can apply through regular channels and we will take his request under advisement. Now if that is all captain?"

"Yes mam thank you mam," the captain said saluting and hurrying away.

"That Gunny was in my second team last year," Rudy said. "He's a good man."

"Got our movement orders Liz," Hank said poking his head out the commander's hatch.

"OK, beam them to the others, LAV in the front, LAVAnti Tank behind it, then us, then the arty, Rudy behind them, a LAVAT and LAV behind Rudy. Should be no problems, but I want everyone ready. Might as well start off like we are in hostile country right off the bat," Elizabeth said as Heidi fired up the Coyote. "Tell the chopper commander to follow as soon as he can. Ignore any orders other than mine and if he gets any static, call me.

"That captain was in a line unit, he should have known better," Elizabeth said.

"It's probably his first time on active duty Liz," Rudy said. "Weekend warrior that thinks he's a hot shot because he's a marine officer. I think you clued him in. Ok I'm off."

"I'll link up with you after everyone is settled in," he said, giving her a quick kiss, then sliding off the fender and walking to his Coyote.

Elizabeth slid into her position in the commander's hatch of the turret and placed her headset on over her cap.

"Tango One, Pav One," she heard.

"Pav One, Tango One, pass traffic," she said.

"Pav One, ground crews are embarking ground transport and we are finishing final check lists. We should be air born in fifteen."

"Roger, Pav One and flight airborne in fifteen, tallyho," Elizabeth said.

"Oh, aren't we just the proper Brit now?" Heidi said into the intercom.

"Rather," Hank said. "We must uphold her ladyships honour don't you know."

"Her ladyship can uphold her own honour I will have you know," Elizabeth said kicking Hank on the shoulder as he hunched beneath her in the body of the Coyote. "You just tend to the radios and the monitors smart ass. And you just drive this thing and not hit anything miss prissy."

"Oh, my, her ladyship is in a foul mood today," the crew chief piped in. "I don't think she got enough last night."

"No respect in this crew," Elizabeth said.

"No respect at all," the crew all said, as Elizabeth shook her head laughing.

"Tango Force, Tango One, ok people we are in country now. Boonie caps off and berets on. It's time they learned who we are."

Elizabeth pulled her dark blue almost black beret out of her pants cargo pocket, replacing the olive green cap with it, angling it to the right so it came almost to her right ear and making sure the regimental crest was centred.

The crew chief gave her a thumbs up as he did the same and resumed scanning the area, his hands on the turret mounted machine gun. Being third in line, their turret was facing right covering the right flank, each vehicle alternating sides, except the first and last ones which were facing forward or to the rear.

"Five minutes to base Liz," Hank said. "The Pavs should be over head just as we get there. Should make for a good show."

"Tango One to Tango Force, laager at base, arty in the middle," Elizabeth said. *"Pavs inbound, be aware."*

"Base commander wants you ASAP Liz," Hank said. "He's got an MP Hummer waiting to escort you."

"Ya well he can wait a bit," Elizabeth said. "We get set up first. Just blow by the Hummer."

"Woa shit!" the MP Sergeant said, as each left hand machine gun trained on him as they went by. "Don't these guys know we're allies?"

"Don't look now," the Lieutenant sitting in the passenger seat said. "That PAV hovering to your left has its guns trained on us."

Another of the impressive helicopters flew over their heads and circled the spot chosen for the regiment to barrack, circling around with the door gunner scanning the area with his weapon. It was soon joined by a second one and as the last LAV passed, the commander waved at them from his turret and the helicopter covering them, flew off to join its comrades circling the bivouac area.

"Don't they know we are still at peace yet?"

"That's the difference between professionals and weekend warrior's sergeant, these guys are always ready. Follow them and let's see if we can talk to their commander."

"Wow, they're already setting up a perimeter," the sergeant said as they drove up. "Look, they have com centre going already and the arty is almost ready. Vavavoom, check out to two lookers coming out of that APC. Wish our admin types looked that good."

"Look again sergeant, they both have crossed rifles on their collars and the one on the right is an officer."

"Excuse me mam, I wonder if you could direct me to Major Bekenbaum?" he said in French, saluting.

"So nice to see the US Army has some manners," Elizabeth said in the same language, returning the salute. "You found me Lieutenant."

"Yes mam, sorry mam. The Colonel has ordered that you are to accompany me to his office mam."

"I will be along as soon as my people are settled in Lieutenant. You can hang around or take off. I am sure my driver can find it."

"Yes mam, I am ordered to provide transport to and from the meeting mam."

"You're going to need another Hummer then lieutenant. My second in command will be coming along and our security detail."

"Yes mam," he said saluting and walking back to his vehicle.

"Call in another Hummer sergeant, we are taking more people than planned."

"If these guys are French, why are all of them talking German?" the sergeant asked.

"You got me there sergeant. I was just told to speak French to them."

"Get me the company commanders for a meeting Hank, then you guys change out of those greens and into the desert cammo."

"Sure Liz," Hank said. "Eagle Two is on hold for you, secure satellite link."

"Hey Pop, how's it going," Elizabeth said into the large telephone hand set.

"Just crossed into North Dakota, Hank says you made it ok?" Paul said.

"So far so good dad."

"Ok keep doing what you're doing. Don't let them railroad you into any missions without them having a good reason and better recon. They're already bugging me about it. You can defend yourselves, but no offensive missions unless you think it is ok."

"Yes sir. How's the train ride?"

"Not boring for me. Paper pushers are trying to micro manage everything from the Pentagon and our Canadian Chiefs people don't like being bypassed. It's a cluster Liz. Your mom sends her love. Keep your head down."

"Thanks pop, love to mom."

"Alright people, everyone changes into desert cammo," Elizabeth said to her commanders. "Get the vehicles and guns under netting and set up a perimeter watch schedule. I want the helos on a ten minute standby. We are weapons free for defence and nobody goes anywhere without my say so. If somebody objects to strongly, you have my permission to arrest them. Questions? No, alright then, Rudy you and your security detail come with me."

"Ok lieutenant, take me to your leader," Liz said.

"We come in peace," Heidi said, flashing the peace sign and smiling at the sergeant as she jumped in the back seat, Elizabeth in the middle with the warrant on the other side.

"What did she say?" the sergeant asked. "Christ they're loaded for bear."

"What did you expect dummy, we're in a war zone," the lieutenant said.

The group drew every eye in site as they came out of the Hummers at the command post. It looked like they were the only ones armed with more than a pistol.

"Welcome Major," the Marine Colonel said in badly accented French, sticking his hand out to Rudy as the two Canadians stood at attention saluting.

"Is there a reason why everyone is speaking French?" the General said in English. "At ease."

"Why, I was told they only understood French sir," the colonel said.

"Explain yourself Major Bekenbaum," the general said.

"Yes sir," Elizabeth said in English. "The Marine captain that approached us with inappropriate manners and orders only assumed we spoke only French as we were ignoring him sir. Luckily his gunnery sergeant saved the day for him by reporting to us in the proper manner sir. We took into account he was only a National Guardsman sir."

"I am also being told you are disregarding orders Major?"

"Yes sir. My people have only just finished unloading from a sixteen hour flight sir, we have been on the ground for just over one hour. We are eight time zones away from home and left minus thirty degrees to plus twenty. We need to set up our defensive perimeter, our aid station and repair facilities. We need to establish comms and intel resources and find out who and where our allies are, as well as any possible enemy threats. We need logistics for our vehicles and aircraft. My air and ground crews need familiarization sorties. We have enough fuel for twelve hours of operations, ammunition, for the artillery, helicopters, vehicles and men is limited to what we could carry. We have fresh food for two days and MRE's for ten.

"So, no sir, my people will not be carrying out any missions at all unless to defend themselves until those issues are rectified. My primary mission is to prepare our base for the rest of the regiment's arrival. To gather intel for them, set up logistical support and then to assist you in recon missions. I understand we will be occupying two of your observation posts, which will result in the loss of use of two of my Coyotes and two LAVs, plus fourteen troopers. I only have at my disposal four Coyotes, two of which are not fully trained. I have two command Coyotes, which will have to serve as our command and control until the rest of the regiment arrives. All of my vehicle crews and air ground crews will have to provide their own maintenance and repairs until the regiment arrives and everyone will be building the base.

"I do not see us being prepared to conduct offensive actions for at least two weeks and as we are not in an active war or danger of imminent attack, I see no reason for this to change. Of course if the situation changes I will reconsider our readiness, sir"

"That is unacceptable general!" the colonel said. "I will report this to Swartzcoff and put an end to this nonsense!"

"With respect Colonel," Elizabeth said. "You may report this to whomever you want. I accept orders from the Regimental Master Warrant Officer, the Regimental General and the Queen. In that order sir.

"I am authorized to receive requests for deployment from my allies and to act on them as I see fit. My terms of engagement at this point are to defend my people at all costs and we are weapons free to defend ourselves at any time. This may be contrary to your rules of engagement, but those are ours. And I will only say this once, we will defend ourselves vigorously if we receive fire from any and I mean any quarter, SIR!"

"Alright relax, both of you," the general said. "I am aware of your orders Major Bekenbaum, as I am aware of the terms of your regiment's terms for deployment. Colonel, I think that once you have worked with these people for a time you will come to rely on and respect their capabilities.

"Major, we will be working to rectify your logistic issues ASAP and I believe the colonel will be ready to provide you with personnel to assist with your familiarization tours. When will you estimate you will be ready for that?"

"Tomorrow morning, I believe I and Major von Hoadle will be available to see the observation posts. Then we will be able to schedule our people to come in and work with your people. My pilots tell me they will be ready to begin flying with your people tomorrow morning as well, for familiarization flights only. My intel and comms officer is ready to meet with your people anytime. But as I said earlier, my primary mission is to set up our base for the Regiments arrival. Everything else is secondary."

"If we were to provide you with some help in that regard, would that be acceptable?" the General said.

"Yes sir. Depending on the type of help and the numbers of people, it would shorten the time a lot."

"OK Colonel, send an engineering officer over there right away," the general said. "He needs to assess the situation and give whatever help you can give them. We need these people fully operational AS-AP."

"Yes sir. Right after this meeting general," the colonel said.

"OK, we all have to make the best of what we have," the general said. "I just wanted this meeting to clear the air and for you two to meet each other. If there is nothing else?

"Alright, you are dismissed Majors. Get back to work."

"Well she certainly can't be pushed around," the colonel said. "And she's right. I would have done the same thing."

"In our army she would be a general already and her husband would be a colonel. They have just under three hundred troopers here and they are better than two battalions of your National Guardsmen. Half of the combat troopers have been in some very nasty places with the SAS, Delta and Seal teams. Or have been deployed in half a dozen hotspots the UN or Nato has needed them. That young lady has more combat time than either of us. Her daddy, the Master Warrant, pretty much developed the counter insurgency and rapid response tactics we all use. Her granddaddy, the general, saved our asses big time in Korea and if you think she is tough, wait until you meet her momma. Her great granddaddy pretty much set up the original special forces group in WW2 and the original SAS copied their tactics in the desert. The whole regiment are born and bred warriors."

"Ok, I get it. How come we never hear anything about them? Do they have a name?"

"I have seen their regimental colours colonel. They have campaign ribbons from before they came to Canada over a hundred years ago. The just call themselves The Regiment and they generally let the regiment they are serving with take all the glory. We just call them the Bears and Eagles because of their badges. Legend has it they were Cossacks, another legend says they were Prussian Hussars. Somewhere in the middle will be the truth."

"Well, I think if you don't mind, I'm going to collect my lazy engineer and head on out there. We need these folks doing their jobs like yesterday."

"Well that went rather well, sort of," Rudy said as he and Elizabeth walked up to the MP Hummers.

"If we let these guys push us around before we are ready Rudy, a bunch of our people will die or get wounded for no reason," Elizabeth said.

"Alright Lieutenant, you can take us back to our new home now," she said in English.

"Excuse me mam?" he said. "You speak English?"

"Why yes Lieutenant, my mother is from California and Quebec is three thousand kilometres from my home and English is the language of choice where we come from. We were only speaking French to be polite."

"Oh. Yes mam, sorry mam," the flustered MP officer said. "Um, I am afraid your body guard disappeared on me mam."

"Well then, they will just have to find their own way back then," Elizabeth said. "More room for us in the Hummer. Major, place Sergeant Zimmerman and Warrant Eichmann under report for being AWOL. Let's go Lieutenant, I am late for my hair and nails appointment."

Camouflage netting was over all of the vehicles and artillery, when they arrived and the camp was a buzz of activity as rifle pits were being dug and revetments being prepared for the vehicles. Troopers were busy with paint brushes changing the vehicles from their dark forest green camouflage to the desert terrain they were now in. Large antennas were already up all around the camp and there were two Hummers parked in front of Elizabeth's Coyote.

"Thanks for the lift Lieutenant," Elizabeth said as she exited the vehicle, walking toward her vehicle.

"That better be my tent over there Hank, or I will have your balls for breakfast!" she said as the MPs drove away.

"No fear my commander," Hank said. "All is in order."

"How much did the Hummers set us back Zimmerman?" she said.

"Two cases of the Regiments best Liz," he said. "Heidi got the paint for two bottles."

"We have any left?"

"Four more cases, but the boys have the still up and running already. We won't run short."

"Low key Warrant, low key. We don't want any trouble with the locals."

"No problem Liz, the boys on the still have been in country before."

"Rudy dear," Elizabeth said. "Please fine the Warrant his desert for this evening and the Sergeant one massage for her commander for being AWOL and we will hear no more of this matter. Then you will go about and see how the troops are making out while your CO gets a well-deserved massage and a beauty snooze before supper.

"Warrant, you are to ensure that your CO is not disturbed unless the world is coming to an end for the next three hours."

"Yes mam!" both men said saluting and walking away.

"Heidi, get your lazy ass over to my tent. My neck is killing me!" Elizabeth said walking to the tent.

Chapter Five

"Richard, put your books away and join me in the office would you?" Nicolas said.

"What's up Oppa, nothing happened to pop or Liz did it?" Rick said, as he joined his grandfather in the office he used on the main floor of the house.

"No nothing like that Gadget," Nicolas said using the nickname the family had given Rick. "Grab a beer and sit down. Your mother's instructions were quiet specific. That I have weekly meetings with you to discuss your school and other activities. It's Friday, so here we are."

"Oh it's just more of the same old boring stuff Oppa, ah fresh cool beer," Rick said. Both of them were speaking German as was normal amongst the colony residence when they were alone.

"Nothing big going on for the weekend?"

"I think there is a party and dance at school Friday night, but I'm going to pass on it. It's my weekend training session."

"So you have made the commitment to serve then?"

"Ya, Liz and I had a good discussion on it when we were in the bush. What she said made a lot of sense. I'm not going to guarantee a top level or even an ordinary Eagle though. I think I might make a Bear though. Just my technical abilities and my fire arms skills and physical abilities should let me pass."

"Your marks are not good enough for us to send you to the RCMC Gadget." Even with his family connections, the Royal Canadian Military Collage only selected the highest qualified. Candidates. "Unless you bone up on them, you will at best only achieve Warrant Officer."

"Hey, if it was good enough for pop, it's good enough for me." Rick said. "Besides, we have enough Bekenbaum officers around here. Somebody needs to do the work. There are also a lot of fellows that need the money and have studied hard all through school to make to be officers. Just being allowed to serve is good enough for me Oppa."

"And your Russian? How is that progressing?" Nicolas said in Russian.

"Slow," Rick replied in a thick accent. "I try and speak it as much as possible. My understanding is not bad. Writing is a chore."

"Keep at it, I think we will be needing it before long. You and I will talk in Russian from now on ok?"

"Sure that will help."

"Alright, here is your first royalty check. It's not much, but you should be able to buy a few toys with it."

"A thousand dollars! Royalty check?" Rick said. "For what?"

"Your father, as your legal guardian, registered a patent on your flight control and video enhancement protocols for the Adlers Gadget. We have sold the nonexclusive rights to those patents to several American, British and German aeronautical firms. In addition, we have a team of the company's electrical engineers working on upgrades to your design. You receive ten percent of any profits generated by those patents and it is placed in a trust for you. The family has decided to grant you a portion of that trust as an income for you. This is a standard agreement the company uses for any patentable designs we receive."

"Can anybody submit? My buddy Harold is working on an updated fuselage design that is showing promise," Rick said.

"Yes and as a referral, we will give you two percent of his royalties. Keep that in mind," Nicolas said. "That's how we generate a lot of the company's income Rick. Bombardier has expressed an interest in obtaining marketing and manufacturing rights for the Adlers as they are. This might be just the right time. Does he have a working proto type?"

"Ya, we can make it fly. I haven't worked out all the finer details on the electronics package yet though. We can take off and land with this one and it is a lot larger and has a more powerful engine package. We think it can stay up for ten to sixteen hours, but we haven't had the chance to test it for that long yet. Fully configured, the video package will be about double what it is now."

"I'll make an appointment for him to bring it by for a test flight for our engineering people." Nicolas said.

"Fantastic! I will be able to buy a few test devices for a further enhancement we are working on with this check. If it works, you might have a second generation bird to test before we head out to basic training this year."

"You are in the same grade? You get along?"

"Oh yes, he's my best bud. He's our middle line backer, both of us get a lot of ribbing about being Geekazoids in the locker room," Rick said.

"A brain and an athlete, just like someone else I know. Speaking of which, why the low grades Richard? Your math and English scores should be much higher. Is being the defensive captain on the football team taking too much of your time?"

"No not really. Maybe in the fall during the season, but not now. School is just boring grandpa. I do enough to pass. I just want to finish and get in the real world. I learn more hanging around the ranch and with you and pop. Now I am focusing on my Russian and getting ready for basic. I hope school is over soon."

"Soon enough Rick, soon enough. I am going to assign you and Harold to the same rifle team. Your whole grade will be one company. Do you know where Harold stands as far as the regiment?"

"Oh he'll be an Eagle Oppa and an officer. He wants it badly."

"OK, get out of here, counselling session over."

"Does he remind you of some one?" Katherine said from the doorway, watching her grandson barrel his way through the kitchen to the outside door.

"Ya, my granddad, he even looks like him more than a bit."

"Really? I haven't seen much of the guts or glory in him." Katherine said.

"You haven't been paying attention at the football games then dear. He's probably the best cornerback in Canada. I have NFL teams and NCAA teams clamouring for a look at him." Nicolas continued.

"Andreas was much more than a military man Kat. He was a farm hand first and an accountant. He had very good business instincts and always had his eye on the bigger picture. That's why we are here."

"Yes and an outstanding leader and family man," Katherine said. "He has passed that on to all of you. I can't understand why Richard has no girlfriends. When I was his age all the star athletes had girls clamouring all around them."

"Liz says he has the pick of the crop," Nicolas said. "All he has to do is look at a girl and she swoons away. She says he's more interested in hanging out with the guys and playing with his toy airplanes. He's had a few casual deals, but nothing serious."

"Sounds like a Bekenbaum" she said. "It sounds like we have to go chasing for you guys if we want you."

"And rightly so. We are the best of the best and a little competition for our attention goes a long way. Ow that hurts! Do you guys learn that or is it a genetic thing. Omma used to punch Oppa the same way."

"That's a trade secret. Now come along with me and I'll show you another one," she said flicking her hair and hitching her right hip, before she giggled and raced up the stairs with Nicolas in hot pursuit.

"Oh Major dear, nappy time is over," a cheerful Heidi said tossing a pillow at Elizabeth. "Your loyal subordinates are waiting your beck and call dearie."

"Argh shit, is it time already?" Elizabeth said.

"Sorry to ruin your dream of Rudy ravishing you, but yes it is time. That Marine Colonel just showed up with an engineering Colonel and the Saudis will be here for your dinner date in three hours. Your desert cammos are on the end of the bed and I have a team pressing another set for your dinner. It's going to be tight for you to do your tour, meet with the Yanks and be ready for the Saudis, so get at it girl."

"I should have done like you, become an enlisted man, gotten married and had a couple of kids."

"But you still would be here like I am," Heidi said. "If you couldn't take a joke, you shouldn't have joined."

"Good afternoon Colonel, good of you to drop by," Elizabeth said, saluting as she came out of her tent. "Would you care to join me on my rounds? I want to inspect our positions before the Saudis arrive."

"This is my Engineering Officer, Major," the colonel said. "He will be evaluating the manpower and equipment needs you will require to build this base. We want it done yesterday. We really need you people in the field major."

"Your people have done a lot of work in a short time Major," the engineer said shaking her hand. "You have dug rifle pits and partially dug in your LAVs, you have a three foot wide and three foot deep trench dug around the camp, the dirt piled up to make a wall and machine gun emplacements all along the wall."

"I wish this was my idea Colonel," Elizabeth said. "But we learned it from the Ancient Romans. We don't usually dig in like this at the end of every day like they did, but this is going to be our permanent home while we are here and we want it as secure as possible.

If we had some heavy machinery, I would expand the ditch to six feet wide and deep with a wall and rampart. But this will do for now."

"I should say so, I'll have a couple of backhoes over here tomorrow."

"If you don't mind Liz, I am going to send some of my battalion commanders over here in the morning. Some of them have been in country for a couple of months and don't have half the defences you have," the Marine colonel said. "Maybe it will light a fire under their butts."

"No problem Colonel. The Saudis have asked us to do some joint training with them. Perhaps a surprise attack or two might be arranged?"

"Oh I like how you think Major," the colonel said. "I have just the unit in mind for that too. Thanks for the tour Major and could you have one of your people send over to the Engineers your list of requirements and priorities with one of those newly acquired Humvees of yours in the morning?"

"Humvees?" Elizabeth said. "We have Humvees now? The Saudis are being generous I guess."

"Ok Major, you stick to your story," the colonel said. "I can't prove it anyway, just keep it low key and not to much, or too obvious, ok."

"Warrant Eichmann, give the colonels a case of the good stuff," Elizabeth said. "Each, then I want to hear about these new Humvees we seem to have acquired."

"Why so considerate of you Major," the colonel said. "It is very difficult to obtain any of the good stuff around here and I hear yours is most excellent."

"All in the spirit of cooperation and free trade sir," Elizabeth said smiling.

"You know, if a couple of six by six transport trucks went missing from the raid, we would have to chock them up as combat loses wouldn't we colonel?" the engineer said.

"Yes I believe you would be correct on that colonel," the marine said. "Vehicles get damaged beyond repair during training exercises all the time. Just make sure you change the vehicle identifications to Canadian next time Major. It's a dead giveaway when you don't. Have a good day Major."

"Yes sir, thank you sir. Zimmerman get your sorry butt over here!"

"What's up?" Heidi said.

"Christ, you left the bloody Yank ID's on those stupid Humvees Heidi."

"Oh shit, sorry Liz, I must be tired. I'll get someone on it right away."

"Warrant, tell Hank I want a breakfast meeting with my department heads in the morning ok? And tell Rudy he needs to be here in an hour for the Saudi meeting."

"I have asked you here this morning to brief you on a training mission our allies are going to be conducting" the Marine colonel said. "It has been some time since they have been involved in large scale operations and have asked for some help from us so they can get up to speed. I have selected your battalion because you are the very best the Marine Corp has in country and they can then gauge how much more training they will require, before we place them on full operational status.

"Marines, I give you Major Elizabeth Bekenbaum of the Canadian Army. Major?"

Elizabeth stood, walked up to the colonel saluted and took her place at the podium, in front of the assembled battalion officers, turning a deaf ear to derogatory remarks about the Canadian army and female combat officers.

"Marines," she said. "At some point this week we will be attacking your base. Our objective will be to incapacitate your ability to function as a combat force. We will be using every weapon we have available. It will be loud, it will be chaotic and it will be as real as we can make it without actually firing real rounds. We are a little rusty and there are not to many of us, but we aim to take this base and render it useless. You had better be good and you had better be ready, or this little incompetent female combat officer from a third world banana republic will have your balls for breakfast. Have a good day now ya'all."

"So, Major, when do you think you will be springing this little surprise?" the colonel asked as he escorted Elizabeth to her Humvee.

"Now it wouldn't be a surprise if I told you would it colonel?" she said. "To be honest I don't really know. My people will let me know when I get back to camp when we will be ready and I will go from there."

"Everybody here?" Elizabeth asked as she walked into the large tent they used for a mess hall.

"Yes Liz," said her Warrant. "Attention, Officer ON Deck!"

"We have been tasked to raid an American Marine encampment as a training exercise. We are a little rusty in these types of operations and can use the experience. Especially from the second battalion guys, they have for the most part not been involved in these types of ops.

"Rudy, you and I will plan the raid and you will lead it. I want to observe this time. It will be a full meal deal. I want artillery and the Pavs involved. The colonel is not happy with how his troops are deployed and wants to teach them a lesson. This is not a reserve or National Guard Unit people, it is a regular Marine battalion and from what I could see they are way over confident.

"What I would like to see, is a similar operation to what NAJ pulled off in Montana in WW2. We have regimental calling cards?"

"Yes mam," one of her company commanders said. "Never leave home without 'em."

"Right same deal then, leave them where they can be seen to the most embarrassment possible.

"The next part of the deal is, I want at least two six by sixes loaded to the nuts with fuel, ammo, food, anything you can think of that we need and can get a hold of fast. Hank, I want the toys air born over that base now and aloft as much as possible. We need hard intel. I want to hit them about three am Wednesday morning. They will be bored by then. Ok make your plans, coordinate with Rudy and be ready. Questions?"

"Yes mam," an artillery captain said. "Will we be allowed to play?"

"Yes they are in range. Smoke and light show only. Rudy will have your targets for you and the time schedule. You Pavs will land an initial strike force just before the main force hits them and then I want you flying top cover. Anything else?"

"OK get at it and let's show them what a third word banana republic can do."

"Colonel, your people seem a little bored out there," the Marine colonel said to the lieutenant colonel in charge of the battalion.

"Oh, we don't expect them until Friday or Saturday Colonel," he said. "Besides, we have recon people watching their base and they will give us at least an hour or two warning. You can't move that many people around without us noticing it.

"No fear colonel, my recon team is the best and my boys won't let you down."

"You better be right colonel, good night then."

"JESUS CHRIST!" the colonel said as he was rocked out his bunk by a series of loud whistles and bangs, star shells exploding all around the base and the sound of machine gun fire and helicopter blades overhead. Already laser hit detectors were registering hits all over the base. He was just tying his boot laces when his barracks door was kicked open and a black faced trooper burst in, fired three quick rounds at him and flicked a card on his chest.

"Bang your dead colonel," the trooper said and disappeared back out the door, gun fire and laser hit detectors going off all through the building.

"SHIT!!" the colonel said, as he heard the roar of engines and twenty millimetre cannon and grenade launchers joined the sounds of crew served weapons and personal weapons going off. Flashes and smoke canisters simulating hits were going off all over the camp and three helicopters were circling overhead, firing at any and everything.

After what seemed to be an hour, a red flare was fired overhead and the attack as quickly as it started, was over.

"What the Fuck just happened!!" the colonel said. "I want a report and I want it right now!"

"Gentlemen," Elizabeth said once again in front of the Marines, this time with Rudy and her command team at her side and addressing the whole battalion from a microphone. "This morning you were subjected to an intense and overwhelming raid. The raid lasted only twenty minutes from the first artillery shell fired to the last. In that time we estimate that you lost sixty percent of your buildings, all of your command and control personnel and equipment and fifty percent casualties. We had two casualties.

"You were over confident and lazy. We had your heavy guns incapacitated within seconds. Your crew served weapons and guard vehicles disabled and we got most of your people and machinery trying to deploy or still in barracks. Had this been for real most of you would be dead right now."

"All this was accomplished by under two hundred troops and ten light combat vehicles from a third rate banana republic commanded by a woman.

"The Proud, the Brave, my ass! The arrogant, stupid and dead Marines, more like. Oh and your high and mighty Force Recon? They are walking back to camp in their shorts and t shirts. Just who do you think trained the people that train them? Next time you people have the privilege to serve with the regiment, recognize it for what it is.

"Colonel at this time I cannot allow my people to serve alongside your people. We don't trust them."

"Major I agree with you fully" said the colonel, who came to attention before her and saluted.

The Colonel looked out at his troops, hands on his hips and a scowl on his face.

"You people suffered a ninety percent loss in heavy guns and crew served weapons, sixty percent loss of vehicles, four trucks and four LAVs totally destroyed and written off the books. Seventy percent casualties in personal. In effect people, you were wiped out!

"This young lady employed almost exactly the same tactics her granddaddy used against the army on a practice raid in Montana during WW2. He achieved the same results and he didn't have armoured vehicles, helicopters or artillery. Tactics he developed fighting the Germans for two years in the desert before America entered the war. Tactics he had modified from the ones his father had used against the Turks and Germans in the First World War right in this very same area you are standing in. Very rarely sustaining more than a few loses. Later her grandaddy saved everyone's asses in Korea. He held the Chinese when everyone else ran, including us, at great cost to himself and his regiment. They say you could walk down that hill and never step on the ground from all the bodies. This regiment received two Congressional Medals of Honour, three Victoria Crosses and a Presidential Unit Siltation for that action. In Vietnam, this young ladies uncle saved our asses more than once and his company was the deciding factor in the taking of Hamburger Hill to his personal cost, as it cost him his career from the wounds he suffered attacking a machine gun bunker and destroying it.

"This is the most highly decorated and professional regiment in North America and possibly all of NATO. If this is what two hundred, half of them support troops can do, I can see why we wanted the whole regiment. In three weeks, three thousand of them will be here, fully equipped and trained. You think on that for a bit and then you think about why they were put with us.

"I have never been so embarrassed," he said holding up a calling card in his hand. "I got this within minutes of the start in my own barrack room. Battalion Attention!"

Then he turned and faced the Canadians.

"Battalion! Salute!"

The Canadians returned the salute, smartly turned and marched off in the stiff high swinging arm march the Canadians used.

"I warned you Lieutenant Colonel. You get these people up to snuff by the end of next week or I will have your ass! A Goddamned National Guard Unit would have done better than you! Get those assholes in the skivvies over here!" he said pointing at the group of bare foot men hobbling into camp as the Canadian command group left in their Coyotes. The Coyote crews calling out insults to them as they went by.

"The mighty Force Recon, the best of the best! What the hell is this, what do I see. The high and mighty SEALs too. Oh my God! Get out of my sight before I lose more of my temper!

"Master Gunnery Sergeant!"

"Sir!" the Gunny said.

"Those people need some remedial training starting in ten minutes. I want them fully clothed with full packs and weapons loads and on the march. Every day for a week, is that clear?"

"Aye Aye Sir!"

"Everyone out of my sight! Now I have to find a way of reporting this to Shwartzcov without making us look to bad. Christ what a cluster fuck!"

"Ok people, tell your troops mama said well done," Elizabeth said. "The intel Hank gave us was spot on, but the arty was a tad slow and the first few rounds were slightly off target. Once we have enough real ammo for practice I am sure that will improve. The Pavs were also a bit late, but they made up for it afterward in top cover. Ground operations went smooth both inbound and out bound, once again, the Pavs covering the exit. Well done.

"Casualty report?"

"Corporal Heinz twisted his ankle repelling out of the helo. When he landed, his right foot hit a bottle laying on the ground. Sergeant Zimmerman slightly jammed her right thumb when the door of the Hummer she was trying to steal didn't open right away. Both injuries that did not stop or hamper their performance of the task mam. But we had to report some casualties or it would have made it look worse for the Yanks," Rudy said.

"We now are the proud owners of four Humvees, two new LAVs, complete with ready ammo for our guns and four six by six trucks loaded with as much fresh food as we could toss into them. We should be alright until the Saudis supply us."

"I have a report from Eagle Base, that an Antinov full of fresh beef, potatoes, small arms ammo, twenty mike ammo, grenades for the launchers and enough artillery ammunition for them to run two major operations is leaving tomorrow," Warrant Eichmann said.

"Ok, Rudy schedule practice for the arty once the shells have arrived. Anything else?"

"Man you should have seen the look on that Colonels face when I tossed the calling card on his lap and said bang your dead," Rudy said. "It was priceless."

"I'll show you video of the chaos Liz," Hank said. "Those guys did not know which way was up down or sideways."

Elizabeth let them banter like this for a while. Laughing about their exploits, both pro and con. This would be going on all over the camp she thought. Troopers bragging and making fun of themselves and their opponents.

"OK people," Elizabeth said. "The Yanks, especially the Marines are proud people, they will not take this lightly, so don't make the same mistake they did and get to cocky or they just might do the same thing to us. Keep on the training and train hard. Hank, I want the toys in the bad guys territory starting today and I want some hard targets identified. Ammo dumps and supply points mostly. Anything else?

"Ok, every Sunday morning here, same time, until the regiment gets here."

"Liz, the Recon and Seals will be marching by in about ten minutes for 'extra training.'" Hank said.

"I would like to see that," she said. "Are you in contact with them?"

"Yes, the Master Gunnery Sergeant is supervising the training from his Humvee, why?"

"Ask him to find a few seconds for me would you?" she said. "I'll be on the wall. Come Rudy dear, let's observe our Allies. Do you think your damaged pinky will hamper you in escorting us Sergeant? I wouldn't want to hinder your recovery now."

"Bloody officers is all da same," Heidi said. "I'll have you know it was my thumb not my pinky and it will take months to get my nails proper again."

As requested, the gunnery sergeant stopped the punishment tour in front of the gate and had them form up at attention inline.

"Arru, Arru, I think I smell seals," a trooper on the gun mount on the right side of the gate joked, his troop mates all laughing at his seal imitation.

"ACHTUNG!" Elizabeth said, "Corporal, front and centre with your team, now!"

She took her time returning the corporals salute, then marched up until she was nose to nose with him.

"I will not tolerate behaviour like that in front of my Allies corporal!" she said in English. "Do I make myself clear?"

"Yes mam! Sorry mam!" the corporal said, also in English.

"Your behaviour has embarrassed me and the regiment in front of the Master Gunnery Sergeant. I will not tolerate it. You and your team mates are fined one weeks pay and you will join the Master Gunnery Sergeant in his training exercises for the rest of the week. You will report to the Master Gunnery Sergeant every morning before he leaves his barracks and you will march to his base and back again after the training. Is that clear?"

"Yes mam!"

"Now get your full combat loads and get after the formation, move! You people on the other gun mount! You will take over this mount as well as your own and it will be for the whole week! I will not tolerate unprofessional behaviour from my people!"

"Thank you so much for stopping by Gunny," Elizabeth said. "It's been a long time. I hope we haven't set your training schedule to far back?"

"No mam, it's a pleasure to see you again mam," the gunnery sergeant said. "I trust Master Warrant and Colonel Bekenbaum are doing well?"

"Yes Gunny, in fact they will be joining us in a few weeks' time. It gladdens my heart that you are wearing our patch on your shoulder and your Eagle on your collar Gunny."

"I earned 'em Major and I'm damn proud of it," he said. "So you made Sergeant, Zimmerman. I thought your ass would have been busted out by now."

"You wish Gunny," she said "And as a punishment for your remark, you get to drive me around all this week on this training exercise. You see, I am on light duty do to the wound I received this morning kicking your sorry asses."

"Ok Gunny, I have taken enough of your time" Elizabeth said. "You are invited to take part in a barbecue we are having this evening. You and any other Eagles you have kicking around over there. We seem to have recently obtained some prime grade A Texas beef."

"You bet Major, there are ten of us in camp mam. Ok Zimmerman, enough chit chat, get your cute butt into the Humvee. With your permission Major," he said saluting.

"Squad left face! Squad at the double quick, March!" the group of SEAL and Force Recon troops that the regiment had captured, took off at a dog trot as the Gunny and the Sergeant got in the Humvee and drove along side. A short time later, the six man Canadian rifle team ran after them, full packs and weapons bouncing.

"Warrant, I want a full report on that team, every day. Let them know I am evaluating whether or not to bust them down to Bears," Elizabeth said. "Now Major, I believe I have two hours of free time. I wonder if you would join me in my tent for some after action sex?"

"Liz, scrambled sat call from Eagle One," Hank said.

"Right," Elizabeth said, putting her cup of coffee down and walking over to the Coyote.

"This a secure line?" she said. "Hey Oppa, how's it goin'?"

"Just fine, it's below zero and snowing," Nicolas said. "Omma says hi and all is well here. I've not had any complaint calls from our southern allies lately. Is that a good or a bad thing?"

"Don't know, things have settled down after we kicked their butts and took over our sector." Elizabeth said. "We had a barbecue with the ones close and in country that passed our training. That probably helped. We've been taking groups of Saudi scout troops and artillery commanders on some of our clandestine ops and we have some of their enlisted troops shadowing our guys to see how we operate. The Eaglets are working well and are extending our hard intel range a lot. The integration with the Coyote systems is seamless. We are experimenting with a few modifications with our antennae arrays to get more range."

"Gadget and his buddy have developed a second generation vehicle that has forward, rear and downward capabilities in infrared and normal colour video," Nicolas said. "It is a bit larger but has a more powerful engine and has longer range and will be able to take off and land. It's in the proto type stage right now. But we are still probably a year or so away from a working model.

"Listen Liz, we have three Leopard Twos arriving in port tomorrow with ammo and spares. Can you arrange some transport for the ammo and spares and round up three crews to get them to base?"

"Rudy is not on patrol tomorrow, or any of his guys, so yes, I think they are qualified. Will four six bys be ok? I'll send them down, otherwise we'll have to make more trips."

"Four six byes? What type?"

"Dodge, I think."

"Deuce and a halfs? Where'd you get those?"

"I could tell you but then I'd have to kill you," Elizabeth said and chuckled. "The Marine Engineer Corp has done a wonderful job getting the base ready for the regiment. It should be completed by the end of the week. We've got running water, barracks halls, mess halls, a gym, repair garages, ammo dumps the whole nine yards."

"How'd you manage that?"

"Won a bet."

"You could tell me, but you'd have to kill me, I know. Good girl keep up the family traditions. You and Rudy still good?"

"Yup, it would have been nice to have a honey moon, but this is all right. We'll go on a long leave after this is over and go see the homeland."

"Ok, I'll break this link down now. Keep your head down and ass up."

"You bet Oppa."

"What're we gonna do with three Leopard Two's," Heidi said.

"I'll let Rudy figure that one out," Elizabeth said. "I'm just a light cavalry gal. Is he on his way back from the OP?"

"Just about to Liz," Hank said. "Oh, and Liz, he confirms the Iraqis are stepping up patrols in the sector and the toys are showing a buildup of artillery. We might need those tanks. I hope it stays cold until the Regiment gets here."

"Alright, go to plan D or F or Q or whatever we're at now. Only Russian spoken on the OPs and radios from now on."

"If the Yanks haven't broken our codes and freque hops, you think the Iraqis will?" Hank said.

"No chance. Let them sweat it out. We have two weeks until the Regiment is here. Right now they can't figure out whether were Krauts or Yanks. Keep them on their toes I say."

"Just got an Email from Division Liz," Hank said. "Arial recon says the Iraqis are deploying portable Scud missile launchers and that they may have chemical warheads installed."

"Great, just what we needed," Elizabeth said, shaking her head. "Ok give everyone a heads up and make sure the chem seals are tight on the vehicles and personal chem gear is functional."

"Brits are sending in three SAS teams to see if they can find them. I'll have the toys looking too," Hank said.

"Have a couple of guns on standby just in case we spot one close enough and they fire at us," Elizabeth said. "Send a message to the Marine Colonel and let him know about the artillery moving in and that it's in range of the oil transfer station on the coast."

"Already let their Intel people know, they are going to confirm and task a battery for counter battery action if it pans out. But HQ is not worried and feels we are over reacting, there will be no offensive movement from the Enemy and if there is, it won't be in this sector."

"Still haven't come to grips with the Arab mind yet I see. Well no matter, we will be ready."

Chapter Six

"Ok people," the training Lieutenant said. "Your official training starts the day after boxing day. We will be humping from here to the firing range for your base competency evals. So when you grab your gear, make sure you have all the right stuff to last two weeks in the boonies. Each of you will be issued a C7 and one hundred rounds of ammo. Make sure you have at least twenty five rounds left when we reach the range so you can qualify and that you can strip it and clean it. You have all had the basics on that. Everything else you require, will be issued and whatever you choose to bring on a personal basis, you will have to hump to the range. After that, you can lighten your loads if you wish. Questions? Ok get at it. Make sure your gear fits and is proper for the conditions. You will only use what you bring. See you after Christmas."

"You going to the grad party tonight Gadget?" Harold said as they left the auditorium and trudged to the armoury.

"Maybe for a bit, I have some code I want to work on for the Adler project," Rick said "I've got the sat link down pat, but just need to tweak the weapons release coding. How's the platform making out?"

"Done, I just have to test it in the air with a simulated payload and then we can try your software to see if it will simulate a fire sequence. After that, we can send her in for eval with the Regiment people. They should be done their tests by the time we finish the training."

"Sunday afternoon then?" Rick said. "I'll be done by then and we can do the party tonight for a bit and sleep in Saturday. I don't know why we bother, it's not like we'll be missed or anything."

"Are you kidding me?" Harold said. "That bunch of babes over there have been eyeballing us all day."

"The head cheerleader and her gaggle?" Rick said "They're probably planning all the nasty shit they want to try and pull on us in the bush. Nah, I'm just going to go and have a few beers with the guys and then head home."

"Ya, well Twinkies wingman has been after me all year. I think I'll have a go tonight."

"Better men than you have tried Harold, good luck. What the hell."

"That which doesn't kill you makes you strong," they both said at the same time, before breaking off in a long laugh.

"I'm sure glad I don't have to go in the field anymore," Nicolas said, as Rick walked into the kitchen, his loaded pack on his back and rifle in his hand. "I don't think I could handle all the weight. I thought the basic loads were getting lighter."

"They are a bit," Rick said dumping the pack and his rifle on the bed. "But we have all this new stuff, integrated coms in the helmets, night vision, crap like that."

"Like I said, a young man's game. You ready?"

"I'll be ok. It will be good to get out of the lab for a while."

"This year we have some Finns, some Ukrainians, Germans, and the usual SAS and Force Recons. Oh ya, some Green Berets this year as well. It's a little bigger group than normal."

"What no SEALs? I guess they're all deployed."

"Oh leave the poor boy alone Naj," Katherine said. "It's his last few days at home. You go to that party tonight and have some fun. Naj, give him the keys to my old truck, just don't let the Mounties catch you driving over the limit young man."

"No fear of that Omma," Rick said. "I'm only gonna have a couple of beer, then come home. I have a lot to do on the Adler before I go."

"Work, work, work" his grandmother said. "I said go have some fun, maybe meet a girl."

"No time for girls right now Omma, now if you two will excuse me, I will have a shower and put on my nice comfortable civvies for one of the last times."

"Kat, don't push him," Nicolas said. "He's only just eighteen. If I had listened to mom, we never would have met."

"And maybe I would have been better off," Katherine said. "But I don't think so. I do miss her some days. She would have been fusing all about Richard and his big party tonight. No matter what he says, I and you, know he will not be home early tonight."

"Well Gadget, every boy in our class has danced with me at least once during high school, except you," the girl he called Twinkie said. She was five ten, blue eyed and had her long blond hair undone to flow down her back tonight.

What? She's talking to me, Rick thought as he eyed her. She was wearing tasteful clothing that showed off her figure and wherever she went she drew eyes, male and female.

"No date tonight?" Rick said. "I guess you want to dance then? I warn you I'm all left feet."

"No date, I like you, am a free spirit. And I have seen you dance, which is why I requested this song for us. Come on then." She grabbed his hand and as she dragged him on the dance floor a slow waltz started to play.

She snuggled him close and he was overwhelmed from the scent of her hair and the feel of her body jammed against his. Wow, a guy could get used to this, he thought.

"Why don't we get a beer and go outside?" she said after three dances. "It's a little warm in here and I'd like to get away from all the eyes for a bit."

"Look at those two," she said as Rick handed her a beer. She was pointing at Harold and her best friend on the dance floor. Still dancing slow and close, even though the beat had picked up. Both looking deep into each other's eyes.

"She's had the hots for him all year," she said.

"Score one for the Geek squad," Rick said. "It's the same with Harold."

"God it's beautiful out here tonight," she said. They had walked a short way away from the hall and she was looking up into the clear night sky. She slipped her arm under the back of his jacket and took hold of his waist with her hand.

"Sandy, is this a put on?" Rick asked softly.

"No," she whispered, turning him around so she could look into his eyes. "Far from it."

She pulled his head down to her and kissed him slowly at first and then hard.

"Oh shit," she said, breaking away from him and turning away.

"That was unexpected, but nice," Rick said. "Are you ok? You're not going to vomit or anything?"

"God no!" she said and laughed, turning around. "I'm sorry, that was awfully forward of me. I know you Bekenbaum's are all conservative and all."

"Hell no Sandy, we invented woman's lib."

"This isn't going to work is it Richard?"

"Oh all formal now Sandra? The only time someone calls me Richard is when I'm in shit. What do you mean by that?"

"Sorry Rick, I didn't mean it like that," she said putting her hand on his arm. "I've had a crush on you since middle school. You were the only boy that never paid any attention to me and you were the only one I wanted to."

"Ah," Rick said. "Look Sandy, I like you and all. You're cute, the head cheerleader, smart as a whip, all the things a guy could ask for and I am flattered, really."

"It's just not there," she finished for him. "Me too. I thought there would be fireworks going off and stuff. But nothing. Well, not nothing, you are a hunk after all, but you know what I mean."

"Oh ya, I am still a guy, geekazoid or not and there would be nothing I would like better than to swap DNA with you tonight. But that's all it would be and you deserve better than that."

"Girls have the same thoughts you Neanderthal," she said. "I hear you and Harold are working on some super secret project together."

"Oh, it's not much," Rick said. "We are just playing around with an unmanned small aircraft and the Regiment took an interest in it. I'm having a little bit of problem with some of the software coding with the satellite up and down link."

"You using c++? Or something else?"

"Something of our own, but close. You know about that stuff?"

"Hell yes," Sandy said. "I'm not just a cute blond you know. I've got my choice of Cal Tech or MIT after my time with the regiment is up. Maybe I could stop by and help a bit?"

"Sure, if being in a confined space with a super hunk won't distract you. I've got a lot to cram into in a couple of days. I have to keep working on my Russian too. I think we are going to need it soon."

"I can help you with that too," she said in flawless Russian. "That's all we speak at home when the grandparents come over."

"Gadget, there is a girl here to see you," his grandmother said over the intercom to his small work shop in the garage.

"Send her over," Rick said, not even looking up from the computer monitor.

"Thank you Missus Bekenbaum, I know the way," Sandy said.

"Was that Sandra Olynick?" Nicolas asked. "Wow, she done be all growed up in all the right places."

"Dirty old man," Katherine said smacking him on the arm. "I'll give them an hour, then break it up. Maybe I should make it sooner, we are related no?"

"If we are it's to far back anyway. I think it was the Countess's sister," Nicolas said.

"Tatiana's sister? I thought she was the only one who got out and that is to close."

"No dear, Tatiana was a Duchess. Grandma Elizabeth had a sister, Katia and I think she married an Olynick."

"Ha, I am such an idiot!" Rick was saying in Russian as Nicolas and Katherine walked in on them. "It was right in front of my face all along. If you weren't so bloody cute I'd kiss you right now."

"Why thank you, I think," Sandy said, leaning back from the key board.

"Harold, Sandy has found the glitch, when can you get over here, I want to test it out right away." Rick had grabbed the telephone on the wall and called Harold. "Yes Sandy, she's more of a geek than you are. Get your ass over here."

"Now that sir, was a compliment," Sandy said and pecked him on the cheek. "Does that mean I am now a part of the Geekazoid club?"

"Hey Omma, Oppa," Rick said, still in Russian. "It took Sandy, girl genius, less than an hour to fix this stupid glitch. I've been on it for a month."

"New eyes Gadget," Nicolas said. "Beer or coke?"

"Coke for me, maybe beer after the test flight," Rick said. "Can Sandy share in the royalties? She not only fixed the glitch, but cleaned up some redundant coding for me."

"We'll talk later," Nicolas said. "Your grandmother here was worried we'd find you in a compromising position. I told you there was nothing to worry about Kat."

"Ew, are you kidding?" Sandy said.

"Why, you're both fine looking kids," Katherine said. "I thought it would be a natural fit."

"Ya, so did we, for what, about ten seconds?" Rick said.

"It was like kissing my brother, no thanks," Sandy said. "You know, if you were like the other football players, I would have gotten over that and not wasted all that time pining over you."

"Since time immortal, the Bekenbaum men have needed help from us women to make up their minds dear," Katherine said. "Why such the big fuss over toy planes?"

"Mrs. Bekenbaum, this toy plane will be able to stay aloft for twelve hours and carry four remote guided antitank rockets as a pay load. It is far from being a toy," Sandy said.

"Need to know Kat," Nicolas said after he saw the look in her eyes.

"Well, Naj," she said, taking his arm. "If you have any hopes of getting any tonight, I better be in the need to know."

"Oh that's cute," Sandy said as the older couple left. "I hope I'm still that much in love at their age. Now what's this about royalties?"

"Every design anyone gives the Regiment and they accept and it's patentable, we get royalties on any sales. It's not much more than beer and toy money though."

"Really? How come I've never heard about it?" she said. "I've got some guidance software I've been playing around with. It would integrate well with your hardware."

"Pop let everyone know about it last year," he said. "That's strange. Hmm. I was wondering why only guys were submitting stuff. I think maybe grandma will be having a chat with some teachers. Tell me about your software."

"Well look at him, smiling from ear to ear, not a drop of sweat on him," Heidi said, pointing at Rudy walking up to the command tent. "Damned if I'd be happy driving around in that big coffin."

"The difference between my coffin and yours dear Heidi, is that mine has twice the amount of armour than yours does and has a much bigger gun," Rudy said, kissing Elizabeth before sitting down. "And like my wife keeps reminding me, size matters. It's nice not driving around in a tin can waiting to get stuck in loose sand with only a little popgun at my disposal."

"You can take the boy out of the tank, but you can't take the tank out of the boy," Elizabeth said.

"Regiment is landing tomorrow morning Rudy. Command group should be here about noon and the rest will be trickling in for the next few days. After that, I am afraid dear, it will back to recon for me."

"About time. You're getting fat and cranky sitting here at base and fighting paper all day."

"Fat am I?" she said, bolting out of her chair and leg looping him to the ground, sitting across his shoulders. "Who's fat and lazy?"

"Hey no fair!" Rudy said. "I'm just a poor tank driver, not a ninja like you. Hmm, nice view."

"Get lost Heidi, I am going to have to teach my prisoner a lesson," she said.

Elizabeth and Rudy were just finishing their ten o'clock coffee, when a dust plume approached, to reveal itself as four armed G wagons.

"Warrant, sound the alarm. The Master Warrant is chomping at the bit and about to arrive," Elizabeth said.

The forty troopers still on base and not on duty, had just barely enough time to arrange themselves, when the small convoy came to a dust and gravel spattering halt. The front passenger door flung open and Paul stepped out, almost before the vehicle had stopped.

"Achtung! Officer on deck!" Elizabeth said. She and the other troopers coming to attention and snapping a salute as Emily exited the rear of the G wagon.

"What's the sit rep Major? I want to get out to the OP ASAP," Paul said, waving his hand at his forehead and then had a puzzled look on his face as the line of troopers still stood at attention saluting.

"At ease. You will have to excuse the Master Warrant," Emily said, returning the salute in the proper fashion. "He has been away from the centre of action for so long he forgets himself at times. Major, the camp looks well prepared and your troops look good. Thank you for the reception. I wonder if we could prevail upon you to bring us up to speed on the local situation and after, perhaps a tour of the front? Is that real Arabian coffee I am smelling?"

"Yes mam," Elizabeth said. "If you and your officers would follow me, we will brief you and give you some coffee. My Warrant will take care of your trooper's mam."

"I am sorry Major, please accept my apologies," Paul said taking his cup of coffee.

"That's ok pop," she said giving him a hug. "I'd be stir crazy too sitting in that ship for two weeks."

"Hell, she's stir crazy here sitting at the base all the time," Rudy said. "Thanks for the new toys, I was getting an inferiority complex driving those little tin cans all the time."

"New toys? What new toys?" Paul said.

"Three brand spanking new Leopards. You didn't know about them?" Elizabeth said.

"I know we are on the waiting list, but we were at least a year away from getting them."

"Grandpa must have pulled some strings then," Elizabeth said. "Ok, if you would take a look at this map, this is what we are facing in our sector."

"You've done a good job here Liz," Paul said as he surveyed across the lines with his binoculars. "The camp is well prepared. How did you manage that?"

"Well, we seem to be having a small potato shortage right now" she said. "It really is amazing what a case of good home brew can get you out here. The Marine Engineers built most of it. We tweaked this OP to suit us, but most of it was already here."

"Are those Iraqis close enough to hear us?" Paul said pointing at the Iraqi post opposite.

"Ya," Elizabeth responded. "We've been switching languages on them every couple of weeks to keep them on their toes. This week it will be English. They don't know what to think, our equipment looks American, but not really, and now there will be more German stuff."

"So you could be Saudis for all they know," he said. "That was a good idea too. Ok I've seen enough, we brought another two Eagles with us. That will expand our intel gathering a lot."

"The Yanks discount it all anyway," Elizabeth said. "Like normal, they are only interested in what they are interested in. We'll be ready anyhow. They are pushing us hard to get behind the lines a bit and now that you are here, I guess I can."

"No rush Liz, after Christmas will be soon enough."

"Sweat heart how have you been doing," Emily said, taking Elizabeth aside when they returned to the bace. "You look like you've gained a little weight. Is everything ok? The clinic should be up and running tomorrow if you need it."

"Everything is fine mom," Elizabeth said. "I've been stuck behind a desk to long is all, that will change now. Only being in charge of my own company will be nice too. I won't have to attend daily brigade meetings and emails and such anymore."

"Yes dear," Emily said. "Our pencil necks will take over and communicate with their pencil necks. That's why I'm here. Your father too I suppose. He was so worried you'd let them push you around and start operations behind the lines. I kept telling him that you were my daughter and if that wasn't enough, that you were his daughter and there was no way that was going to happen. But I think sometimes he looks at you and still sees little Lizzy and to tell the truth, so do I sometimes."

"Oh mom," Elizabeth said and hugged her mother. "I know. I hope Rudy and I love our kids as much as you and pop have loved us. Come on now, back to work don't you think Colonel?"

"Not just yet Liz. We haven't seen each other for quite a while and once things get heated up, we will not have any time later. So is Rudy as dreamy as he looks?"

"MOM!"

"Well a mother needs to know these things you know. Now I know he's not as dreamy as your father, who could be, but when I was newly married, my mother heard all the stories. It's mandatory dear."

"BS mom, you just want a juicy story. I will have you know he is dreamier than Pop, has all the right parts and knows how to use them, thank you very much. Oh I wish we could have had more time alone together, but we will make it up once we get home."

"During the long and boring boat ride over here," Emily said. "A bunch of us got together and decided we needed a big time Christmas Day party. Do you think we could manage that?"

"Sure, the Saudis owe us a few favours," Elizabeth said. "I am sure if pop talks to them they will take over our sector duties for a couple of days. We helped them out the same way for one of their festivals."

"Good, we have all the fresh meat and veggies, being flown in from home. Do you still remember how to roll cabbage rolls and pirogies? We are going to need a lot of help."

"Heidi, get your butt over here!" Elizabeth said.

"Yes your Majorship, how may I assist you your Majorship?" Heidi said. "Morning Colonel. May I say how invigorating you look today mam?"

"Heidi, Heidi. Never change, the world would be worse off," Emily said.

"Listen dummy," Elizabeth said. "Mom is planning a big Christmas dinner, fresh food and all, right from home. Get the lads working overtime on the booze and I want all the girls, especially you, to help fix pirogies, cabbage rolls, stuffing and like that. You know, normal girl stuff for once."

"All depends your Majorship. I'm supposed to be on OP for Christmas, so are you by the way. Not fair if I make a shit load of my award winning cabbage rolls and I don't get to eat them fresh."

"Her Majorship assures me the Saudis will be happy to take over for us for a few days, Heidi," Emily said.

"They better, we did all of Ramadan for them. Ok Mrs. B. you got a deal. When do we start?"

"Plane's supposed to be here tomorrow Heidi," Emily said. "We need to get the stuff here first."

"No problem Colonel, it's all under control," Heidi said. "You came to the right person. With your permission ladies? Warrant, a word if you please. Now!"

"Oh, by the way mom," Elizabeth said. "We have about fifty eagle grads in country. They should be invited as well."

"Get me their names and unit numbers Liz, I'll make it happen."

"Already done Colonel," Hank said poking his head out of Elizabeth's Coyote. "I'm not just another pretty face behind a gun you know. And yes Colonel, the Saudis are more than willing to take over our duties for the whole week mam and it's all been ok'd by brigade."

"No wonder you get a lot done around here," Emily said. "Your people are amazing."

"We've had to be mom. To tell you the truth, we can use the time off, we're all getting burnt out."

"Going somewhere special general?" the officer of the guard asked, eying the generals dress air force uniform. There were an impressive array of ribbons, two sets of wings and a shiny brass eagle, wings outstretched on his right collar. On one shoulder he had a blue, yellow and red shield crest with a maple leaf in the centre an eagle on the right, a bear on the left with a beaver on top. The Captain of the guard had never seen that crest before and wondered what unit it represented and why the general was wearing it. Then the general put on a strange shaped black beret with the same crest, but in brass in the centre of it. 'That looks like a Canadian beret,' he thought.

"Nothing special Captain," the general said. "Just a little Christmas reunion."

The captain escorted the general to the door and opened it for him to the sound of "Attention On Deck" and a number of highly polished boots hitting the ground in unison, as an astonishing group of men came to attention and saluted the general, who came to attention and crisply returned the salute in the old open handed British fashion. Lined up in their best dress uniforms in groups of ten, were sailors, marines, air force special services and army troopers. Most were sergeants, petty officers and warrant officers, but there were a few officers among them. Along with all of their authorized US decorations and it was an impressive array, each man had an eagle on his collar, a black Canadian beret on his head and the same crest the general had on the beret and the shoulder.

'Holy shit,' the captain thought. 'That's almost the whole Special Forces group there and these guys are the best of the best.'

"Ok Chief Petty Officer," the general said. "Where's the wheels, or are we supposed to walk there?"

"Well Spanky," the Seal said. "All they said was to be here, so here we are."

The general walked up to the now disintegrating line of men and was shaking hands and slapping backs, with a few special men giving and receiving long hugs.

"Do you see what comes from not allowing women to serve in the front lads?" a female voice with an upper crust British accent said. "Will the Yanks never learn? How are you Spanky, it's been a while."

"Christ! Trust the Canuks, they'll let anyone into their parties," the General said as he hugged the older woman and lifted her off the ground. "Don't ask don't tell, that's our motto Maggy. God it's been a long time. Your sis let you come here?"

Another highly decorated group of troopers joined the laughing, back slapping and hugging group. There were a few in red jackets a few in Horse Guards blue, but most in RAF blue, except for Maggy, who was wearing a dark, almost black, blue uniform with a wide red stripe down the centre of the outside of each pants leg, which were tucked into tall dark brown riding boots with laces up the front. Like the Americans, they had eagles on their collars and the same crest and badge on the black berets.

"Well, we did send for them and I am the honorary colonel you know," Maggy said. "Of both Regiments."

"Both regiments?" the general said.

"Yes, the Alberta's are here too, with their Leopards and their guns. It's the first time they've been deployed since Korea. Their PM is not pleased I can tell you."

"Oh Jazzus," an American from the group said. "Now the flippen neighbourhood has gone all to hell."

Another ten troopers sauntered in, wearing the understated dark green Canadian uniforms, one of them in the Red Serge of the RCMP. Not one of them were officers. They too had the same berets, eagles and crests as the others.

"Well somebody has to come and be the peace keepers around here, that's what we're famous for," a Canadian said, as they too joined the now large group of impressive soldiers.

Then four six by six deuce and a half trucks pulled up and two troopers from each vehicle came out of the cabs and silently lined up in front of the milling group of super soldiers. They were wearing the same uniform as Maggy and all of them were armed with side arms, buttoned down in shinny brown leather holsters, butt first on their off hip. On each chest were twelve shinny 7.62 bullets, six to each side, placed in blood red bullets loops sewn onto the tunic. All of the troopers had parachute wings on their chests, rifles on their left collars and eagles on their right. The only other decorations to be seen were their understated rank badges, the same tri colour crest on the left sleeve and an under stated maple leaf flag with the word Canada in a curved brass badge above it on the right.

Glancing at the trucks, the captain saw the butts of what looked like M16's poking over the dashes and twin fifty caliber machine guns mounted on a ring on the top of the cabs, belts of ammo fed into them.

A striking blond, with her blond hair pinned up behind her head and major's insignia was in the centre of the small silent group slowly uncoiling and shaking out what looked to be a six foot long whip. She stood watching the group for a moment and then began to slowly whirl the whip around her head and then cracked it in what sounded like a pistol shot.

"OFFICER ON DECK!" an SAS man yelled and the group of revellers immediately lined up and came to attention, all countries and units mixed together in a colourful perfect two lines in front of the small group.

The general marched forward two steps and saluted in his Air Force Academy best salute.

"Party reporting mam! All present or accounted for mam!"

"Very well recruit," the major said, not raising her voice and recoiling the whip and sticking it on a loop on her right side. "Nice of

JTF to show up. We weren't sure you could make it. Ten against one. Not bad odds wouldn't you say sergeant?"

"Ah come on Liz, you only gonna let me have ten?" another smaller blond said from the ranks of the newcomers.

"OK, sergeant, you can have the JTF, they might prove a little more challenging. Ok recruits into the trucks! The other buggers are already tying into the beer and vodka and I want to make sure I get my share. General, you ride in the cab in Heidi's truck. Maggy, you're with me. Let's go people, if I miss out on the beer I'm gonna be pissed!"

The groups of troopers piled into the back of the trucks with one of the new group joining them, passing out bottles of clear fluid to his group, to the joy of all.

"The only way you're riding with me," Heidi said to the general, "is if you man the gun."

"No prob sergeant," the general said and did just that, sticking his head and shoulders out of the turret mounted on the cab and charged both fifty caliber machine guns, as the vehicle roared toward the gate.

Then the shocked captain watched as the general pushed the beret back to the crown of his head, reached down into the cab of the truck and saluting the gate guards with the bottle, took a deep pull from it, dropped it down back into the cab, griped the handles of the twin fifties and let off a burst into the dirt alongside the truck.

"Fucking eh!" the Captain heard the general say. "Nothing like a twin fifty gun salute!"

Chapter Seven

Nicolas stood on the podium with Katherine on his right and his staff officers behind and to either side of the colour party behind him. He looked down at the one hundred new candidates with their new equipment and pristine and freshly pressed dark green battle fatigues and highly polished boots. Some of the faces he saw were happy, some sad, some serious. All young. He couldn't help but remember his own first day, eager, young and full of wonder, looking up at the veterans on the podium in awe.

"Candidates!" he said. "Right now, you are trained well enough to join any of the front line battalions of any army in the world. By the time you reach the training area two weeks from now, you will be good enough to be their best troopers. The other trainees you will be joining will be the very best troopers their countries could send us. At the end of the next six months, you will be as good as they are. Six months after that, those of you who choose and are successful at becoming eagles, will be better than them. The next month will be hard, you will miss home, you will be cold and wet and hungry and tired. The bonds you form among each other will be stronger than anything else that you ever form. You will truly become brothers and sisters, but more than that, you will become Cossack. True Cossack, not the want to be militia gangs in Europe. You will be Andreas Host Cossack, worthy of all the name implies.

"It is time, who will be first?"

One by one, each candidate came forward and first took hold of the Canadian flag with their left hand, raising their right and swearing their oath of allegiance to Canada and the Queen. Then taking hold of the Regimental colour and swearing allegiance to the Regiment and Nicolas, as the head of the Host.

Nicolas took note that Rick was not the first, allowing one of the others to have the honour, nor was he the last. After the oath taking ,the group saluted the podium, donned their packs, formed columns and marched off into the wilderness. Not to be seen by family and friends again for the next six months.

Rick sat hunkered down in the listening post out beyond the temporary camps perimeter, just his white toque covered head poking over the surface. It was his turn for duty tonight and he had drawn the first shift, until eleven, to be the one awake. The bonus to that was, that he would get six hours of uninterrupted sleep. Out of the wind in the hole, the sub zero temperature was bearable, just. At least it was not the mind numbing minus thirty of the week earlier. It got dark early up here in the mountains, just before five and the sun would not break the horizon until nine the next morning. Meanwhile, the full moon and the clear star lit night reflecting off the snow, almost made it as bright as day. It was deadly silent, almost soul crushing silent. He could hear the breathing of Harold, his team mate for the evening, quite clearly and knew that any sound in the cold still mountain air would travel a long distance. He let his mind wonder as he scanned the area in front and to the sides of him. You had to stay awake and alert out here, you never knew when one or more of the instructors would pounce on you.

The first week had been a killer. They all had thought they were tough and in shape, but marching thirty miles a day with full loads on their backs had been brutal. After the first few days, anything that was not absolutely necessary had been jettisoned. They had been taught that first week how to properly pack and position their loads so they were the most comfortable. How to place and position their rifle pits for maximum protection, from an attack and from the elements. And how to leave the position afterward, to leave as little as possible behind to betray their presence after they left. Every few days, on an intermittent and ever changing schedule, they received a resupply and a rest day, where they would repair broken equipment or clothing, replenish used food and ammunition and get rid of garbage and spent shell casings. These days were looked forward to with relish, as they gave everyone a chance to rest wary backs and legs and to get warm and dry out clothing by the fires in the fire pits that were always waiting. Not tonight though. Tonight they were in a cold camp.

It had taken them two weeks of heavy slogging to find the enemy camp. The first week, they had just headed in the general direction they had been provided by division. Then they had homed in on the sound and sight of the enemies resupply helicopters until finally, the smell of their wood stoves homed the candidates into the right position to find the camp. The camp had been under surveillance, night and day for three days now and tomorrow, the candidates would move into positions for the attack for the following morning. So far their observations had gone unnoticed, but the enemy was well dug in and supplied with all the latest gear. Night vision and infrared detectors, motion sensors, mine simulators and these troopers were well trained and mostly vigilant. It would not be easy getting into attack positions. The candidates had all of the locations of the sensors and mines located and routes planned to infiltrate and disable the devices.

Rick had been chosen as one of the first assaulters and he was impatiently waiting to get underway. His task was to neutralize all devises on his attack route so the follow on troops could traverse it quickly. But there was always a chance that a new unmapped device had been placed or one had been over looked. It would take him and his teammate all night to creep up to the listening post they had been assigned to neutralize and capture. They had been told the attack would take place on January eighteen. Seventeen days since they had left home.

"The Iraqi air force is no longer functional," Paul said to the assembled officers of the Regiment. "The Coalition has complete control of the air and has now shifted its focus to ground targets. Command and control centres, vehicle formations and targets of opportunity. The Eagles, our sensors, and other forms of intel, are telling us the Iraqis are massing a large group of armour and troops to the south of us and that they plan on hitting the oil transfer station on the coast. The same facility they have been trying to shell the last little while. This information has been passed up the line, but has been discounted as a diversion, so we are pretty much being left to our own devices out here. The only support we can count on is our own and that of our neighbours and a few National Guard A10's for air support if they are not needed elsewhere.

"The Iraqis are not being left alone however. There have been a number of interdiction air strikes conducted on the formation, but it is still very large and very capable. We feel the main thrust will be along the coast with the aim to capture the town and the loading facility and to destroy the facility. In an effort to secure their flank, the enemy will hit us and try to dislodge us. We will do our utmost to prevent that from happening. As of now, each OP will be augmented by three Leopards. You people out there, hold them up as long as you can and then get out of the way. You are out gunned and out manned. We will make it look like the OPs are manned, but I want the positions shifted a couple of hundred yards to the rear, dug in and camouflaged tonight. We feel the attack will proceed in the next few days. Be alert, be safe, good luck."

"Liz, Rudy? A moment?"

"I want both of you up on the OPs" Paul said to them after the rest of the officers had left. "Liz, you will be local Command and Control, Rudy, you for the tanks under Liz. Take your best equipment and troopers. The only air assets I can guarantee are our three helos. We have three more on the way, but I don't think they will get here on time. When the shit hits the fan, let them know you are there in a big way and we will send whatever arty we can to you as well. As soon as you are in danger of being overrun, get out of there and regroup to keep harassing them. It's not going to be like we faced before in Afghanistan, South Africa and Korea. These guys have modern armour and weapons and there are a lot more of them than there are of us. Make sure all of your IFFs are functioning properly, your radios and comms are fully operational and your vehicles are fully fuelled and armed. When it comes down, it may take us some time to reach you and you will be on your own. Standard procedure, knocked out vehicles and the dead are to be left in place. Focus on the mission and the living. We will retrieve the fallen after. Questions? Requests?"

"I want two LAV Anti Tanks and two with twenty mm mounts on each position," Elizabeth said. "Two Javelin crews and two mortar crews. Leave the crews currently manning the positions in place until tonight, then have them cammo the position and withdraw. We will be ready by morning."

"Done. Ok get going, round up your people and move out at dusk."

"Ya baby, time for the big boys to play!" Rudy said, lifting Elizabeth off the ground in a bear hug. "You spot 'em for me and I'll take 'em out for you."

"Ok big boy, just you keep up and out of my way," she said, hugging him in return and then kissing him long and hard.

"You keep your head down, you hear?" she said looking him in the eyes.

"Hey no fear, we have better optics, bigger guns, better targeting systems and armour than their T72's Liz. Not only that, but we run faster backwards than they run forwards. Ok let me go, I've got to round up my guys."

"Alright people," Liz said to her officers and crew commanders. "Load your vehicles with fuel until it overflows and take four full Gerry cans of fuel and another four of water. I want to refuel once we get into position. I want every square inch of space not occupied by crew loaded with ammo, personal as well as vehicle. Make sure your IFF's are working and a full load of coloured smoke. We don't have to worry about detection from the air, so once we are in position, just cammo for anti ground detection. We want to be able to react as fast as possible to any threat. Once we get mobile, place your dismounts to best effect and be ready to retrieve them on a moments notice. Any KIA, vehicle, or human, are to be left in place. Hit and run people. Hit and run, just like the old days against Napoleon and Rommel. Leave the tanks to the tanks unless you have no choice. We want to hit fuel, personnel and light armoured vehicles in that order. Anything, and I mean anything, that fires on us is to be fired upon. Anything not coalition is to be fired at on sight. When I give the word to leave, you leave, no questions asked. We are out gunned and out numbered. Mortar crews, find a position and set up and fire as quick as you can, then shift. Everyone has fall back position coordinates for rendezvous, so if we have to scatter we can link back up again. Get cracking, we are out of here at dusk."

"I don't feel good about leaving you guys out here alone Liz." The captain manning the OPs said, as his crews were pulling out just before day break. "More bodies is a good thing. There are a shit load of them just out of range."

"Thanks, but get back to camp. Get some grub a shower, clean cloths and ammo up. Regiment will be needing you guys more. We are just here to delay them, not stop them," Liz said, patting the captain on the arm.

"For all we know this might just be a feint to draw attention away from our main thrust. We have all your remotes up and running and will deploy them to good effect before we let the Iraqis know we are here. Now get out of here."

An hour later the first artillery rounds hit the observation point.

"What have we got Hank?" Liz said.

"Just like Regiment briefed Liz. They are aiming for the flank. The main thrust is up the coast. Looks like we are on the edge and they just want to pin us down. They are hitting the Saudis hard and that seems to be the main thrust."

"OK, data burst to Regiment and command. Tell command to mount up, lock and load. No engines until we are sure where they are going to hit."

"No doubt about it now Liz. They've got one T72 and four BMP's heading our way, the rest are heading for the Saudis. We should be able to hit them in the flank to good effect for a while."

"Rudy," Elizabeth said over the command net. "One T72 and four BMP's targeting our position. Take them out. You need any help?"

"No, I'll deploy one tank, the rest of us go with you."

"Roger, ok gang fire 'em up. This is for real and those guys will not be firing lasers at you. Hit them hard and keep moving."

As they began to move out, one Leopard moved out on its own half way to the OP and as it moved, began firing. After four shots, it turned and pursued the rest of the group proceeding at the highest speed possible.

"Squash four, confirmed," came the report.

"Holy shit!" Hank said. "Target rich environment!"

"Open fire at will and when in range," Liz said on the command net, arming her twenty millimetre and swinging the turret to cover a BMP disgorging its troops. Two rounds later the BMP was smoking and she was just about to fire the fifty caliber coax when Heidi started firing hers.

"Tally ho!" Heidi shouted into the intercom.

"Target left, BMP cannon! Armour piercing up!" the warrant said.

"Target acquired!" Liz said and pulled the main gun firing device. "Target neutralized."

"BMP ahead!"

"Rearm!" she said after what seemed to be an hour.

"Two A10's on the way Liz. They know we have IFF and are waiting the smoke."

"Purple smoke on the way," Liz said. "All crews purple smoke three hundred meters in front."

"A10's acknowledge purple, target rich to the east Liz."

"Woo hoo!" Heidi said. "Shake and bake time!"

"What the fuck!" Hank said. "They just hit one of our Leopards and a LAV!"

"A10, A10, break off, break off!" Hank yelled. "You are blue on blue, I repeat, you are blue on blue! Targets east of smoke, I repeat targets east of smoke! Shit here they come again!"

Liz swung her turret and placed the fire controls on anti air, targeting the first A10 and flipping the arming position to fire both the twenty and the fifty. The crew chief flung open his hatch and grabbed his C6 on the turret and swung it to cover as well, charging the gun as he swung it. As the first rounds left the A10 and Elizabeth saw they were targeting another Leopard, she fired and kept her finger on the trigger targeting the wing root. Other LAV's and Cougars did like wise, with the aircraft Elizabeth was targeting blowing up and the other breaking off and smoking badly.

"Fuckers!" Heidi said as she threw open her hatch and left her position, sprinting towards the second Leopard, which was just catching fire, a number of the crew trying to bail out. They didn't make it, as with a roar, flames shot out of the hatches.

Heidi could see what was about to happen and sprawled on the ground just as the Leopard exploded sending shrapnel everywhere.

She was just about to get up and run back when she was hit by enemy machine gun fire walked up to her from a BMP.

"Warrant, man the drivers compartment!" Elizabeth said scanning her friends body for signs of life, knowing from her condition that if she wasn't dead yet, she would be in minutes.

"Driver up!" the warrant said taking the controls and slamming the hatch shut.

"Shift position, one hundred meters to the right. Engaging BMP cannon left!"

"Saudis are bugging out Liz, we should too. All vehicles reporting low on ready ammo."

"Roger, fall back to position three. Driver, break off attack, reposition to position three. Hank, three smoke rounds to cover, driver make smoke as soon as you can. T72 left engaging!"

She fired both the twenty millimetre and the fifty caliber at the tracks hoping to do some damage and at least distract it from the target it was acquiring. Both seemed to have worked, as the near track came flying off and the turret swung around looking for her when it was hit by a Leopard round, putting it out of action.

Very soon they were out of the enemies range and repositioning to hit them again and rearming as they went.

"The arty is hitting them hard Liz and a couple of F18's and a few more A10's are inbound. Our Helos are hitting them as we speak and will be covering our withdrawal."

"Roger. We need a new driver Hank, I need the warrant up here with me."

"Roger, ones coming over once we stop."

"OK, I want a sit rep by that time. Get me Regiment."

"Brigade is hollering for you too Liz."

"No time for Brigade right now. They can get their info from Regiment."

"Regiment up Liz."

"Engaged hostile vehicles, large numbers destroyed. Hostiles are moving south, target appears to be the loading facility. Two Leopards, one LAVAT and one trooper confirmed KIA, by air blue on blue. Hostile vehicles engaged include one A10 destroyed and one damaged. Friendlies are redeploying to provide screen, over."

"Roger, multiple enemy targets destroyed, including one A10 destroyed and one damaged. Two Leopard, one LAVAT and one confirmed trooper KIA. Friendlies redeploying to provide screen. Enemy advancing on loading facility and town. Give us more info when you get time Liz," her father said.

Liz kept scanning her displays for threats keeping the turret in constant motion.

"Any other casualties?" she said.

"No Liz," Hank said. "Ah, Liz...that Leopard was Rudy's."

"I know, damn you, I know!" she said, tears streaming down her cheeks. "Keep doing your jobs God damnit, or we'll all get killed!"

"Paul pull her out for God's sake!" Emily said.

"She would ignore me if I ordered it Emm," Paul said. "She knows what's at stake here. You do the best you can here, I need to go. Once we hit the enemy, I'll send her back, you'll need the help here."

"What the hell are you banana republic soldiers up to Colonel!" an irate American army colonel with flight wings said. "You people shot down and killed one of my pilots and wounded and damaged another!"

Paul took the foot he had placed in his command Coyote out and turned around to see the American nose to nose with Emily.

"Well Lieutenant Colonel," Emily said quietly. "It seems to me that you came out the winner. One dead, one wounded and one vehicle lost and another damaged. We lost two tracks, an armoured vehicle and seventeen dead. You win. Now get the hell out of my camp, I have one hundred and fifty thousand Iraqis bearing down on me and don't need this shit right now!"

Paul wasn't sure if it is was the tone of her voice, the look in her eyes or the fact that she withdrew her pistol and pointed it at the American that made him back off.

"I'll be damned if I send you any more support!" the American said.

"Ya, we won't be so nice next time, get the hell out of here!"

"Crank em up" Paul said as he took his place behind the electronics consul. "Tally ho, the hunts a foot!"

"New driver is here Liz," Hank said. "The rest of the LAVs are headed back here and the Leopards to meet up with the Regiment. I dumped what little fuel we had left in the Gerry cans into the tanks and got rid of them. All vehicles are rearmed and deployed or deploying."

"OP One to Beaver Base," Elizabeth said on the command link.

"Beaver Base, to OP One, secure link established. How's it going hun?" Emily said.

"As good as it can be right now. Task force has left I take it. Sit rep follows. Two, I repeat two Leopards, Major von Hoadle's command track and his wingman destroyed, all personnel presumed killed. One LAVAT destroyed, crew and dismounts presumed killed. All by friendly fire. Sergeant Heidi Zimmerman, confirmed killed by Iraqi heavy machine gun. We are up linking gun and Eagle footage of the action as well as telemetry and voice to Regiment for dissemination. We are deployed in our primary secondary position and waiting further orders mam," Elizabeth said.

"Very well Major. Tango One will contact you with further instructions."

"OP One out," Elizabeth said, leaned her head against the turret wall and closed her eyes.

"Is that the group that engaged the enemy?" an American print journalist who was embedded with the regiment said. "Is it true that they shot down two American A10s?"

"Yes, our rules of engagement are very clear," Emily replied. "Anything that shoots at us will be shot at in return. Our people were squawking the proper IFF codes, we were on the right side of the coloured smoke, yet the A10s attacked them anyway. At that point the A10s became the greater threat and they were dealt with."

"So is that why you wanted to pull them back? To face a court of inquiry?"

"There will be no court sir. Now, how would you feel if you lost your wife and your best friend and sixteen others within minutes of each other? That's why I wanted to bring my daughter and her group home. Unfortunately, we, and they, are all that is keeping the Iraqis from over running this whole sector right now, so she has to stay in place. It's her job, it's what she has trained her whole life for and her country and the coalition on counting on her. She knows what she has to do."

"Tango one on secure link Liz," Hank said.

"Tango One, OP One on secure link sir," Elizabeth said.

"Good work Major," Paul said. *"We are two miles east and parallel to you. We want to use Rommels tactics on this one. Position your dismounts and all anti-armour units along the ridge to the rear. Take your armoured vehicles to a hull down position behind the hill in front of you and draw them onto you and then start to fall back on your dismounts. Once you join your dismounts give them hell and about that time we should be hitting them on your right flank and the helos from your left. Once they react to our bigger threat and ease off pressure on you, withdraw back to base. The only thing we have defending the base are your mother's clerks, medical orderlies and the helo maintenance people. Once you get back to base, rearm, and refuel yourselves and your vehicles in case some of these enemy break through.*

"We have two CF18s, Two Italian Tornados and four British Harriers at our disposal, but they won't be coming in until we have the enemy on the run. Once we have them on the run and they begin to fall back from you, fall back, I repeat fall back, under no circumstances are you to stay where you are. Is that clear Major?"

"Yes Master Warrant, engage using Kassarine Pass tactics, once the enemy disengages, fall back to Beaver Base, regroup, rearm and provide defence of base."

"Very well Major, Tango One out."

"Looks like a battalion of mounted infantry, two T72s and four T50s coming in range Liz," Hank said pointing at his monitor.

"OP Four, OP Eight," Elizabeth said after she switched to her company frequency. *"Take out those two scout vehicles once they get into range, then shift position. The rest of you, wait until they dismount from the BMPs and then take out as many BMPS as you can with the two first rounds. After that take on the infantry, as soon as we are in the T72s range, we bug out in over watch to the next position. Dismounts, you stay out of sight until we join you and the T72s are in your kill box. Then I want every anti tank rocket position to fire at first the T72s and then the T50s. after that we can start taking out the BMPs and the infantry."*

"Lock and load people."

"Hank, pull down the mast once the two scout vehicles have been fired on, we'll be joining in on this one. Master Warrant, I want armour piercing first, then we'll shift to anti personnel, ok? Driver, after we pull down the mast go to the top of the hill and be ready to pull us out at high speed, got it?"

"Scouts destroyed Liz," Hank said as he hit the button to retract the surveillance mast. Sticking his upper body out of the turret to observe the progress, he hung the blue, yellow and red flag with the battalion crest in the centre on the rear radio antennae before ducking back into the Coyote and slamming the hatch shut.

"Good to go!" he yelled.

The driver immediately gunned the vehicle into motion and sped up to the top of the hill. Elizabeth didn't know it, but she had started to sing the Regimental song. She also didn't know that Hank had keyed the tactical and command net radios on, as he and the rest of the crew joined in the song. He kept it keyed until she fired her first shot, then cleared the airwaves.

"Target, BMP gun, right!" the crew chief said.

Elizabeth found the enemy vehicle and targeted it. "BMP gun, target hot, on the way," she said and fired the twenty millimetre. The BMP came to a dead stop as rounds walked through the drivers compartment and the turret. She then switched to the coaxial machine gun and sprayed the infantry scattering around the BMP with a few short bursts. Out of the corner of her eye, she saw a dust plume from a missed shell.

"T72s engaging, everyone back to secondary lines," she said on the tactical net. "Driver, take us back when I say so. Warrant, targets?"

"BMP left, T50 right, your choice."

The BMP was only mounted with a machine gun, so Elizabeth shifted her focus to the medium T50 tank and fired six rounds into it, one of which penetrated the lighter armour of the turret causing a catastrophic fire in it.

"Over watch we are clear," Elizabeth heard on her head set. "Driver fall back now! All over watch fall back."

Half way back Hank swore.

"Shit, OP4 just took a hit, they are bailing out Liz."

"OP2, pick up OP4, we will cover, driver stop."

OP2, a regular LAV, sprinted over to the stricken vehicle and opened the hatch in the rear loading ramp. Several troopers ran out of it and assisted the four wounded members of the OP4 crew. The last trooper was barley inside, when OP2 took off, headed for the secondary line. Elizabeth targeted the open rear hatch of OP4 and let four rounds fly into the interior, blowing the vehicle apart from the inside.

"Driver get us out of here" she yelled.

She had the driver stop at the crest of the hill, turned around so the more heavily armoured front of the vehicle was facing the enemy and they waited.

The Iraqi battalion took the bait and came poring over the hill, troopers on foot jogging behind and beside BMPs. Seeing only three LAVs before them, they sped up to get into range. Elizabeth waited until they had passed the burnt out Coyote then ordered her troops to engage.

The T72s were hit by multiple anti tank rockets and ceased to be a threat, smoking and burning wrecks and Elizabeth searched out and destroyed any BMP with a cannon as did all the other LAVs and Coyote, leaving the T50s to the LAVATs and the anti tank rockets. Any vehicle that moved became a target and the driver started firing his C6 as did the Crew chief from the turret top.

"Regiment is engaging Liz," Hank said from the interior, grabbing his C7, intending on opening his hatch to join in with his personal weapon.

"You stay put Hank," Elizabeth said. "I need you on the radios and the monitors. Make sure nothing gets behind us when we bug out."

As soon as it started, it was over. Iraqi troops were throwing down their weapons and raising their arms all over the destroyed vehicle strewn field. Any vehicle that could still move was running to the rear followed by tracers of twenty millimetre and fifty caliber bullets. Only a few BMPs made it back over the hill, none of the tanks did. The field was littered with burning or smoking vehicles and bodies of dead Iraqi soldiers were everywhere.

"Disengage," Elizabeth said into her tactical network. "Remount the troopers and let's get out of here. We've done enough today."

"Tango One, OP1," Elizabeth said switching frequencies. *"OP force is disengaging."*

"Roger OP1, OP1 disengaging," she heard her father say, his vehicles cannon could be heard firing as he was engaging targets as he spoke.

"All dismounts, remounted Liz," Hank said.

"Ok, back to camp, driver, get us the hell out of here!"

"OP1, this is Bravo Six, be advised we will be over flying you in two mikes. We are a flight of coalition fighters and we would like to stay air born long enough to kill some Iraqi tanks please. We have you on IFF."

"Ok, Zoomie, no problem. Give the Iraqis all the best from Cold Lake for us eh?" Elizabeth said.

"Well we can't have Central Alberta having all the fun now can we? Bravo Six out."

Two minutes later, 2 CF18s flashed over head at low level, wing mounts loaded with anti tank missiles.

"We're in the clear Liz," Hank said after that.

"Ok, pop the hatches let's get some air in here" she said, flinging her hatch open and sticking her head and shoulders out into the clear non gun smoke tainted air. That's when she saw the battle flag.

"What the fuck Hank!" she said.

"Hey, the Warrant said to draw them onto us. It worked," he said.

"Oh gezzus," she said. "He didn't mean it that way. Ok leave it there. We deserve it.

"Beaver base, OP1.

"Be advised Beaver One, we are in bound your location, you can't miss us, we have a very big tricolour flag on our radio mast. We have four wounded, I repeat four wounded. We estimate our time of arrival at ten minutes. Hot coffee and donuts would be appreciated."

"Roger OP1 is inbound eta ten minutes. Look for large tricolour flag. We are ready to receive four wounded upon arrival. Coffee and glazed donuts waiting for you."

"Oh shit Liz, you've got to see this," Hank said five minutes later.

Hank started a replay of two American transport supply tanker trucks driving down a town street being ambushed. The rear truck was able to reverse, turn around and escape, but the lead truck stopped. It's occupants were dragged out of the cab, roughed up and tossed into the back of a BMP, which took off at high speed.

"The drone operator is following that BMP Major."

"OK, tell him to stay on it, I want to know where they are dropped off and he is to stay there to get more evidence and to keep the place under surveillance until otherwise told differently by us."

Five minutes later, they slowed down and entered the base to the crews of guard posts cheering and raising weapons in the air in salute.

"One coffee and donuts as ordered," her mother said, as Elizabeth came out the rear hatch of her Coyote, kicking spent twenty millimetre shell casings out in front of her.

"Just what I needed," Elizabeth said after taking a long pull of the coffee and a big bite out of the donut.

"Hank, assemble two assault teams and we are going to need two helos and their crews when they get back in. This is priority one for us now. Colonel, an American transport vehicle was captured and it operators captured. We have them under surveillance and as soon as we can have intel on where they were taken, we will retrieve them."

"But Elizabeth dear..." Emily said.

"The mission comes first Colonel, I shouldn't have to tell you that. Hank, send the team over to my command post. Warrant you're with me. If you would excuse me Colonel? I have a rescue operation to plan."

"Wow a Major tells a Colonel what to do?" the American Journalist said.

"Yes, in this, she outranks me," Emily said. "I can only advice, not order, during combat operations. She is the senior ranking combat officer here right now."

"Can we have a talk with her?" he said.

"Not right now she is busy. We have some video for you to see of her latest action if you wish and we are starting to get some from our main thrust, it is going extremely well."

Emily glanced back at her daughter with a look of concern as Elizabeth took long strides back to command post, she had her C7 on her shoulder and tossed the empty coffee cup into a trash can as she walked by, issuing orders to Hank and the Warrant Officer as she went.

God I hope she can hold it together, Emily thought. I don't think I could if I was in her shoes.

Chapter Eight

"General, the Earl is here to see you sir," Nicolas' aide said from the door, before he was shoved out of the way by a burly large man. The large man surveyed the room with a look of disproval on his face as he took in the Spartan business like office.

"Get out of the way you fool!" an old mans voice said from the hall. "Do you think I am going to be murdered in my own kinsman's house?"

A wheeled walker proceeded a frail older man through the office door and Nicolas rose to greet him. The old man shared the Bekenbaum's features, but the natural lankiness had been supplanted by an almost skeletal set of features. The hairless head, almost skull like and the bones of the hand that he proffered to Nicolas were prominent. The old man was followed into the room by two more men, one of whom was hovering, as the Earl deftly spun his walker around after shaking Nicolas/ hand, set the brake and sat down.

"My Lord," Nicolas said. "If you would have asked, I would have been happy to come to you, instead of you coming here."

"Nonsense Naj! I'm not dead yet. A little fresh country air and exercise never hurt anybody," the Earl said.

"You two," he said, pointing at the burly man and one of the others. "Get out of here, it's crowded enough. You mister lawyer, you stay. Close the door behind you.

"So Naj, what progress in the Gulf?"

"Have a seat please," Nicolas said pointing at a spare chair for the lawyer to take. Nicolas remained standing.

"My Lord," he said. "The sector we were assigned was attacked four days ago by an over whelming enemy force. Our initial forces held them off long enough, along with our Saudi allies, for us to mount a planned counter attack, but not before sustaining casualties and the Saudis lost a key town with an oil tanker loading facility. Air superiority and our allies superior training and equipment, saw the Saudis retake the town and the regiment has pushed the enemy back across the border with much loss of equipment and manpower destroyed and captured.

"Our casualties in people and equipment were minimal. Seventeen dead, all from the initial blocking force, two leopard tanks destroyed, one LAVAT destroyed, six lightly wounded."

"Any civilian casualties?" the Earl asked. "And I heard that our people were killed by friendly fire?"

"The Saudis, unlike the Americans, took our warning of the enemy buildup seriously and had evacuated the town before the attack, so there were no civilian casualties. But there is significant damage to the loading facility. An overzealous American piloting an A10 attack aircraft killed, or was responsible for killing our people."

"I hope he is going to pay for that?" the Earl said.

"He already has, my granddaughter and her people shot him down sir."

"Repercussions? I will express my anger if there are."

"There were some initial expressions of concern from the American military and State department, but Colonel Bekenbaum reaffirmed our rules of engagement, which the Americans had signed off on, as well as reminding our allies that we had followed all the proper protocols and that all of our equipment was functioning properly at the time. In addition, the Colonels father is a member of the Senate House Committee and demanded immediate answers. It did not help that the same squadron did the same thing to the British a few days later, during the main Coalition push. Our Defence Department, after hearing the evidence has no problems."

"Just so." The Earl said. "Ok Naj, I see some fine Vodka in your cabinet there, how about a glass for us and the good barrister here, hmm? Then down to the business I came here for."

The three men raised their glasses and saluted the fallen, then the lawyer opened his brief case and laid some papers on Nicolas' desk.

"As you know, I am dying from cancer and will soon be incapacitated," the Earl said. "As a result, I will no longer be capable of maintaining my responsibilities as Earl and as head of the family trusts. Not having the stamina to be able to function in our armed forces, our fathers agreed to split the Earls duties so that you took over the armed forces and I the Earldom and family trust. This has worked well, until now.

"My two daughters have, unfortunately, been spoiled by my dear departed wife and overindulged their whole lives. They have lived pampered and privileged lives with no thought given to family tradition or responsibility. They have married American men of similar backgrounds and have no intention of fulfilling the family obligations or responsibilities that come with the title. All they are interested in is the money and the status that comes from being landed gentry. I have consulted the original charter and Andreas's wishes and have come to the conclusion that it was never the intent to have the two parts of the Earldom separated and that the hope was that my offspring would be able to resume both sets of duties upon my death.

"Therefore, I am going to abdicate the Earldom in favour of you assuming the titles and responsibilities thereof, thus reuniting the Earldom as it should always have been."

"Are you sure Wilhelm?" Nicolas asked, after a moment of thought. "You would take the legacy away from your family?"

"Why not? They never cared about us or our people. Their sons are already spouting off about how they are fancy Earls and will never leave America anyway. They would just ruin all we have built here. No, your family has kept our traditions and customs. This is as it should be."

"Well I thank you for your thoughts. Unfortunately I must decline," Nicolas said. "For reasons I cannot disclose, I am unable to be the Earl. Paul, as my designated heir, is also not able to be Earl. My other son George, is not of true Bekenbaum blood, he and his offspring are also ineligible. My granddaughter Elizabeth, is now Countess of Olds, inheriting her husbands Earldom on his death and cannot hold two Earldoms. That leaves my Grandson Richard, who is underage."

"That will not be a problem sir," the lawyer said. "A regent can be appointed to perform the duties until such time as Richard is deemed ready to assume the title. But as his father's heir, will not the same restrictions you have, not also govern him?"

"Not until I die and precedence has already been established that will allow him to assume the Earldom."

"Very well then," William said. "Make it so, right now. Nicolas and his heir is to be named Regent until such time as Richard is deemed fit to assume the title and responsibilities. He has the proper temperament?"

"Yes I believe so," Nicolas said. "In fact, I believe he is almost exactly like Andreas himself. He just doesn't know it yet."

Richard and his partner had taken two days to get into position, moving slowly in the daytime and not at all at night. They had slowly crawled up from where they had been, behind their targets until they were within touching distance of the two British soldiers in the listening post rifle pit. In fact, both men now had the regiments calling cards pasted on the backs of their jackets. Four other listening posts had similarly been targeted and now the initial assault force was just waiting for the ambush they had set up a half mile away to be triggered.

The ambush was staged to resemble a camp, fires burning and tents erected, just like the attackers would expect from rookies. Other than smoky fires and crudely constructed dummies, the camp was empty. A small stay behind force was ready to ambush the ambushers and were just waiting for the enemy attack to begin, which should be soon, as they had left their main camp three hours earlier. As soon as that attack began, the main attack on the enemy home base would begin.

As if on cue, the still night quiet was disrupted as American and Russian small arms fire erupted. This was soon followed by a number of bright flares being fired and the booms of anti personal mines going off. Then, the two and three round measured bursts that made the regiments C7's distinctive of their American M16 counter parts began.

"Caught them napping, just like planned," one British trooper said.

Richard and his partner fired one simulated round at each of the British troopers, triggering their laser responders to let them know they were dead.

"Bang, you're dead," Richard said quietly to the two surprised men, before he and his partner quickly strode off to target one of the guard towers, flipping up their night vision glasses and closing one eye as they hit the ground.

As the firing was dying down at the ambush site, a group of bright white flares illuminated the enemy camp, followed by smoke shells hitting machine gun emplacements. Richard and his mate opened fire on the now blinded guard tower, nocking it out of action as the other four assault teams did the same. Then they shifted their fire to the tents which were now full of men trying to escape and take up firing positions. Next came the whole assault team, firing as they came, rushing up in three or four yard bursts, laying down firing as their partners rushed forward, then moving again. C6 machine guns followed suit and the night was filled with the sound of automatic weapons and laser designators shrilling, as the defenders were over whelmed. It was soon over. Surprised umpires calling a halt to the attack just as dawn was being hinted at.

Half an hour later, sullen and dejected Russian and American troopers flanked by smiling Canadians, ten to a side, walked into camp and the groups were called together for a debriefing.

"Lesson learned I hope?" Katherine said. "A hurried assault plan is almost as good as no plan at all. You people were led by the nose to your destruction. You did no scouting and made your plan on faulty assumptions. Your assault team was completely destroyed in seconds."

"Next. You regiment people were over confident. A number of your main assault team were killed because you failed to neutralize two listening posts which you wrongly assumed during your planning would not be a factor in the assault. Both sides made mistakes that cost lives or critically wounded people. In the case of the Regiment, this cannot be tolerated. You should have known better. Now in time honoured tradition, the losers get to set up the winners camp and cook breakfast, while the winners get to stay cozy and warm and lick their wounds. Where's the booze?"

The two groups of troopers were soon mingling and joking with each other, comparing notes and in the killed listening post troopers case, proudly displaying the calling cards that had been placed on their backs. Everyone was enjoying themselves when the sound of a helicopter approaching drew their attention and it landed, disgorging Nicolas and several other officers, including a priest. Katherine and the other Regimental officers, knowing something was up, hurried over and a quick conference was held. Katherine walked back to the camp.

"Regiment assemble! Now!" she said.

The Regimental candidates scrambled to gather rifles and line up in formation, Katherine and the officers standing at ease until all was reported as assembled. Then she called out twenty names and marched them over to where Nicolas and the other officers were waiting. The rest of the candidates, Richard included, were put at ease and they looked at each other, questions in their eyes. This turned to concern, as several of the female troopers who had been separated broke out in loud cries and a number of the male ones sank to their knees, heads on hands.

Katherine, marched back up and called them to attention once again.

"One week ago, the Iraqi army attacked our positions in Saudi Arabia with over whelming force. Seventeen of our brothers and sisters were killed. In the ensuing counter attack seven others were wounded. The Regiment and our Saudi allies have defeated the invaders at great enemy cost and the main invasion by the coalition is now in the final cleanup stages. The Iraqis have ceased to be an effective fighting force and been heavily defeated. As a result, training has been suspended and transport has been dispatched to return us all back to main base."

The foreign trainees had come forward in a loose group to hear what was going on and as they heard what was being said started forming lines themselves.

"As to our guests," Katherine said. "I do not have the figures of casualties suffered by coalition forces. They were light, but there were casualties. By the time we reach base, we should have the numbers and names for you. By all accounts, it was an overwhelming victory. Gather up your gear, the trucks should be here within the hour. Candidate Bekenbaum a word?"

"Mam!" Rick said saluting.

"Rick, Rudy was killed," Katherine said. "Liz, Emily and Paul are fine."

"Shit!" Rick said. "He was a good guy. How's Liz taking it?"

"She is still in the line doing her job, I hear. What else could she do? She killed the SOB that did it and carried on. That's what we have to do Rick, otherwise it all falls apart and more people die. She's going to need us after."

Another two helicopters landed and took the grieving troopers away. It was a long, somber, quiet trip home for the rest.

"No, I do not need your permission. You people have been after us for months to do this type of work. We have identified a target, it has been confirmed and the Saudi King himself has signed off on it. We will be assaulting the target at those coordinates at that time. We will be inbound with six helicopters. Three CF18's and three Saudi F15's have been tasked for cover should we need it. I am merely informing you of the mission and reminding you of our rules of engagement. Have I made myself abundantly clear?" Elizabeth was trying valiantly to hide her frustration from her voice and was almost succeeding.

"What part of that is hard to understand sweetheart? I know this is hard for you to comprehend, but I am not a clerk or an admin officer like you. I am a fully trained and qualified assault commander and I intend to do my job," Elizabeth said to the American female officer on the other end of the telephone.

"I do not need or require your permission. If any of your people interfere or fire upon us, I will, as I have done in the past, destroy them!"

"God Damn bureaucrats!" she said as she slammed the telephone down and hung up. "Ok, suit up and let's get out of here. I want to hit that building the same time the Yanks hit the one they think the prisoners are in."

She buttoned up her flack jacket as she walked out and after plunking her beret on her head, she went through all of her magazine pouches making sure they were all full and that a full magazine was in her rifle. The rest of the assault team hurried behind her as she strode quickly to the waiting helicopters. The three Saudi Apache attack birds were sitting beside her three Pavlovs and all the helicopter crews began to run to their birds to get them ready to go as she approached. The second the last trooper was seated the pilot started the machine and in a matter of moments they took off headed for the border.

It had been a week of frustration as they had waited for the Americans to do something, but they had been convinced the prisoners were being held elsewhere and had insisted on intensive training before they would commit to assault the false target. Elizabeth was going to hit the real target at the same time as they hit the false one.

They came in low and quiet. The Regiments helicopters had especially designed rotor blades that made them much quieter than normal helicopters and the Apaches would only hit after they had started to hit the target. One helicopter, Elizabeth's, would descend onto the roof of the building and enter it from there, while another would land its troops in the front while the third circled to provide cover. Then it would land its troops in the rear and the apaches would take out any threats. Elizabeth stood, attached her repelling rope to its hooks and stepped out onto the skids, leaning back to keep tension on the rope. Four troopers on each side would do the same. The helicopter swooped to a hover and she released the loose end of her rope and was flying the last ten feet to the roof top. She quickly disengaged her rope and went to a crouch pulling her modified C7 to her shoulder and sighting all around the roof top as other troopers did the same or hit the door to the interior.

Gunfire erupted in the street below as her troops eliminated surprised guard posts and assaulted the front door. Shortly after the same happened in the rear. The Apaches found targets in the surrounding areas and started firing. From the secondary explosions, the targets must have been armed vehicles. Elizabeth wished she could be inside with her troopers, but she needed to be on the roof in command, not inside.

"Bravo Four to Echelon Three, party has begun," she said into her helmet mounted microphone.

"Team one, party guests have been found, transporting to roof now," Hank said.

"Bird one copy?" Elizabeth said.

"Roger, on our way in. No targets close by."

"Team two, team three, parties over, time to go home."

"Big Bird One, Little Bird Two, two T72's about a mile away heading our way, can you help us out? We are almost out of ordinance and have a couple of BMP's to handle."

"Roger, we have them painted as well as a convoy of bad guys heading your way. It would be best if the party guests left in a hurry."

As the helicopter came to an expert hover just above the roof, Hank and the assault team burst into sight, each prisoner held in a fireman's carry over a troopers back. One of the prisoners screamed as she was dumped into the machine and the waiting medic pulled her further inside, ripping clothing off to begin treatment. Elisabeth waited until all her people were on board before jumping head first into the loading bay and yelling go go go go.

"How's the other one?" she said to Hank.

"He's beat up pretty good, but no where near as bad as she is. Nobody else was hurt as far as I know."

The medic finished doing what he could and had a female trooper holding an iv bag for him.

"They worked her over pretty good Liz. Looks like they used her for their play toy. I have already contacted the base and they are waiting for us. I've given her a sedative to calm her down. The other one is beat up, but he should be ok."

Elizabeth exchanged a long knowing look at her female trooper. They well knew what they could expect if they were ever captured. This poor girl had never been trained for it. Elizabeth traded spots with another trooper and bent to yell into the male trooper they had rescued's ear.

"How you holding up?" she said. He was a tall African American and welts and bruises could be seen on his face.

"I've had worse in the Hood back in LA, but not many," he said. "Who are you guys Delta Force? I didn't know they had females serving."

"Something like that," Elizabeth said. "We are Canadians."

"Didn't know Canada was here. Thanks, I didn't think we were ever gonna get out of there. The bad guys were hard on my partner. They took turns using her. She's a good kid, from the suburbs just outside of LA. She didn't deserve this. They gave us the wrong directions and sent us right into the middle of it. Shot us up good. I dunno what happened to the other truck, do you?"

"It was pretty chaotic at the time. We were right up at the border when it hit. Fun times. Your other truck was able to turn around and get out. They are fine."

"Major," Hank said. "I have informed brigade and they have medical standing by. Surprise, the Yanks found nothing on their raid but an empty building. Big birds are out of bad country already and we will be in about ten minutes."

"Thanks Hank. Let the medics know we will most likely need a psychologist on hand ok? A female one."

Elizabeth knelt down beside the female trooper laying on the floor of the helicopter and took her hand.

"How you holding up trooper? My name is Major Elizabeth Bekenbaum of the Canadian Army. I command this motley group of misfits and we are taking you to our base. We have doctors waiting for your arrival." she said.

"Oh God, thank you Major," the trooper said. "I was praying they would just kill me. Thank God you're a woman, you understand."

"I'm right here and I'm not going anywhere just yet. If I do, Master Corporal Lisa Ackerman is right there on the other side of you. We will take good care of you, don't you worry, right Master Corporal?"

"You got it Liz," Lisa said. "All of us here will make sure of that."

"Liz, got a priority for you from Division," Hank said.

"Bravo Four here," Elizabeth said, triggering her helmet mounted radio.

"I hear you have two of our people. We demand you divert immediately to our facility and we will take over from there."

"Bravo Four to whoever the hell you think you are. I do not recognize your authority."

"I am Colonel Alfred Blacksmith from the United States Army in the Pentagon and I am ordering you to take our people to the nearest United States military base."

"Bravo Four to Colonel Alfred Blacksmith of the Pentagon. I and the rest of the world are resting easy today, sure of the security of the free world when a high ranking senior officer not only discloses his name and rank, but his location for the whole world to hear in the clear over an unsecured connection. I still do not recognize your authority and disregard any orders given to me. Any further transmission other than by secure means and from my regiment will be ignored. Bravo Four out. Oh, kiss your career goodbye Colonel, God Damn pencil pushers anyway."

"Bravo Four to all Bravo units, switch to tak freq three, now."

All the troopers had large grins on their faces and gave Elizabeth the thumbs up. The conversation had been heard on all their radios.

"Brovo Four, Brovo two. Well done, out."

"What was that all about?" the wounded female trooper asked Lisa. "And who is Bravo Two?"

"One of your chair warming Colonels in the Pentagon is about to lose his job. Nobody tangles with us. Bravo Two is our Boss and her father. If you have our regiment and her family in your corner, you have nothing to worry about trooper. Ever."

"That true," the other trooper asked Hank seated next to him. "She like that for every body?"

"I tell you what, I'd go through hell and more for her, or any of our officers and they for us. If you can pass our physicals and basic minims, we are always looking for good people."

"Even a Black Getto kid like me?"

"I don't see no Black people here," Hank said. "Hey Phil, there any Black people in this chopper?"

"Dunno, I'm colour blind myself. See a lot of ugly Catholic Krauts though."

"Ya well, I see almost as many ugly Catholic Rushkies."

"You guys all Catholics? Shit maybe I will join up. Where do I sign up? You don't care that I'm Black and a Catholic. That's a new one for me."

"Well if you would have been a Baptist or an Anglican that may have been a problem, for you. We don't care. Think we can tolerate another Yank Bill?"

"Why not, you tolerate me," Bill sitting across from Hank said. "Bill, I'm from South Carolina originally. I met these yokals on a mission in Chad a few years ago. I was a clerk working for a jerk like that colonel we just heard. I applied, took the training and was good enough to get an eagle. Now I get to play with the big boys instead of hanging around in the back. I warn you though, these people are the best of the best and not everyone gets combat duty."

"Good enough for me. I don't mind driving trucks for a living. Where you guys based out of?"

"All in good time my friend, all in good time," Hank said. "You heal up first, then we'll talk ok?"

"Bravo Four, Bravo Three." Elizabeth heard her mother say on the radio.

"Trooper, do you think you can sit? You can look out the window next to Lisa if you want. I have to take this call."

"I'll take over Liz," Lisa said. "Come on up here trooper. You ever been in a chopper before? The view is fantastic."

Lisa helped the trooper off the floor and onto the chair by the window. *She's tougher than she thinks,* Lisa thought.

"Do you always address each other by first names?" the trooper said.

"No, just in the field and only in the same unit. It's like everything else, it has to be earned."

"You allow females in the front lines? We don't."

"Only if I am tough enough love. Just like the boys, I have to carry my own weight, or I'm out, just like they are."

"Bravo Three, Bravo Four." Elizabeth said into her mike.

"Bravo Four what's your ETA? Regiment has returned and is waiting on you."

"RTB twenty. The whole Regiment?"

"Roger Bravo Four, the whole regiment. Copy RTB twenty."

Liz spent the rest of the flight in quiet contemplation, not even looking out the window as they slowed and came in to land. Had she, she would have seen the whole regiment, lined up in front of their vehicles, parked on both sides of the main road in the camp. With seventeen vehicles, each with a flag draped body on top, waiting outside the gate.

"Right let's get this over with, then we can all get a shower and some sleep," Liz said as the helicopter blades came to a stop. "Everybody out and assemble in column of two. Can the wounded walk? Ok, wounded in the middle, let's welcome our trooper's home."

Joined by the pilots and air crew, they formed a double column and marched to the end of the line of vehicles, as they passed a helicopter, the occupants joined their line, even the Saudi crews. The rest of the regiment had cleaned up and were in new clean uniforms, Liz's group stood out in that they were still in combat uniforms and gear, weapons and ammunition festooned all over their bodies. Liz marched them in front of the whole regiment to the head of the line where the colour party was, lined them up and saluted smartly.

"Bravo team, with a party of two, all present and accounted for Mam!" Liz said.

"Thank you Major," Emily said. "Your people will have the place of honour major. The last troopers were all under you command."

"Yes mam, thank you mam. Column, about face!"

One by one, the seventeen vehicles with the flag draped bodies on top, slowly made their way down the main street of the camp. As they passed each group of troopers in front of their vehicles, all came to attention and saluted, holding the salutes until the last vehicle had passed. As the first vehicle came up to them it stopped and four troopers picked up the stretcher on top of it, moving it to the ground.

"Bravo Team, Present Arms!" Liz ordered, those with rifles, Liz included, presented the rifle salute and held it as each vehicle drove up, dismounted its stretcher and moved off.

A lump hit her throat as the second last vehicle pulled up. Along with the Canadian Colours, the Regimental colours were on the other half. *That's Heidi* she thought as the stretcher was put down. Then the last vehicle pulled up and she had a hard time keeping it together. This one had the Von Hoadle flag draped over it.

"Bravo Team, Attention!" she said, then about faced and presented arms once again.

"Regiment assembled mam! All present and accounted for mam!"

"Very well. Master Warrant?" Emily said.

"Regiment!" Paul said. "Form on the Colour!"

Starting by the gate, troop by troop they merged into companies and marched to the front of the line behind the stretchers and formed up. Elizabeth's company formed around her Bravo team who had about faced and were facing the review stand and the national and regimental flags.

"Regiment! Attention!" Paul ordered and stepped back saluting, as an older man wearing traditional Saudi clothing approached the microphone.

"On behalf of my people, I personally thank you for all you have done for us and our people. We will forever be grateful for your help and your dead will be honoured forever," the King said and stepped back to be replaced by a slight oriental woman, dressed in her official Governor General of Canada robes.

"A message from Her Majesty, Queen Elizabeth the Second. Once again you have come to our call and once again you have made us proud. From the Prime Minister of Canada. Well done, all of Canada is proud of your achievements and your efforts in upholding freedom. From my self and the other members of the Canadian armed forces, I say thank you, job well done."

Now Paul stepped forward.

"Regiment, once again you have performed as we expected. You have upheld our traditions as your forefathers have done. They are looking down on us with pride! Once again we have lived up to our motto! Once again tyranny has been defeated, once again the oppressed have been freed. Once again the world can sleep safe at night. Well done!"

"In the name of the Father the Son and the Holy Spirit."

The regiment as a whole made the sign of the cross went to one knee and bowed their heads.

"Father, we ask that you grant the souls of our fallen access to your bosom. They fought to protect the innocent and to free the oppressed. We thank you for our deliverance from harm and we ask that you grant the families of our fallen grace and relief from their sorrows. In the name of the Father, the Son and the Holy Ghost, Amen."

"Let it be known, that the Actions of Tango Company and their leader Major Elizabeth Bekenbaum, made possible our victory and that her bravery and that of her company have been noted in dispatch to the Queen and the Department of Defence. Let it be known that Major Bekenbaum is relieved of her duties as of now. Not because of any dereliction, but for compassion. Major, by order of the Queen and your Ataman, you are hereby relieved with our gratitude and may join your family."

"Sir!" Elizabeth said performing once again the rifle salute and walked over to Rudy's flag draped body.

As Paul began to sing the Regimental song in the customary Russian, the whole regiment immediately picked it up and sang as well. Liz could not hold the pain and the grief back any longer. She dropped her weapon into the dirt of the street and grabbed Rudy's flag draped body and let out all her grief and anguish in one long and mournful wail. The first one to her side was her mother, who joined her on her knees, tears streaming down her face, then her father also crying as the regiment kept singing.

"What's that all about?" the female American trooper asked Lisa.

"That's her husband. They were married just before we shipped out. He was killed on the first day of fighting and she is three months pregnant."

"Oh my God," the American said, as she rushed over and joined the group of family members, putting her arm around Liz and her head on her shoulder. "I am here for you as you were there for me," she said.

Then the tall American soldier, hobbled forward and picked up Liz's fallen rifle, came to attention and performed the rifle salute. Then he smartly about faced, brought the C7 to port arms, assuming the guard position. One by one, the wounded of the regiment stood from wheel chairs, taking rifles from comrades and positioned themselves in front of one of the fallen, placing the barrels on the ground, folding their hands on the rifle butts and bowing their heads in the

Canadian tradition. Meanwhile the regiment kept singing the regimental song, slow and long. Tears freely flowing down cheeks as they shared the family's grief and their own. Finally Paul stood and motioned the stretcher bearers forward.

Escorted by Tango Company, the group moved to the hospital, Liz supported by her mother on one side and the wounded American girl on the other, with the Black soldier standing guard over them. Unbidden, the song began to pick up pace and soon the sorrow was replaced by joy. The joy of survival. The joy of living to see another day. The joy of realizing that soon they would be home.

Unknown to them, an American news camera had caught the whole thing on camera and the next day it was all over the world.

Chapter Nine

It had taken a lot of coordination and planning, but as Nicolas surveyed the assembled regiment, it was well worth it. Two thousand troopers stood assembled in their troops beside their horses or their horse drawn gun carriages. Dignitaries were assembled and beside their carriages. Now they were only awaiting the arrival of the caskets, which would be placed on the gun carriages for transport home. They were assembled in a field north of the Calgary International Airport where eleven jumbo jets had landed one after the other to unload the Regiment after their long trip home. Now the Regiment was dressed in their traditional dark blue, almost black uniforms with lambs wool caps. Rifles were slung over backs as was their tradition and the Regimental Colour was uncased, its yellow battle honour ribbons flying freely in the wind.

They would make the sixty kilometre trek to the Regiment on horseback, up the west ditch of Highway Two. The procession would be proceeded and followed by a Leopard tank and two Coyotes. In front of them would be three RCMP cruisers and three Alberta Sheriffs vehicles. The highway had been shut down from Innisvail to Calgary to prevent any traffic from interfering. They would have the whole road to themselves. The RCMP had provided their ceremonial mounted party to escort the federal dignitaries and the Lord Strathcona Horse theirs for the Provincial dignitaries. The Red Serge of the Mounties and the dark green and brass helmets of the Strathconas, clashing brilliantly with the dark blue and scarlet red of the Regiment.

Seventeen hearses pulled up alongside the gun carriages and troopers pulled the flag draped coffins from the backs and securely fastened them to the gun carriages, then mounted the carriages. When that was done, the order to mount was given, then troop by troop, the regiment swung first onto Country Hills Boulevard, then north onto the main highway. When Nicolas received the signal that the whole regiment was on the highway, he signalled for the trot and the country side was soon filled by the sound of two thousand horses hooves hitting the ground like thunder.

At the first over pass and every one there after banners, welcoming them home were strung out, fire trucks and their crews, lights flashing with Canadian flags blowing in the wind were flying. Police officers, local and RCMP stood and saluted as they passed. People holding Canadian flags and miniatures of the regiment's colours lined the road at intervals. All were quiet, some saluting, others with their hands over their hearts as the regiment passed. Some calling out thank you, but mostly just standing in quiet respect. Until the young Major, her long blond hair tied in a ponytail down her back and over her rifle rode by, escorting her husbands coffin. Then they cheered and clapped for this brave woman, whose grief they had shared on the nightly news.

When they reached Airdrie, both sides of the highway were lined by the residents of the city and in the centre were a group of almost a thousand Alberta war Veterans, some in old uniforms, all wearing their campaign medals, saluting as the Regiment passed. North of Airdrie, the Regiment was joined by the Second Battalion of the Princess Patricia Canadian Light Infantry. Their polished LAVs escorting them on both sides of the highway, dark green dress uniforms crisply pressed, then they were joined by the kilted Calgary Highlanders in their spotless LAVs. Both units having served with the Regiment in the past.

"I didn't know you Canucks were much into the military," one American news caster asked a Canadian counterpart. "And the people are so quiet. In the states, there would be more soldiers guarding the route than in the parade."

"Well, you ain't in Kansas anymore Toto," the Canadian broadcaster said. "From what I hear, we ain't seen nothin yet."

Four hours later, the Regiment was coming up the last hill into Didsbury when the broadcasters saw what was awaiting them. Ten thousand dark blue uniformed troopers, all with rifles at their sides, lined the street in formation. Some of the rifles and the troopers holding them were old and ancient, but all stood tall and performed the rifle salute without orders as the Regiment passed. Another ten thousand were waiting at the barracks.

"Christ, I thought you Canucks only had three thousand combat troops total," the American said.

"Ya, we do. But these people are not part of the regular army. You Yanks had the opportunity to have them when they came to North America, but you blew it."

Willing hands took horses away as the weary riders dismounted and two American Army soldiers, both dressed in dark green American uniform, rushed to Elizabeth's side as she dismounted. One male and black, the other female. Both of them were sporting the Regiments patch on their shoulders and both of them flanked her, two steps to the rear as she walked to the front of her troops.

Nicolas and the dignitaries rose to the reviewing platform and one by one the dignitaries made their speeches until only Nicolas himself was left.

"Welcome Home!" he said. "Dismissed! Parties On!"

Pandemonium broke loose as family members and friends descended on them. Nicolas and Katherine came to Paul and Emily and hugged them and Rick who came up as well.

"Well, well, look what the cat dragged in," Elizabeth said. "Since when are candidates allowed to join in formation?"

"Sorry mam, won't happen again Major," Rick said coming to stiff attention.

"Get your sorry ass over here Gadget and give your sis a hug!"

"God I am so sorry Liz. Are you ok?" Rick said.

"Ya I'm fine, or almost fine anyway. You're going to be an uncle in a few months."

"What? How? Oh shut up recruit, you aint that dumb. Do mom and dad know?"

"No and don't you tell them. These are my two new friends. Your task, little brother will be to test them and let me know if they can pass minimums, ok? You take them with you and your buddies tonight and clue them into who we are. Then if they pass and still want to, they will join us."

"Omma, oppa, you look great!" Liz said.

"Good tailors," Nicolas said. "You putting on a little weight?"

"Something like that," Elizabeth said. "Can we go up to the house? I have something to say. Are Rudy's parents here?"

"Yes, but they want you to spend some time with us first. The funeral is tomorrow, that's when they are going to need you."

"No, they need to hear this as well, please have someone bring them up to the house father? You two, go with candidate Bekenbaum here. He will introduce you to the other candidates and they will clue you into what you are getting yourselves into ok? Then you get your ass back home candidate, right after you pass my friends off to your buddies or I will kick your ass around the block. Got it."

"Godamn officers, is always the same. You two sure you wanna join? That Major can be a real bitch."

"I'll show you a bitch you little shit!" Liz said, raising her fist in mock anger as Rick scurried away.

"How can you get away with talking to an officer like that?" the female American asked.

"Well it's a fine line. You have to figure out when she's your commander and when she's your sister. Right now she's being my sister. Come on I'll introduce you to the gang. We have a couple of weeks off then we are back out to the bush. I'm Rick by the way, no rank yet I haven't graduated yet."

"How is my little brother doing out there?" Elizabeth asked.

"Very well," Katherine said. "He came up with a novel new idea on our classic raid the aliens scheme. It was an overwhelming success, he did take a few casualties, but that is a good learning tool as well.

"What he did was, to construct a fake camp about a half mile from the enemy camp, let them discover it and set up an ambush for them. The Americans and the Russians bit on it, the Brits stayed back at their camp. When the ambushers set off the ambush, Rick hit the main camp hard with his main force. As usual we beat the bad guys overwhelmingly."

"Before he left for training," Nicolas said, "he and his two buddies, Harold and Sandy, came up with a bigger and improved drone aircraft that can be armed. It uses satellites for communication and guidance. The tests have been very successful. They and we, are going to make a lot of money from this."

"Sandy Olynick?" Elizabeth said. "I was hoping those two would get together. She's had the hots for him forever."

"Not to be granddaughter," Katherine said. "Sandy said they got together at the grad party and it was like kissing her brother."

"So he does like girls," Emily said. "I was beginning to wonder."

"Oh mom!" Elizabeth said. "He's had other girls! He just doesn't brag about it."

"As well he shouldn't," Emily said. "I thought your father was a saint too when I first met him."

"Well, my man was," Katherine said. "Weren't you?"

"Yes mam, anything you say mam?" Nicolas said. "Tatiana ran them all off as soon as they came near anyway."

"Oh come on, grandma wasn't that bad," Paul said.

"Yes she was," both the elder Bekenbaum's said at the same time.

"When she found out about Katherine," Nicolas said, "she hired private detectives to find out all about her. Then she went down to Billings after I shipped out to Italy and saw for herself. But grandma here won her over with ease."

"Ah Earl and Countess von Hoadle, welcome. Some wine?" Nicolas said as Rudy's parents came into the kitchen.

"Are you sure this is alright?" Rudy's father said. "You do not need some time together?"

"We are all family now my lord, lady. Besides, Liz wants it."

"In that case, I will have some of your famous vodka."

"I as well," Rudy's mother said undoing the top button of her uniform tunic. "Mine Gott, I forgot how uncomfortable these Gott Ver Damnt uniforms were."

"Well we all have put a few pounds on since we were kids Helen," Katherine said. "Except for Emily that is. How the hell she can look so trim and thin after two kids is beyond me."

"Hard work, exercise and three in one rations ladies," Emily said and they all laughed. "I recommend the diet and exercise routine. Maybe I should make a video and sell it. I'd make a fortune. Only Liz seems to have gained any weight over there."

Everyone but Liz, who drank a pop, had a good shot of vodka and were laughing and joking when Rick came in and Liz put down her pop and stood as soon as Rick sat down.

"Helen, Kurt, I was a quarter of a mile away from Rudy's tank when it got hit and saw everything. It was instant and catastrophic. The tank blew right apart on the spot. If any of them felt anything it wasn't for long. They had taken out four T72s and a couple of BMPs before that happened. They did their jobs and did them well. He was a beautiful loving man, an exceptional officer and would have made a perfect father. I and his child will miss him dearly."

"Thank you Liz, we knew he was a good man and leader. And he proved he was brave and courageous. Father?" Helen said.

"Yes, I am four months pregnant."

"What?" all the Elders said.

"You're four months pregnant, led that raid to rescue those prisoners and rode for six hours today in your condition!" Emily said. "Are you insane? You could have damaged yourself or your unborn child."

"Oh mom," Emily said squeezing her mother's shoulders. "I am not a porcelain doll you know. Nor a pampered sorority girl. Today we celebrate the new life that will be coming to us. Tomorrow we celebrate Rudy's life. The day after, I start my new life in Olds. We all knew this day would come and it has."

"One small bit of business first," Nicolas said. "The two Americans. The girl's parents are here and they want to speak with us and her Liz."

"After the funeral then general," Emily said. "After the funeral, I start my new life and they theirs."

The seventeen had been laid to rest among those who had fallen in earlier conflicts. The artillery had fired the salute, the flags been handed out to family members and the last post played. Veterans had moved among the graves visiting old comrades and the mood had slowly shifted from grief to joy as was their way. Soon everyone was gravitating to the armoury or private homes to carry on with the celebration. The Bekenbaum's were no different.

Nicolas, Katherine, Emily, Paul and lastly Elizabeth, sat behind the large table at the front of the briefing room and the American girls parents were seated in the front row of the rows of empty chairs. They were dressed in their Sunday best, but from the cut of the clothing, the family could tell they were not well off.

The door to the briefing room was flung open and the two American soldiers marched in. Their caps under their left arms, they marched to the front of the table and saluted. Nicolas stood and returned the salute, then sat back down.

"Lance Corporal William Henry Jackson reporting sir!" the man said.

"Private First Class Julia Smith reporting sir!" the woman said.

"I am General Nicolas Bekenbaum, I am the commander of the Regiment. You have asked to join the Regiment and this board is to determine if you are qualified and if you are suited to join. If you do join, you will be required to serve full time in the Regiment for five years and if required, to serve a further five years full time. Thereafter, you will be given the option to remain full time but in any case will be required to serve in reserve and full time three months per year for the following twenty years. All members of the Regiment, no matter the age, will be called up for duty at anytime in case of emergency or need of expertise. This is a lifetime commitment people.

"After your first five years of service, you will be granted Canadian Citizenship. After you're twenty, you will be granted full membership in the Andrea Host and classed as Blood Cossack and members of the Earldom of Didsbury. We take ten percent of anything you make, in the Regiment or outside, as dues, or taxes if you will. As long as you stay within the Regiment or the Earldom. That is all the taxes you will ever pay.

"We provide all the medical you will ever need. Any education requirements you have and are qualified to receive. We will start up a business in partnership with you, or provide a means of employment for you if you wish. Housing for veterans is provided prorated as to years of service and these services and privileges are provided to off-spring and spouses of all members of the Regiment. Every position in the Earldom is open to anyone, regardless of sex. The only requirements are the ability to do the job.

"Questions?"

"Lance Corporal Jackson, your records state that you qualified as an expert marksman and that you completed basic combat training at the head of your class, yet you selected to serve on supply and services as a truck driver. Explain."

"Sir, serving in the infantry as a combat soldier would not help me find a job after I got out sir," Jackson said. "Being a truck driver, I could buy my own truck after I got out and have a real job sir."

"Private First Class Smith, what are your real reasons for joining. The work is hard and far from being romantic."

"Sir, in America, women are viewed as being weaker and not allowed to do many of the things that men do. When I was captured, my own country would not come to my aide, but yours did. Not only that, but the Major disobeyed orders to do so. Your people have treated me with nothing but kindness and respect. They treated me like an equal, not a lower class nothing. For the first time in my life I feel like I am a valued member of society sir.

"I know I will never be like the Major sir. I don't have the education or the skill set. But I can still be a valuable member of the Regiment sir and your community, if given a chance sir."

"Private First Class Smith. The Major speaks highly of your courage and compassion. The fact that you finished basic training in the American Army and that you have qualified on the basic American Army rifle course, should qualify you for membership in the Regiment. Not everyone in the Regiment is a combat soldier, but everyone needs to be ready to be one. The Colonel here is an example. So was my mother. If you can make our minimum physical and fire arms qualifications you will be granted membership. We will provide the training for anything you are suited for after that. Have you spoken to your parents about this?"

"Yes sir I have."

"Mr. and Mrs Smith do you have any questions or concerns you would like me to address?"

"Mr. General sir," Mr. Smith said, he and his wife stood. "If everything you say is true it is far better than our daughter could ever expect back home sir. The only hope of a job that she had was in the Army sir. The short time we have been here, why you people are from a different planet. Everyone is friendly and helpful. People stop and say hello and we are strangers here. The only concern that we have is that we may never see her again."

"There will never be any reason that you cannot come and visit Mr. Smith. Well other than she may be on duty or deployed. But that is no different than what she was doing before. She will have three weeks minimum leave every year and she can go or do whatever she wants with that. I am sure that we can arrange for you to immigrate to Canada if you wish. I believe you are an automotive mechanic? The dealership in Olds is always looking for good people. Mrs. Smith? You are a certified health care provider? We can use the help for our older folks here.

"Our forefathers, like yours, came here for a better life. All that you see here was built by us. There was nothing here before we came. The difference is, that we were able to keep our traditions and values and customs. The people you saw today are farmers and trades-men, janitors, street cleaners, businessmen, retail clerks, store own-ers, whatever. But when they put on these blue uniforms, they are all the same. That is what we can offer. We give everyone a chance to be what they want to be, the rest is up to them."

"Thank you general sir. That's all we wanted to hear."

"Lance Corporal Jackson. If you join the Regiment, you will be placed in the level of service we feel you are qualified for, not what you think you want to do. At this point it would seem to be combat arms. Are you prepared to do that? To be placed into harms way and maybe die for a country not of your birth?"

"Sir, yes Sir! After what you people done for me already and what you promise to do for me in the future, yes Sir, no problem sir!"

"You both will be willing to swear allegiance to the Queen, Canada and the Regiment? To drop your allegiance to the United States of America?"

"Sir, yes Sir!" both of them said.

"Show in Candidate Bekenbaum," Nicolas ordered and his aid opened the conference room door and beckoned to Rick waiting outside.

Rick marched to the front of the table, came to a halt, raising his right knee almost to his chest and stomping it on the floor, standing at attention, his eyes focused two inches over Nicolas' head.

"Candidate Bekenbaum reporting as ordered sir!" he said.

"Candidate Bekenbaum, due to your outstanding record in the field and the classroom, it is deemed that you have done enough to graduate. You are relieved of training duty and assigned as training officer to these two new candidates. You are to immediately evaluate their qualifications and report back to us this afternoon with your findings and recommendations. At that time, we will implement your recommendations and fast track them so they graduate with the rest of your class. Is that clear?"

"Sir, yes sir!"

"All right. Get the hell out of my sight and take these two with you. Mr. and Mrs. Smith have a party to attend. Get!"

"Ok," Rick said, after he, Bill and Julia had gone outside.. "When the General says this afternoon, he means this afternoon, not this evening. That means we have to be back here no later than 16:59. It's now 10:30 so we have to hustle. Follow me to the armoury and we will get you kitted out." He was talking as he was walking and he was walking fast.

"You will have a full combat load when we leave and we will be going ten kilometres to the rifle range where you will fire your weapons to qualify. Then we will march back. Do you have boots that you want to use instead of the new ones you will be issued?"

"Ya, mine are in my room beside the bed," Jackson said.

"Mine too," Julia said.

"Ok, I'll send someone for them. Look this is not going to be easy. Our combat arms people are better trained than your Special Forces people and our service arms people are trained as well as your regular army people. Those are the minimum requirements. My evaluation today will determine only if you will meet the minimum requirements with minimal training. Clear?"

"If you don't mind sir, you seem awfully young to be Special Forces," William said.

"We start our training as cadets when we are thirteen, candidate. Last week I planned and led my classmates on an assault and ambush of a number of Special Forces people from different countries and soundly defeated them. And we are no where near as good as the Master Warrant and the Major are. Half of my people don't even want to get their Eagles. That is the level you will be competing against."

"Sir, candidates Bekenbaum, Jackson and Smith reporting as ordered sir!" Rick said at exactly 16:59.

All three stood once again in front of the panel at the briefing room. They were in battle dress, minus weapons and packs. All three were dusty, boots muddy and hair mussed. Nicolas noted the Americans did not salute this time.

"I see you have coached the new candidates on how to report properly in the Canadian Armed Forces," Nicolas said. Saluting indoors was frowned upon.

"Report."

"Candidate Jackson qualified expert on the range with the C7, grenade launcher and side arm, first time out sir. Candidate Smith Qualified expert in the C7 and passed on the grenade launcher, but was subpar on the side arm sir. Both candidates, will, I fear, pass minimum standards sir. Candidate Smith shows stamina and determination sir. I am positive she will qualify expert in fire arms after a bit of training. Candidate Jackson, I feel, will qualify combat arms with further training sir, no doubt about it."

"Candidate Jackson," Elizabeth said. "Do you know how to ride a horse?"

"No mam. Only ever seen one on TV mam," Jackson said.

Elizabeth looked down the table at Nicolas who nodded his head.

"Candidate Jackson, it will be to late for you to graduate with this year's combat arms class with the amount of training you will require. We do however have a qualification exam, which if you pass, will short track you into the combat arms. You will have three months in which to train for this qualification exam. Are you prepared to undergo this training?"

"Yes mam!" Jackson said.

"Candidate Smith, you have indicated that you do not wish to be in the combat arms. I will extend the same training opportunity for you if you so wish."

"No mam. I only wish to serve in whatever capacity I am qualified for mam," Julia said.

"Very well Candiate Smith," Emily said. "I myself have no wish to be in the combat arms and have risen to be a Colonel in the Regiment. Up until five years ago, the Colonel there also did not have her eagle. Each year you will have the opportunity to qualify for your eagle should you wish to do so."

"Candidate Bekenbaum," Paul said. "You will provide the necessary training for Candidates Smith and Jackson to qualify in their chosen area of service. In addition, in order to fully graduate, you will also have to pass the qualification exam. Is that clear?"

"Yes Master Warrant, very clear."

"Candidate Jackson," Paul said. "Your service record says that you have completed your High school equivalency and that your induction test scores indicate that you could well do better. We will expect you to do your utmost to fulfill your full potential.

"Candidate Smith, you do not have your High School equivalency and you will be expected to do so before the three months training is up. Each day from nine until eleven, the colonel will be teaching you those requirements. During those same hours Candidate Jackson, you will be given horsemanship and cavalry instruction by candidate Bekenbaum. Both of you will be given fire arms training for one hour in the afternoon. Then candidate Smith will return to her studies and Candidate Jackson to his. After evening mess, both of you will receive German language instruction. It is the language of choice among us and we revert to it automatically in times of duress.

"As of now, both of you are accepted as candidates and will receive one thousand five hundred dollars per month in wages. You will be issued a full complement of clothing and equipment, which you will be responsible for as to repair and replacement. You will be provided with a barracks which candidate Bekenbaum will share with you. We are co ed here people. Get used to it. Training begins in earnest Monday morning, so you have the rest of today and all of tomorrow to get your selves in order. Dismissed."

"Mr and Mrs. Smith," Nicolas said. "Your daughter will be free in about an hour. You can have her then. We will arrange for your trip home and your trip back here in three months when she graduates and graduate she will. She wants this badly."

"I am sorry to put you through all this trouble candidate Bekenbaum," Jackson said.

"Are you kidding me?" Rick said. "I get hot food every day and a nice cozy warm bed at night. My buds are heading back out to the bush on Monday for the next three months and when they stop freezing their butts off, they will be slogging through mud and fighting off mosquitos. No, I thank you instead. Not only that, but it is a great honour for me. It's not every day we get outsiders wanting to join. My name is Rick and we are all the same rank now. It's only when we have official crap that we have to do all the formal crap."

"I'm Bill," Jackson said sticking out his hand. "You not going to have a problem bunking with a black man?"

"The only problem I'm going to have is if you keep bringing it up. I only care about what you have in here," Rick said poking his heart. "Both of you better get that right away. There were twenty girls with us in the bush. You pull your weight, do your job as best you can, that's all we care about. You're not the first of your kind here Bill. The man that started Olds Collage was a Buffalo Soldier. Nobody cared then and nobody cares now. Come on, I want to get some beer and food before it's all gone."

"How the hell can you do that?" Bill asked. "I can hit the target most times at a walk, but at a gallop? No way."

Rick had just finished putting five rounds in the bullseye of his target with his C7.

"It's actually easier at a gallop than at a walk," Rick said. "At a certain point, all four hooves will be off the ground. That's when you pull the trigger. You aim where the bullet will be, not where you are now. If you do that, you will always be behind. It's like trying to hit a fast ball. You start your swing early. You played baseball no?"

"A little not much. I was a football guy."

"Ya, me too. What position?"

"Quarterback."

"Even easier then. Receiver is going full out down the side line and he breaks inside. Do you throw the ball where he is?"

"Hell no, I'd be five yards behind him. I give him a five yard lead and throw as he makes his break."

"Same thing here. Give it a try and I'll mark where you're hitting. Then you make your adjustments."

Bill trotted down to the end of the laneway and brought his horse to a gallop, stood in his stirrups and as he came level with his target let fly with five single shots, pivoting as he went.

"You were right, it was a lot easier to get a sight picture and keep it," Bill said.

"OK," Rick said. "You were on target with all five. But just at the trailing edge. Shift your aim about six inches and try again."

Once again Bill made his run, this time hitting all around the bulls eye.

"Much better," Rick said. "You only need three in the bull Bill, we have a week left, you should do ok. The lance work is fine and your sword is ok. What works for the rifle will work for the pistol. You will ace it anyway, you're under the time limit and can always dismount to fire."

"That what you're going to do?"

"No, I have a tradition to uphold. It's not easy having a sister like Liz sometimes you know."

"You gonna be an officer like her too?"

"Na, some of my classmates need it more than me. That and the eagle. If I get one I get one. They finally forced my dad to take his, he kept refusing it. I'll probably do the same thing. I don't really want to be an officer anyway. Don't need the hassle. They'll probably force the old man to do that next. He's pretty much the commander anyway. Enough for today. It's Friday and I want to go to town and have a couple of beer. It's your turn to buy too."

"You think Julia is going to pass? She's trying real hard."

"You know, I think if she could ride, she could get an eagle. Maybe next class she can do the full training if she wants. I put in that recommendation for her already. Just don't you tell her though. She is some tough cookie."

"Never used to be," Bill said. "She was your typical bubble head. Only thought about guys and looking good. Your sister had a big impact on her."

"She had a big impact on Liz too. Both of you coming to her like you did right after landing like that. You didn't even know her."

"Didn't have to. She went above and beyond to help us and we both knew it at the time. Then we found not only was she pregnant, but her husband had just died. When she let out that wail, well it was the least I could do. I would have died for her then and probably still will."

"Ya, I think everyone would. She took all of our emotions then. Enough already I'm thirsty."

"Well Bill, it's the big day. You better be ready for it." Rick said as he looked at the gathering crowd.

"As good as I'll ever be. Thanks for all the help." Bill said. He too was looking at the crowd absently rubbing the brand new parachute wings on his chest. He, Julia and Rick had performed their last qualification jump the day before. The wings and the crossed Winchester badges on their collars were the only decorations they had.

"You see Julia? She said she was going to be here."

"Nope," Rick said. "She's not up with her parents and I haven't spotted her in the crowd yet."

"She better hurry up. I can hear the choppers," Bill said.

Sure enough, the beat of helicopter rotors could be heard and the last of the crowd hurried to their seats in the bleachers just as ten Blackhawks, on loan from the US Marines, came into view coming to a hover ten feet off the ground. No sooner coming to a forward halt when ten troopers, five to a side, slid down ropes to the ground and just that fast the helicopters were gone as the troopers formed a perimeter and started firing at targets.

Right after that, a series of pops could be heard as one hundred parachutes opened above the crowd and the rest of the training group hit the ground, dumped their chutes and joined their comrades in a simulated assault. The crowd loved it.

"Who was who?" Bill asked as the troopers formed up and began receiving their Eagles and patches.

"The helicopter troopers were regular army special forces types. This year we had Delta, Spetsnaz, JTF, Bundeswer and the usual SAS. The parachute troops were our people."

"Wow, exclusive company I'm joining."

"Yup. Hey come on, I want to introduce you to my buddies."

"Yo, Harold, Sandy, those Eagles look good on you." Rick said. "This is my new bud Bill."

"Hey Gadget, good to see you," Harold said, shaking Bills hand while Sandy hugged Rick.

"Gadget?' Bill said raising his eyebrows.

"Ya, he's always tinkering with shit,' Harold said. "I wish Sandy would hug me like that."

"In your dreams bone head. Nice to meet you Bill," Sandy said. "You going to try the qual run?"

"Rick convinced me it was a better way than freezing my butt off for three months next year," Bill said.

"Too right," Sandy said. "Oh I miss my nice cozy bed!"

"That and a shower," Rick said holding his nose. "You two are getting right rank."

"Ya, like your shit don't stink!" Harold said.

"You should go for your Eagle Rick," Sandy said. "I know your stupid reason for not getting it, but we are four slots short. Everyone that wanted one this year got one. Bill gets his and there are still three left."

"I agree Corporal Olynick," Paul said, walking up behind them.

"OFFICERS ON DECK!" Sandy said, the four of them coming to attention and saluting.

"At Ease," Katherine said. "Yes Richard there is no reason not to. You and everyone else knows you deserve one. There is no reason not to this year."

"You sure pop?" Rick said.

"Yes, I am sure Rick, just don't be a show boat about it? Have you seen your mother around?"

"No, Julia is missing too. Oh, there's Liz, she finally showed. They are probably right behind her."

"Funny, Liz isn't coming over here. Oh well, she will probably be meeting with the big shots on stage anyway."

"Do your best, both of you," Paul said and he and Katherine hurried off to the reviewing stand to join Elizabeth.

"It's time guys," Sandy said. "Good luck."

"Ok big guy, show time," Rick said. "Remember, block out the crowd, just focus on the targets. Keep him reined in until the last moment, we have lots of time. I'll be thirty seconds behind you ok?"

"No prob Rick. Thanks for everything."

"Ok, get going before you make me bawl."

Bill mounted, walked to the start line and at the designated time, trotted off. Thirty seconds later so did Rick.

As he rode down the line and toward the lances a kilometre away, Rick thought it odd that four sets of targets and four lances had been set up, but put it out of his mind and focused on the task at hand. He gave Bill a quick wave as he was going the other way, then pulled his lance out of the ground, deftly reversed the tip and stuck the butt in behind his right leg. Bringing his horse from a trot to a canter, he made sure his sword was loose in the scabbard and his pistol was in a good spot for a quick grab. Then all thoughts were pushed out of his head and he let the horse have its head, dropping the reins on its neck and guiding it with his knees, he brought the lance out and levelled it at the target, holding it away from his body and letting the impact pull it through his hands, then he pulled the sword and decapitated his three heads, before letting the sword go to land on its rope and rising in the stirrups as he pulled the rifle from his back, he levelled it at his target and fired three measured rounds. Flipping the rifle back on his back he let the horse go twenty yards before turning him back and kicking his left leg loose of the stirrup, he hooked his knee over the saddle horn and leaned sideways under the horse, aiming his pistol under the horses bobbing head and fired three fast rounds at his target then deftly flipped back up on the saddle.

"Shit, shit, shit," Bill said. "I think I blew it."

"Not a chance Bill," Rick said pointing at the umpires who were waving the good shots signals. "Welcome to the Regiment Bill."

"Holy shit! I thought for sure I blew the pistol shots," he said, accepting Ricks hand and pumping it, before grabbing him in a big bear hug.

"I wonder what's with the other two targets?" Bill said.

"Ya me too. There are two spots left, but if somebody wants them they better hurry up. Times running out."

Just then two female voices could be heard yelling and horse's hooves were thundering as two women, rifles slung on their backs and old style Stetson campaign hats jammed on their heads, came flying down the track at full gallop, crossing the start line with seconds to spare. The two riders, one with a dark haired pony tail bobbing at her back, slowed to a tot and continued down the course grabbing their lances and side by side trotting back.

"You don't think?" Rick said looking at Bill.

"No way, she's never even seen a horse, not a chance. When would she find the time?"

The riders urged their mounts to a gallop, still side by side, splitting wider so that one would take one side and the other the other and then the hats fell off to fall on their backs just as the lances struck the targets.

"Shit, isn't that the Colonel?" Bill said.

"Ya, it's mom and Julia," Rick said.

Both women pulled the rifles from their backs and slid down the side of their horses firing at the opposite targets as they went, then dropped the rifles to hang by the slings and flipped backwards on the saddles and fired facing backwards at the pistol targets. The crowd went nuts as the umpires singled good shots for all the targets. Both women were hugging as they walked the horses back to where Rick and Bill were waiting.

"Anything mans can do," Emily said in a thickly Russian accented English.

"Womans do too," Julia said in the same accent.

"Sometimes womans do better," they both said at the same time.

"When did you find the time Julia?" Rick said. "My God that was wonderful."

"School studies pass early I," Julia said in heavily accented German. "Major says, work hard we, pass test make. Work nine, ten hours day us. Sometimes home dark was."

"She is really motivated Richard," Emily said, the conversation completely in German now. "She really wants that Eagle bad."

"You little Vixen!" Paul said rushing up and swung Emily around, her feet off the ground. "I don't know how you managed to keep this secret but you did. Who taught you to shoot like that?"

"Your daughter of course you big Neanderthal. Now put me down before you break something you might want to use later tonight," Emily said, kissing Paul long and hard on the mouth.

"Oh, get a room you two!" Elizabeth said walking up to the group.

"We plan on it, first opportunity we find," Emily said making Paul's ears turn red.

"Good job, all of you," Elizabeth said hugging all four of the contestants. "The ladies were a little free with the ammo, but we felt the effect was more important than the amount of ammo used."

"Well Rick, totally unexpected, by me at least. You are the top of the class. I thought you would just go through the motions," Elizabeth said.

"I was, but that talk you and I had in the bush and then one I had with Oppa after you guys shipped out, changed my mind," Rick said.

"So grandson, top of the class. You get to pick your crew and your specialty, as if any of us can't figure that out," Katherine the training commander said.

"Coyote, with a little something extra," Rick said. "I am also going to need another crew member to run the something extra. Harold and Sandy of course. If Bill agrees, I'd like him as my gunner and Julia as our driver and backup gunner."

"It's not going to be a bit crowded in there?" Paul said.

"The new equipment is smaller, lighter and more robust, so no. and one extra person on lookout and protection will be good."

"Done," Nicolas said. He handed two boxes to Katherine and one to Paul, keeping one for himself.

"Welcome to the Regiment," Katherine said pinning Eagles on Julia and Bills collars.

Paul and Emily were already kissing, Paul having pinned hers on.

"Richard, this is Andreas' Eagle," Nicolas said quietly pinning it on him. "The Earl wants you to have it. He said that his offspring would make fun of it and that he knew you would not. Prove him right Richard. It is a great honour he does you."

"Damn!" Rick said. "That's it. I'm not going to risk our last prototype. Test is over."

The second drone, like the first, crashed to the ground, pieces of shattered fibreglass scattering everywhere as the right wingless bird impacted.

"The back blast from the rocket is just to great. We have to come up with some way of protecting the wings from the heat without adding to much weight or compromising aerodynamics."

"Well, come on then," Harold said. "Let's see what little we can salvage from the two birds."

Sandy, Harold and Rick started climbing out of the Coyote with green garbage bags in hand.

"Have you guys thought of programming in a delay for rocket engine start up?" Julia asked.

All three of the designers stopped and looked at her.

"The type of rocket you are using, is generally shot out of launcher, so back blast is not an issue. Once the rocket fires up, it is down range far enough not to damage anything. You can't use that type of launcher here because of the weight."

"Here, let me see," Bill said, gently pushing Sandy from her consul. "How do I access the parameters?

"Ok, there we are. Three seconds be enough delay you think?"

"What?" Sandy said.

"After launch, a three second delay will let the rocket drop clear of the wing and the drone will have moved ahead of it."

"Shit!" Harold said. "To flippen easy. Fire up the last drone Rick."

Rick sat back down at his consul and started the engine on the last drone, Harold took control and the white ugly remote controlled aeroplane bounced down the rough clearing and became airborne. Sandy started flipping switches on her consul and a black and white display came alive as the rocket she had selected started transmitting video from its camera. Five minutes later, the drone was at five thousand feet and headed toward the four old pickup trucks they would be using for targets.

"Target lock," Sandy said as a beep on her display went from intermittent to solid. She hit a button on her key board and the rocket video showed the rocket falling. Three seconds later as the motor ignited, it picked up speed, rapidly heading toward the old Ford pickup she had selected as a target. She hit some more keys and selected two rockets on the other wing, waited for them to lock onto their targets and fired them both at once. An explosion was heard outside as the first rocket impacted the Ford and Sandy targeted the last rocket at the same spot. Then she watched the Coyotes large video screen to see all three rockets impact.

All five crew members looked at each other for a second.

"Bird still flying?" Rick said.

"Oh ya!" Harold said. "We have a winner people!"

The interior of the coyote went from silence to bedlam as the five crew members started yelling and high fiveing. Five minutes later, the drone was on the ground and shut down and all five of them clambered out and ran over to it inspecting the wings and fuselage for heat damage and finding none.

"Ok, trial is a success," Rick said. "Sandy, you send all the data to the Regiment and the rest of us will see what we can salvage from the failures."

An hour later there was four green garbage bags with bits and pieces of salvageable electronic parts stacked against the rear door of the coyote.

"May I have a word with the two lieutenants?" Rick said. "Gunner, driver, you two load the junk inside and pack the bird on the roof would you?"

"It would have taken us months to figure that out don't you think?" Rick said after the three of them had moved out of earshot.

"Ya I think so," Harold said.

"You mind giving up five percent?" Rick said.

"It's only fair," Sandy said.

"Yo, you two flunky corporals get your butts over here," Rick said.

"'Sup?" Bill said.

"You two are now fifteen percent owners to the patent rights of the Adler project." Rick said. "Without you two, it would have been months or years before we figured out the problem. It isn't much, but we get some spending money out of it usually."

"What?" Julia asked. "What are you talking about?"

"The Regiment trust will register our design for a patent. Then they either licence the design out, or in this case, they will hire a firm to build it and then sell it to other countries. We get ten percent of the profit of the licences or product sales. The Regiment keeps fifty percent of that in a trust for us and we get the other fifty percent. Last year we got enough to build these three drones and arm them with enough left over to buy three new trucks to replace those three trucks we just blew up. Like I said, we get a few bucks. You guys will have a fifteen percent share. The last five percent we will put into refinements or new projects. Fair enough?"

"We are full partners?" Bill said. "For what? We didn't do much. You guys did all the hard work."

"Without both of your input, this project was a bust," Sandy said.

"Ya, shut up dummy, take it," Julia said. "We can use the money dummy. I'm tired of bumming rides off of Sandy."

"Ya," Rick said. "Shut up dummy, take it. Oh and by the way, new partners buy the beer."

"Ah shit, thanks a lot Julia. Do you know how much Harold drinks? I'll be broke for years."

The joking group was half way back from the firing range to the barracks when they were ordered to prepare for a full test of the design for the regiment the next morning.

Chapter Ten

"Join the army and see the world," Bill said after the Coyote had hit a vicious pothole, bouncing his head off the side of the turret. "They didn't tell us this shit hole country with its crappy roads was part of the deal."

"At least we're warm and dry," Sandy said. "Not like those shmucks at that road block."

It was cold and damp in the mountains and the troopers manning the road block had their jackets done up to the neck, gloves on and you could see their breath. A cloud of black diesel smoke coming from the exhausts of the two T72 tanks, one on each side of the road, and the turrets swinging to cover Ricks little convoy of two enhanced Coyotes, a regular Coyote, one LAVAT and three LAVs, as they came into sight of the road block.

"If you couldn't take a joke sergeant you shouldn't have joined" Rick said. "Sandy, get a lock on those two tanks and the BMP in the rear. Harold tell the rest of the group to fan out as soon as we hit the clearing and for the LAVAT to target the two BMPs in front. Bill target the twenty on the right machine gun post. Julia, stop two hundred yards away from the road block."

A month earlier Rick, and his crew had been summoned to Regiment. Rick had been promoted to Warrant Officer and Sandy and Harold to Captain. Julia and Bill were now sergeants. They had been transported with their equipment to Germany and had been on the road ever since. Rick was in de facto commander of their little task force, while Harold was the on paper commander. They were the spear head of a NATO task force that was coming to put an end to the genocides occurring in the Balkans.

Rick climbed out of the small man door at the rear of the Coyote as it came to a halt and walked to the front of it, making a grand show of pulling the kinks out his back for the watchers at the road block, making sure his helmet mounted radio system was working before he walked toward the road block, armed with nothing but his side arm. He stopped a hundred yards from the road block, put one foot forward and crossed his arms across his chest.

"All targets locked and acquired," Harold said over the radio.

A burly man with long moustaches, flanked by two trooper's, rifles at the ready, approached Rick from the road block. Ten yards away the man, an officer of some sort, ordered his two men to stop and he continued to where Rick was standing.

"No one passes without permission," the man said in heavily accented English.

"I am Warrant Officer Bekenbaum of the Canadian Army and require clear passage to Saryavo, as guaranteed under the UN."

"I am Colonel in Serbian Army and I no recognize your right to passage. If you do not go back I will shoot you dead."

"Are you threatening violent action against me sir?"

"No threat, fact. I wave my hand and your puny force disappears, like that," he said snapping his fingers. "You can do nothing. My tanks destroy you, you can do nothing."

"Very well sir, you have just committed an act of war against a NATO signatory country. In effect Colonel, you have just declared war on NATO. Weapons free Sandy."

Three seconds later, in half second intervals, both T72 tanks and the rear two BMPs were smouldering wrecks. The LAVAT let go with a salvo of rockets that put the other BMPs out of action and the twenty millimetre cannons of the rest of the group had chewed up the machine gun and infantry positions. Julia stitched the two armed soldiers that had come with the Colonel and Rick had his 45ACP levelled at the Colonels nose.

"You were right Colonel. Just like that," Rick snapped his fingers. "It's all over. The next sound you will be hearing is our CF18's hitting your supply base."

"But, UN not supposed to do those things," the Colonel said.

"I'm not part of a UN force Colonel. I told you, I am the Canadian Army, which is now at war with Serbia and you are now my prisoner. Harold, tell the column it is clear to proceed. Now if you would be so kind as to give me your side arm and move off the road, I must proceed to my destination. Some one will be along to take care of your dead and wounded. Good day sir."

Harold and Rick were relaxing, their backs against the turret of the Coyote and their faces upturned to catch the sun's rays. It was their turn to man the Eagle that was circling a distant suspected target and Sandy was letting Julia have a try at the controls while she supervised the monitors, occasionally referring to a road map and jotting down some notes onto it. It was Bills turn to cook today and he was brewing up some coffee and frying up some bacon and eggs he had picked up locally on a Colman stove that had been 'liberated' from someplace. Usually they took their meals in the US Army mess with the rest of their team, but it was their turn for duty and all of them would rather have their own cooked meals rather than the dried three in one meals out of the packet and cooked over the exhaust manifold of the Coyote.

Rick had just finished eating and was lighting a cigarette to go with his after dinner coffee, when a US Army MP Humvee, followed by a white G wagon with large UN lettering on it, came up. Two blue beret members of the second battalion PPCLI got out of the G Wagon and came up to them. One was a Major, the other a Lieutenant.

All five of them stood up and saluted the senior officers.

"Looking for Captain Hassman," the major said.

"You got me Major, what can I do for you?" Harold said.

"You are to accompany me to my headquarters for a briefing," the Major said.

"Right," Harold said, picking up his C7. "Warrant, you're with me. Captain you're in charge and I will need that map."

As Rick picked up his C7, making sure it had a full magazine and buckled on his pistol belt, pistol and spare cartridges attached, Sandy handed the street map to Harold, who put it in a cargo pocket on his pants. The two then followed the Major to the G Wagon and piling in the back seat, took off.

"You shouldn't need those weapons," the lieutenant said.

"Are you kidding me?" Rick said. "I hear it's open season on the UN around here."

"Oh, they usually leave us alone," the Major said. "The general has a bad habit of letting us shoot back, unlike the other UN troops."

Shortly, they were ushered into a briefing room. The general, flanked by two colonels, one a German, the other an Italian, rose to greet them.

"It's good to see the Regiment is involved in this, if only a scout troop. Welcome, have a seat."

"After your little show, the smarter of the so called freedom fighters have turned in their weapons and quit. The show of force from the Americans has been impressive so far. But the Serbs I think, you will find are stubborn. But that is not what I have called you here for.

"The Croatians have taken one of my officer's captive and I have been authorized to have your people get him out. When can you be ready to do that Captain?"

Harold looked over to Rick who nodded. Harold took the map and spread it out so the general could see it.

"You might be able to find someone stupid enough to try it, but it won't be us," Rick said standing. "There are four radar controlled twenty millimetre anti aircraft guns, located here, here and here. Fifty caliber machine guns mounted on these three roof tops and another four covering the ground approaches. So far, we have counted six man portable SAMs. There are approximately five hundred heavily armed troops protecting the area if, by some chance, an attacking force manage to get in close enough."

"I guess we will be forced to pay the ransom then," the general said. "You are confident in your intelligence?"

"Yes sir," Rick said. "We have had the area under constant aerial surveillance since we arrived sir."

"That would cost fortune. Are you sure?"

"Yes sir I am sure. Our Eagles are very small and very quiet. They are seldom spotted. I might have another idea though sir if you are interested. How much ransom are they asking for?"

The two LAVs stood idling ten yards in front of the check point, a white flag prominently hanging from each. Finally a BMW screamed around the corner coming to a halt and three heavily armed men in uniform clambered out, dragging the Canadian officer out with them. Rick and Bill walked over to meet them, Bill carrying a large duffle bag.

"UN finally want to pay?" the leader of the group said.

"Not as far as I know," Rick said. "I'm not with the UN, but I have been authorized to negotiate."

"No negotiate. 1.5 million Euros, you get your man back," the man said.

"We have several options," Rick said. "We can mount a rescue mission, which would most likely kill the hostage, a lot of my people and a lot of yours, not the preferred option. We could just hit you with a massive airstrike which would kill the hostage and a lot of you which would cost a lot more than 1.5 million Euros. We could give you the 1.5 million Euros and all three of you would die within the year from some 'accident'. Or you could give me my officer and his vehicle and I give you this five hundred thousand Euros and we all walk away. Choice is yours. You have three minutes."

Bill opened the duffle and tossed it over to them.

"What stops me from killing you and taking the money? Your little LAVs not make much trouble," the man said.

"There are six CF18's and six Tornado's orbiting the area," Rick said. "They would much rather hit you people and be back at base by lunch, than to have to go to Belgrade for their mission. Two minutes."

"OK, deal. Take officer now, we bring vehicle tomorrow."

"One minute. We take the officer and the vehicle now."

"Times up. Let's go Bill," Rick said. *"Tango Four to Bird Three, commence bomb run. Tango team prepare to mission."*

The turrets of the LAVs swung to cover the group and the crew chiefs could be seen arming the turret mounted fifty caliber machine guns and pointing them at the now very nervous troops manning the check point.

"Wait, wait!" the man said. "Call it off call it off! Deal deal!" Then he yelled some orders to the check point in his own language and a trooper picked up a telephone and made a frantic call.

Just then a CF18 screamed overhead just above the rooftops and just below the speed of sound. The missiles and bombs loaded on it clearly visible as it rotated and went back straight up, after burners full on.

"Just in case you thought we were bluffing," Rick said.

"No, no," the man said. "We have been warned to watch for the ones with the bear and eagle on the shoulders. We know you don't play round. You probably have rest of group hidden around corner and little bird with big punch overhead. No we take deal."

Just then, a little worse for wear LAV with UN markings drove up. The man driving it clambered out and ran back around the corner. Rick waved to his troops and three of them came over and manned the vehicle.

"Do, I need to warn you what will happen if we are fired upon when we leave?" Rick said.

'No, no go," the man said. "You safe."

"A pleasure doing business with you," Rick said, gathering up the dazed Canadian officer. "Welcome back sir."

"OFFICERS ON DECK!" Bill said, as the general flanked by an American Colonel approached. Rick and his crew stopped what they were doing, lined up, came to attention and saluted.

"That was a good job you did there Warrant Bekenbaum," the general said. "I knew you guys were good. I only wish you could have got my vehicle back for me too, but it seems to have disappeared."

"Funny how that happens sir," Rick said. "But I am sure DND will get the UN to pay for it sir."

"Yes, I am sure. Just as I am sure that somehow the Regiment will be reimbursed the money it spent to get my Captain back. Now the Colonel here and the reports that I have received, tell me that you have a couple of interesting toys with you. I wonder if I could have a look at them."

Rick walked the general and his group over to where the two Adlers and the backup Eagle were parked.

"The smaller one is the Eagle sir," Rick said. "We use it for surveillance and long range scouting. The larger ones are the Adlers. They do the same job, but can be armed with four antitank or antipersonnel rockets. All the units are remote control, have built in GPS guidance systems and high definition colour and infrared cameras. If the general wishes, we can show the general what one of our Eagles is looking at right now."

Harold took the general and the Colonel into the Coyote and turned on a monitor, then played with his keyboard for a moment bringing the feed of the airborne Eagle to the monitor.

"Right now, we have it orbiting a suspected target about a hundred miles east of here," Harold said. "It's being controlled from the other Coyote, we take turns. If we had been authorized and if we had found a suitable target, one of the Adlers would be armed and able to take out that T72 over there. But as you can see, they are moving out towards the border, so we will just monitor their progress at this point."

"What's the range of one of these things?"

"About a thousand kilometres sir, but they are slow. What we gain in stealth we lose in speed. If we need a target hit in a hurry, we still call on the zoomies sir."

"Impressive," the General said. "Don't you think so Colonel?"

"Yes sir," the Colonel said. "I have already sent a report to the Pentagon requesting they have a look at procuring them."

"How much would one of these units cost us Captain," the General said.

"Gee I really don't know General," Harold said. "The Regiment just gives them to us. Much like a C7. I don't ask how much they cost, I just use them."

"It was the first warm spring day, the sun was shining and the temperature was warm enough that we had taken off our jackets and rolled up our sleeves."

Rick looked down from the school gymnasium stage at the one hundred fifty or so grade twelve students assembled the week before their graduation. His company had just returned from their duty in the Balkans the week before and were winding down the end of their five years of mandatory service. He had been asked to address the next graduating class, so here he and his four troop mates were, standing in front of these oh so young and oh so eager faces.

"A cease fire had been declared and honoured for over two weeks now and the town was coming alive once again. The shops were re-opening for the first time in months and people were hitting the streets to buy fresh food and to talk to friends they had not seen for a long time. A young mother, about twenty five or so, around eight months pregnant and pushing a baby carriage with another young child, began to cross the street with her mother. Both of them smiling broadly and chatting happily as they crossed the street in safety for the first time in a long time.

"And then the sniper fired. First one shot. It struck the young mother directly in the womb. Then another shot took out her mother and finally a full burst into the baby carriage. My troopers opened up on his position and took him out, but the damage had already been done. A young mother, her mother and her unborn and living baby had died in less time than it took me to tell it.

"Two days later, we were deployed to an area about twenty kilometres north of that town. A large armed faction had refused to stand down and we were being sent as part of the assault force being sent down to confront them and make them comply with their governments orders to disband or to take them out. Our company was to scout the positions, report back to the main task force and to hold them in contact for as long as we could. This we did and somewhat to the chagrin of the main force, we broke them after about an hour's heavy fighting. During that time, we endured a sustained artillery bombardment, until we took out their batteries and several waves of assaults. We were almost ready to disengage because of a lack of ammunition when the enemy broke off and scattered.

"The next morning, as the main battalion entered the town the enemy had come from, we found out why they had been fighting so hard and had refused to stand down. They had not yet finished burying the inhabitants of the town they had destroyed, hoping to conceal their crimes before we appeared on the scene.

"People will ask you and maybe you have asked yourself, I know I did when I was your age. Why would you want to serve in the army? Canada has done nothing since Korea. We are a peace loving people. A polite people who go out of our way not to upset other people. Why join the army it is a waste of time?

"Ask the husband and relatives of the women that were killed by that sniper. Ask the relatives of that town that had been massacred. Ask the people of that country what we did for them. How we stopped the indiscriminate killing of non-combatants, of children. How we arrested those responsible for the genocides, the rapes and the murders. How we treated the injured, not carrying what their nationality or religion was. How we, Canadians and members of this regiment, came from so far away to help people we did not know. And then we went back home. We did not stay and occupy their land. We did not tell them how to live their lives. We did our jobs and we went home.

"We put our lives on the line so that others may have peace and security. So that others may sleep safe at night. So that their children and someday yours, can live a life free of the types of things we fight against. So that the rest of our brother and sister Canadians don't have to ever experience what you will be fighting against. This is why we and this Regiment and our people, join the army. This is our people's commitment to the Canadian people. Whatever branch of service you choose is important. Not everyone has the temperament to be a front line infantry soldier. But we all must be prepared to do our duty and if necessary to put our lives on the line if necessary so that we can save other lives.

"I and my team mates would be proud to serve alongside of each and every one of you should the opportunity present itself. I am Warrant Richard Bekenbaum and five years ago I was sitting right where you are right now, thinking many of the same thoughts you are thinking right now. We survived. Some of us did not, some of us were wounded. It will not be easy, but at the end of your five years, hopefully you will be proud of what you have accomplished, just as we are.

"Thank you for your time and the opportunity to say my piece."

"Captain Hassman," the thin young man at the head of the line to ask questions said. "You graduated at the head of your class and are a recognized computer genius as is Captain Olynick, and an accomplished aeronautical engineer, yet you serve as a front line combat soldier."

"Well someone has to keep the riffraff under control," Harold said. "God knows what those bone head enlisted people would do to my little pets if I was not there."

That received more than a few chuckles from the crowd.

"You have some bad data there my friend. Captain Olynick was at the head of our class, I was second and if Warrant Bekenbaum had spent more time on the books and less time on football and playing with radio frequency control systems for toy airplanes, he would have been at the top of the class. You also seemed to have missed the fact that I too am a jock. I played wide receiver on our football club. Academic standing in high school, while admirable, really has little to do with much of what you will face in real life. Sergeant Smith only has a GED and she only received that after she joined us. Sergeant

Jackson had his grade twelve, but life's circumstances made it impossible for him to go to university. Yet without both of the sergeant's valuable input, the Adler project would be only an interesting failure.

"The founder of our regiment was a geek. He was an accountant. If you want to enjoy the full benefits of our unique society, you are required to serve. That does not mean you have to be a front line grunt like us, but you will be required to pass a minimum of physical, mental and martial requirements. Throughout the regiment's history, we have been on our own and many times the Bears have had to stand in the line along with the Eagles. I think that once you become involved, you will see why."

"Captain Olynick," a tall brunet said. "What are your plans now that you have completed your time in service?"

"The Regiment is sending me to MIT, where I plan to further my understanding on the newest computer coding and language systems, go to a lot of parties and maybe find a cute hunk to play with."

Sandy let the laughter settle down and continued.

"I plan to continue full time in the regiment. Unfortunately, the Warrant will have to find a new systems operator, because the regiment has given me command of my own Coyote crew which will be made up from you people once you graduate. So be nice, I am to be the commander of some of you. I also want to be a mother someday, so at some point, I will have to find a cutie to settle down with. But at this point, I am married to the regiment."

There were ten in all and most of the questions were not deep ones and the final student came forward. She was almost six feet tall and by her clothing, she was not part of the affluent part of society. She came forward with her head down cast, then stood tall and looked each of the team mates in the eyes before starting.

"All of you have done well and all of you come from the affluent part of our community," she said, a look of defiance in her eyes. "What can the rest of us expect?"

"Oh you poor hard done by thing," Julia said. "You live in a community where you can be anything you want. A community which rewards achievement, not on who you are but on what you are.

"I joined the American Army to get away from a dead end low caste life. The only hope I ever had was to join the army or get knocked up and marry some drunk looser. Or a man like my father who worked hard, but only ever had enough to barely pay the rent and buy food for us. But the Army was just like it was at home. I had a job I hated and never would have made it to sergeant because of who I was and where I came from.

"The Regiment offered me the opportunity to prove I was better than that and I have. The regiment has asked me to go to university and to become an officer. I have no wish to do either. I am where I want to be. Doing a job that almost everywhere in the world is forbidden to females. I will, despite what the captains have said, never be a scholastic genius. But I am damn good at what I do and I plan on getting better at it. I will stay full time in the regiment as long as they will have me and I hope my children will too.

"The question for you young lady is. Do you have the balls to back up your defiance, or are you just going to blame class differences for your failures for the rest of your life? You work hard you go places. You sit on your ass and complain, you will go nowhere. Choice is yours."

"Young lady," Bill said standing up. "I grew up in the Hood in LA. Being a black man from the hood in the US, you die young or become a drug addict or a drunk. It is a never ending cycle of destruction. I was brought up by a single mother and grandmother, both of whom worked two jobs to support us. I would have ended up the same, so I joined the army, to get a job and to get training to be a truck driver so I could support a family some day and not live in the hood. That was the only dream I ever had. Be a truck driver, find a nice lady and buy a nice little house in the suburbs and hope my kids could go to college. Being black in America is about the lowest a human being can get, so when the regiment offered me the chance I jumped at it. Here I am not black, I am Bill. I am respected for who I am, not the colour of my skin or where I came from.

"All of you know Mr. Bekenbaum's background. He could have made Eagle easy, he could be an officer, in fact he should be. He was tasked to train me personally, so that I could graduate with an Eagle with the rest of the class. I asked him if he would have a problem with being with a black man for the next two months. He told me the only problem he would have is if I kept bringing it up and to lose my attitude. That he bleeds red blood like I do. That when he takes a dump, it stinks like everyone else's does and that if I had a problem with that I should resign and go back home.

"If you ask anyone in our company, they will tell you that if anyone deserved an Eagle it was Rick. Yet he was more than prepared to flunk his exam and serve as a Bear. He said the important thing was to serve, not to be an Eagle. That there were only so many open slots to be Eagles every year and that others, not as affluent as himself could use the extra money that comes with the Eagle. The only reason he agreed to test for it was that there was a vacant spot that had not been filled. Only then did he prove that he was more than worthy to wear that Eagle.

"So young lady, do you have what it takes? Are you tough enough? Are any of you tough enough? This Regiment is the best of the best. The Bears are good enough to serve as front line and Special Forces troopers in almost any army in the world. The Eagles turn down more jobs than we go on. There just are not enough of us to go around. Before you latest group of candidates are allowed into the field full time, you will get to spend a little time with Mr. Bekenbaum, Sergeant Smith and myself for some enhanced training. We will be looking for ten people to help us. Young lady, I sincerely hope

that you are one of them. I can use someone with your fire and determination."

"You get the names of the first one and the last one?" Rick said.

The five of them were enjoying a beer together. It would be the last they would be together as a group for some time.

"Ya," Bill said. "I figured you would want that. I'll keep tabs on them."

"I suppose you are off to Europe for a holiday Gadget?" Sandy said.

"No Twinkie," Rick said. "I and my pony have an appointment on the Panther we want to make. After I spend a few days at home. I need some me time."

"I'm picking up my folks and taking them on a motorhome holiday for my two months," Julia said. "Master Warrant said he has cleared it with Canada Immigration for my folks to come here if they want and I think they will. I have my eye on a nice house in town that I think they will like. Then I am off to Petawawa for a bit of training with JTF before I link back up with you guys."

"That's what you get for missing training," Harold said. "Now you get to hang out in Pet with JTF. You heading home Bill?"

"Taking Mom and Grandma house hunting in the burbs. I have tutors lined up for my little brothers and sisters so they can catch up. Schooling in the hood sux. My little bros want to come up here for a visit, so I think Gadget will have some company up on the Panther."

"How many siblings do you have?" Sandy said.

"Two bros and two sisters," Bill said.

"So, is there something wrong with girls coming up to the Panther or are you being racist?" Rick said.

"Touché," Bill said. "I never thought about that. I'll ask them."

"Well enjoy your time at university, Geekdoms," Rick said. "While you two slackers are enjoying the warm sun and leisure life, the three of us will be toiling away training the new kids to be the saviours of the free world."

"Ya and loving every second you torment them," Harold said.

After that, the rest of the company joined them and to soon, they went their separate ways.

Rick had just come back to his camp, unsaddled and groomed his horse. It was still cool up in the reaches of Panther Mountain. He had woken up to frost this morning. The spring fed lake had yielded three two pound Rainbow Trout and he stoked up his smouldering fire, before setting about cleaning the fish, rolling them in a batter of flour and butter and then placing them in his cast iron frying pan. He set the frying pan across two rocks of his fire pit and then dumped two cans of beans into a cast iron pot, placing it on two rocks across from the frying pan. Picking up the blue enamel coffee pot, he trekked the short distance to a brook that emptied out of the small lake, filled it, came back to the fire and dumped a handful of coffee grounds into the pot before placing it on a small rack across the fire. That completed, he pulled his saddle over to the fire and leaned it up on its horn, using it for a back stop as he sat down on the ground heavily. Pulling his cowboy hat down over his eyes, he leaned back and went to sleep.

"Look at that," Elizabeth said. "The super trooper asleep while four noisy horses ride up on him unawares."

"My Lady Countess had better get her ass off that horse and check those fish before they burn," Rick said from under his hat. "Those two old codgers you have with you better have some booze on that pack pony, or they ain't welcome in my camp."

"Oh and who says I have to cook?" Elizabeth said.

"I caught 'em. I cleaned 'em, I got the fire goin'. Rules are you cook 'em."

"Oh little brother never change," Elizabeth said giving him a big hug.

Rick hugged her back and then got up and helped his father and grandfather unsaddle and unpack the horses.

"Is that coffee ready?" Nicolas said. "I'm getting to old for this shit."

"He said, after trotting all morning to get here," Elizabeth said. "Ya, pots boiling, bring your cup."

Nicolas dug his beat up blue enamel cup from his saddle bag and waddled over to the fire. Taking the leather riding glove off his right hand, he put it inside his right hand and rapped the side of the coffee pot sharply on the side three times with his cup to settle the grounds before he poured himself a cup. Then he rapidly put the pot down and flung off the gloves from his right hand.

"Goddamn that's hot!" he said.

"Dummy!" the other three said in unison.

"Ya, ya," Nicolas said. "No respect."

They bantered back and forth while they ate lunch. This was the first time in five years the four of them had all been together in one place and not on duty or at some function. Now they could let their hair down and act like normal people.

"What's with all the paper work in the packs Oppa?" Rick said. "You didn't bring work up here did you?"

"Yes and no Gadget," Nicolas said. "I have some letters here for you, one from your uncle George and some things for you to sign. It's family stuff."

Nicolas got up and dragged his saddle bags over to the fire. Rummaging through them, he came up with a file folder and handed Rick one letter out of it. "This is George's. Read it first."

Rick tore it open and began to quickly read it. He rarely had the opportunity to see his uncle being down in Billings full time as he was. As he read, he became confused at what he was reading and at the end he looked up to see his grandfather, father and sister in a line in front of him, down on one knee and very serious looks on their faces, hats in one hand.

"I am Elizabeth, daughter of Emily, daughter of Katherine, daughter of Tatiana, daughter of Elizabeth, Countess of Olds," Elizabeth said looking Rick in the eyes. "What is done to you and yours is done to me and mine, so say I in front of God and those here."

"I am Nicolas, son of John, son of Andreas, Ataman of Andrea Host," Nicolas said. "What is done to you and yours is done to me and mine. So say I in front of God and those here."

"I am Paul, son of Nicolas, son of John, son of Andreas, messenger for Her Royal Highness Queen Elizabeth the Second," Paul said standing, holding a pendant on a sash. He came forward and placed the sash so that it hung from Rick's right shoulder to his left hip, then stood back, unrolled a parchment and began to read.

"Be it known that We hereby decree, that Richard Paul Bekenbaum, shall henceforth rule in our stead over the Earldom of Didsbury and is named Richard, Earl of Didsbury."

"Be it also know that the Earl of Didsbury is made Knight of the Bath with all the rights responsibilities and privileges and that he is named Sir Richard, Earl of Didsbury."

"Sir Richard is to present himself to Our presence on July first for formal investiture at Our estates in Windsor."

"Signed, Elizabeth Two, Queen of Great Britain, Canada and the head of the Commonwealth of Nations."

"There is a personal notation" Paul said.

"Congratulations Gadget, Naj speaks highly of you as does my daughter. I am looking forward to spending some time with you here at Windsor. Your cousin Liz."

"What the hell kind of joke is this?" Rick said.

"No joke," Paul said handing the parchment to Rick. "You need to make the proper responses Sir Richard."

Rick looked from one to the other and then took off his hat and went to one knee in front of them.

"I am Richard, son of Paul, son of Nicolas, son of John, son of Andreas, clan of Bekenbaum, Earl of Didsbury, what is done to you and yours is done to me and mine, so say I in front of God and those here."

"Now we have a couple of hours before the others get here so we can answer your questions and drink some of this lovely bubbly your sister insisted we bring," Nicolas said.

"Before the old Earl died, he bequeathed the Earldom to you Richard," Nicolas continued. "None of us, for reasons we won't get into now, are eligible. I have been administering as regent in your stead until now. It mostly runs itself Gadget, every five years or so the Peers get together in England for a dog and pony show or if somebody important dies, you have to show up for the funeral. Technically you are my boss, but we seem to have separated the Ataman position from the Earl position and if it's all right with you, I would like to continue in that role, with your father taking over after me and you after your father."

"Are you kidding me?" Rick said. "I barely know enough to command a company let alone the whole Regiment. Will this mean I can't go out in the field anymore?"

"We would prefer if you carried on the way you have been son," Paul said. "Outside of the Regiment, all this Royal stuff doesn't mean much. So keep it quiet and carry on, just like we have been."

"You have alliances all over the world you can call on should the need arise," Elizabeth said. "All of them quiet, but with the same oath that you just spoke. For now it is important that you keep doing what you are doing and gaining experience along the way. The Regiment has always been at the forefront of technology and techniques and what you are about to embark in is a modern version of what we did for centuries. It's what we excel at and what is expected of us. Korea and the Gulf were exceptions."

"Most of what we did in my time was behind the lines Gadget," Nicolas said. "Except at the end of WW2 and Korea and Paul's was all behind the lines or small recon tactics until Desert Storm.

"The past was the two major super powers funding surrogates in mostly small conflicts involving regional factions. Now Islamic radicals have taken it to another level, funding and training small cells in guerrilla warfare. Like the IRA, bombings, assassinations, hit and run attacks on major public areas. Unlike the IRA, the Islamic people don't care how many or who they kill and don't much care if they survive themselves," Paul said. "You saw the extreme of that in the Balkans. Mix religion with age old ethnic hatreds and it is one hell of an explosive combination. For the most part in its history, Canada has avoided that kind of nonsense. Once in a while Quebec, or a Native group, will get a little bit out of hand, but nothing like anywhere else in the world including the US. This regiment right from its inception, was raised to combat those kinds of things.

"A convergence of Islamic fundamentalists in the middle east and centred in Afghanistan after the Soviets were kicked out is where we feel the next hot spot will be," Elizabeth said. "All the major Islamic powers are pouring money into the region and setting up training areas all over the country. Pakistan, Iran, Syria, Libya and even our friends, the Saudis, to a small degree, are involved. You, Bill and Julia, will train ten picked people from the upcoming class in the new hit and destroy tactics and those ten will form the leaders of the next groups. We want a hundred of you trained and ready to go at short notice."

"As far as logistics end of things go," Nicolas said. "We have good people in the Bears and they are just as professional as we are at what they do. One thing about how this regiment is set up, the logistics and admin people, train in the field alongside of us and know what we do first hand. So, unlike other regiments, the admin people focus on what we need to function instead of what they need to function. In other regiments, two thirds of their organizations is noncombat bureaucrats, while ours is maybe one third and made up of physically handicapped or severely wounded veterans. Or like myself, to old to serve in the lines, but still willing to serve in whatever way we can."

"The biggest and hardest task you will have to learn Rick is to delegate and trust those beneath you are just as good at what they do as you are," Elizabeth said. "That comes with time in service and experience. You didn't make Warrant on your last name Rick, you got it on your abilities. The old Earl knew he didn't have the capability to function as a soldier, but he was one hell of an administrator. Unfortunately because of his temperament and his choice of spouse, his children became spoiled elitists, more interested in looking good and lording it over those they felt were inferior to them. Just like the old Russian aristocracy that we came here to get away from."

"We, all of us, have been raised differently," Nicolas said. "This was a conscious decision made by my father. Stephan saw the mistake he had made bringing up the old Earl and concurred, he agreed to separate the Earl from the Ataman, with provision that it be reunited at some point. That time has come."

"What's with the cousin reference from Her Majesty?" Rick said.

"At some point in history," Nicolas said. "All the old royal families in Europe were related one way or another. It's not important how, but it is nice that the Monarchy takes a special interest in us. Now let's polish off this bottle of bubbly before our wives get here and start nagging."

"Hey, I'm a mother you know, be nice," Elizabeth said.

"And so it starts," Paul said. "Nag nag nag."

"No respect," Elizabeth said. "Pass the bloody bottle."

"Does your family understand what is involved Bill?" Nicolas asked. "I mean fully understand. We have no exceptions to the membership rules."

"Yes sir," Bill said. "They have been working hard getting their marks up to standard. We even hired a Canadian studies tutor. It will be hardest for my next brother, he will have only grade twelve to get his military training as close to your people as he can. But with my help, he should make it. We have had other relatives that moved to Canada and they tell us all the time how great it is here. What you people offer is even better."

"He's going to have to be tough," Rick said. "All those kids have been together for their whole lives some of them. He is in for a rough time."

"No worse than he was getting back home," Bill said. "He'll be ok. Just being out here doing what we are doing is incentive enough."

Bills whole family, his mother, grandmother two sisters and two brothers had come on horseback up to the camp spot on the Panther. They had never before been in the wild and were enjoying every minute of it.

"As a veteran and a member of the host, you are entitled to a quarter section of land Bill," Nicolas said. "We have a number of vacant ones at this time. One is fairly close to town and I think perfect for you. All but the five acre homestead is farmed or in pasture and rented out. The old house and buildings are pretty much shot, but we can help with low interest loans to build new ones."

"Sounds good, let me take the family to see it and if granny and mom say it's good, it's a go," Bill said. "How much of the rent will I get?"

"We only take ten percent," Nicolas said. "We only ever take ten percent, even if you farmed it yourself."

"What a city boy from LA be farmer? Ya, right." Bill said.

"You never know Bill, the option to rent or farm is yours," Nicolas said.

"Ut oh," Rick said. "Fish Cop approaching at high speed."

A white and green Ford 4X4 pickup was approaching at a high rate of speed, throwing its two occupants around the cab as it bounced over the rough trail.

"Hey Emm. Bobs got a rookie driving," Paul said. "This should be fun, you handle it."

"What's going on, are we not allowed to be here?" Bill's mother said.

"It's all fine," Emily said. "Bob's an old friend."

The truck slid to a stop and the driver came piling out, clearly upset.

"What are you people doing here?" the Fish and Wild Life Officer said. "You are not allowed to be up here on this Crown Land."

"My understanding is that this is public land and only closed to vehicular traffic," Emily said. "The only vehicle I see is yours and we are members of the public."

"This is Crown Land, not public land and subject to the rules and regulations covered under the Alberta Environment Act. I am going to ask you to leave and fine you for being in an unauthorized area," he said, pulling out his ticket book.

"We do not recognize your authority, now please take your noisy smelly vehicle and go away," Emily said.

The rookie looked back at his trainer who just motioned him to carry on.

"I am afraid I must insist that you vacate the area immediately or by the Authority of the Crown I will be forced to arrest you," the rookie said.

"As the representative of the Crown responsible for this property I order you to stop your harassment of these people," Elizabeth said.

"Well that is not strictly true sis," Rick said. "Young man, I am Sir Richard Bekenbaum, Earl of Didsbury, by order of Her Majesty Queen Elizabeth. So technically you are my employee and this is my land. I commend you on your diligence and sense of duty, but I fear in this instance it is misplaced. Bob get your ass out here and quit laughing your head off in that truck."

"He wouldn't listen Rick," Bob said still smirking. "I told him you had every right to be here and had let us know you would be here. Give him a break, he's from Edmonton."

"Look son," Bob said. "This land is Crown Land only for convenience and at the bequest of the Bekenbaum family, who are the deeded owners of the land. In the old days, he could have had you shot for your impertinence. You handled yourself fairly well otherwise, like the Earl there said. By the way, the other lady is the Countess of Olds and she has the same arrangement for the forestry reserve as the Earl does here. Now that all this crap is done, Nicolas where is the bottle? I fear the drive up here has unsettled me and I need some medicine to settle my stomach down."

Chapter Eleven

"Hey Bill," Rick said as the two men broke their hug. "Get the house built?"

"Yup," Bill said. "Grandma is finally almost happy. Mom has learned to drive and has a cute little Rav4 to bomb around in. My youngest brother and sister have joined the 4H and we are trying our hand at raising some cows. I'm glad we are going back active, I was getting bored."

"You're getting bored," Rick said. "At least you got to play weekend soldier and spend two months at Wainwright in maneuvers. I had to hang out in wet and damp England attending boring parties and giving lectures on small unit cavalry tactics to oh so superior RMC students."

"Well you got to hang out with the Royal Family that must have been nice."

"Ah, they try to act like normal people, but they can't. Different life style over there. Young Harry has possibilities though. He wants to be a regular army officer and not being in realistic line for the throne, is more normal."

"By the way," Rick continued, "here are some do dads to add to your uniform. One for the paper cut you got in the Balkans, a couple of mentioned in dispatches, a unit citation, a NATO Balkans Medal and a Meritorious Service Medal."

"What's the unit citation for?" Bill asked.

"That little nonsense we were playing with against the Croats. The Pixlies are getting it too, they were the hammer to our anvil on that deal. Please to have the ribbons on in time for graduation. Your brother got his Eagle?"

"Barely, but yes. Big Sis is in this year's candidates. We getting our new crew member anytime soon?"

"Ya," Rick said. "She'll be joining us for the graduation ceremonies with Julia. Both of them got back a couple of days ago from Fort Benning. She'll take over Julia's job as driver and Julia will take over Twinkies job. Her name is Patricia Stewart. Her family was one of the original settlers and her forefather started what is now Olds Collage for us. She's the first one in her family to want to be a combat trooper."

"Great. Another female officer. I suppose she's blond and cute too?"

"Nope, she's still a Master Corporal, but I'm positive she'll be promoted to Sergeant soon. You are now a Warrant like me and Julia is a Master Sergeant. Until Harold gets back from MIT, we won't have an officer with us. I am working on getting him his own crew, so we will be back to four crew members and no officers."

"Won't matter much for the next little while anyway," Bill said. "We have to train up this next bunch and then rumour has it we go active."

"That's the rumour all right," Rick said. "Thanks for picking me up. The folks don't even know I'm coming in today. Make sure your wearing all the do dad ribbons at graduation Bill. Julia was awarded hers at Benning in an official ceremony with the GG and DND there and all that. I can arrange that for you if you want."

"Not unless you force me to," Bill said.

"Just what I said to Her Majesty when she gave me mine. They can't get over how we don't like making a big deal over this. Anyway, thanks for the lift and I will see you after the grad ceremony."

"Look at our little girl. All growed up and full of piss and vinegar, coming back from snake eater course," Rick said, holding Julia at arm's length after hugging. She like Bill, had her citations arranged on the left breast of her dark blue undress uniform. She had one more Mentioned In Dispatches than Bill had, but was missing the Wound Badge.

"How are your folks settling in?"

"This is from mom," Julia said, hugging him again and kissing his cheek. "Pop is really happy and his shop is getting some good business. Word is getting around about the hot shot mechanic from LA. Oh, this is Sergeant Stewart Rick."

The Sergeant came to attention and saluted. She was just over six feet tall and slender. The fruit salad on her uniform said she had been in Somalia and the Balkans.

"You don't salute me Sergeant, I work for a living," Rick said. Sticking out his hand. "Rick Bekenbaum. Welcome to the crew."

"Thank you My Lord," Patricia said. "Patricia Steward, My Lord. I'll do my best to be a valuable member My Lord."

She took his hand then resumed the at attention stance.

"She always this prim and proper Jules?" Rick said. "I might have to revaluate my decision to include her in our crew."

A look of concern came into Patricia's eyes as she saw Rick's easy grin turn serious, as he looked into her dark brown eyes. If anything her stance became more ridged.

"Are you kidding me Gadget?" Julia said. "She drank even the old timers' at Benning under the table. Then I had to spend the rest of the night holding her head as she puked it all up. Lighten up will ya Pat. Gadget here puts his pants on the same way we do."

"Jules baby!" Bill said grabbing her and swinging her around in a huge bear hug. "Long time no see. How ya been?"

He put her down and looked at Patricia, now at the at ease position her arms behind her back.

"Who's the prissy sister Gadget?" Bill said jerking his thumb over his shoulder at Patricia.

"The prissy sister is our new probationary driver," Rick said.

"I am not your bloody sister!" Patricia exploded. "Nor am I bloody prissy! I'm a damn good driver and a combat trooper just as damn good as you two assholes are!" she was in a fine rage now.

"Oh my William. We may have made a bad judgment call here," Rick said.

"Just because I have the same skin colour as you does not give you the right to call me your sister. I am not related to you, nor have been in battle with you!" Patricia said.

"And you!" she said looking at Rick, pointing her finger at him. "I give you the respect you deserve as my Ataman and Earl and you mock me for it!"

Rick put his hands behind his back and looked down for a second. He took a deep breath, held it for a second and then let it out. He stood up straight, came to attention and saluted the fuming girl before him.

"Sergeant Steward, I apologize for my behaviour and welcome you to our crew," Rick said. "This is Warrant Jackson our crew chief. Warrant this is Sergeant Steward our new driver and team member."

"Sergeant Steward, I also apologize for my behaviour," Bill said. "Sometimes the Ghetto still comes out. Thank you for pointing that out for me."

"Easy girl," Julia said. "My Lord there does not stand for to much ceremony, especially in the field and with us. You have to learn things are different in the field. Give her a break guys, she was stuck in an admin position before. She's damn near as good as we are. Give her a chance. She's my bud."

"Look, Sergeant Steward, I really am sorry," Bill said. "I'm not used to seeing any Blacks around here and I just reverted to old habits. I didn't mean any disrespect. Can we start over?"

"Ok Bill," Patricia said sticking out her hand for him to shake. "To be honest, I don't think I'm black at all. I just have a superior tan than the white girls."

"Ya rub it in Pat, thanks for bringing that up," Julia said. "That and being taller than most of us."

"Well, all of you are buying the booze as punishment for how you have welcomed me. Except you Jules, you stood up for me like a good bud should."

"All right, all right," Rick said. "We surrender. Bill, Miss Prissy's booze is on us tonight."

"No, no way," Patricia said. "You're not hanging that name on me. No way." Patricia said.

"And just like that, a new legend is born," Julia said. "Miss Prissy. I think it sounds good."

"Not you too!" Patricia said punching Julia on the arm. "Shit!"

"Well come along now children," Rick said. "We have to join in welcoming the boots to the Regiment. After that, we must make a suitably impressive impression on our ten comrades for the next year."

"Yes My Lord, of course My Lord," Bill said bowing and scraping before Rick. "Whatever is My Lord Gadgets pleasure My Lord."

It was with considerate effort that the group of four kept from breaking down in complete laughter during the graduation ceremonies.

"Ok, go hang out with your family for a bit Bill," Rick said. "You have an hour, then we have to get to work with the new guys."

"Right," Bill said. "See you guys in a bit."

"Oh my, he does look good in those blues," Julia said, as Bill walked away to join his family.

"Sure, just like all the brothers we met at Benning," Patricia said. "Good looking and cocky. Nothing I'd want to take home to meet mom."

An hour later the four of them were standing in line abreast at ease as the ten troopers marched into the room, formed two lines of five and came to attention before them. There were four women and six men. Three of the troopers were newly minted Lieutenants, one of them the defiant blond from the grade twelve lecture Rick had given earlier, the rest were corporals. As Rick held them at attention he saw the trooper's eyes going over his and his teams I Was There, ribbons and then back to their serious faces.

"So. You think now that you have your Eagles and have completed a year of advanced training, you're tough guys?" Rick said quietly. "The two ladies with me here just finished number one and number two at Delta Force training in Fort Benning. The Warrant there has just finished advanced training with the SAS. Oh I'm sorry, he just finished *instructing* advanced training for the SAS. You people have a ways to go yet.

"For the next year, you will be receiving instruction unrelated to what you have learned so far. Small unit counter insurgency tactics. Advanced deep recon tactics and deep behind the lines combat training. You will learn to act and perform as insurgents. That is the only way you will learn how to defeat our opponents. At the end of the training, we will be deployed somewhere doing one of those tasks. After that, you will be broken up and you will form your own groups and training them. The Regiment wants ten teams of ten ready to go at any time. You are the beginning of the one hundred.

"We will muster at the helipad at 04:00 tomorrow with full combat loads and provisions for two weeks in the field. We will be dropped in an undisclosed location for the purpose of eliminating a terrorist training camp and the taking of a few prisoners and whatever we think is important for intelligence purposes. Once we are on the ground we will be given the general coordinates of the camp. Dismissed!"

"Where the hell are we going anyway?" Bill asked.

"Deep inside CFB Suffield for a rendezvous with your ex-students Bill." Rick said.

"Oh shit," Bill said. "We're gonna get our asses kicked."

"That's the whole point Bill."

Rick sat in the middle of the table surveying the two separate groups before him. The British had given him access to the All Ranks Club for his debriefing. His troopers were sitting in a quiet dejected group. Their dirty rumpled uniforms reflecting the drooping shoulders and hung heads.

The SAS on the other hand were boisterous. Slapping each other on the backs and toasting their victory. Not shy about taunting their victory over the hapless Canadians.

Rick sat watching for some time. His sweat stained and very dusty forest green battle dress, still had pieces of hay and straw in it and it was hard to tell it was dark green under it all. Unlike his ten troopers, who stood out because of their dark green uniforms. After ten minutes he had had enough and banged his empty bottle of beer on the table hard until the room quieted down and he had everyone's attention.

"I estimate that the Regiment had ninety percent casualties, SAS thirty percent. The Regiment did not complete ninety nine percent of it's objectives," Rick said. "Congratulations to SAS. Well done."

"What do you mean ninety nine percent? You didn't complete a hundred percent of the stated objectives," the SAS commander said.

"Really?" Rick said. "My troop completed theirs." He put two fingers in his mouth and whistled. Bill and the two girls marched in, their uniforms as dirty as Ricks. In the lead was Patricia with the SAS banner on a broom handle, flanked by Bill and Julia.

"Bullshit!" the SAS commander said. "I've got that banner in my lockup and it hasn't left my sight."

"It's right here inside this box," he said holding up a wooden box with a large lock on it.

"Well open it up and prove me wrong then," Rick said.

The man pulled a key attached to a cord from around his neck, unlocked the lock and flung open the box. Several dozen spring loaded snakes sprang from the box startling everyone near the box. A little spring loaded flag popped up. It read, Bang Your Dead.

"I think you should check your back pocket while you're at it Captain," Bill said.

"Ah crap!" the Captain said pulling Ricks calling card out of his pocket.

"You people," Rick said pointing at his troopers. "Went in over confident and unprepared. You did not adapt to the situation and used tactics that may have been ok back home in the woods, but got you all killed here. And you Captain, forgot to keep situational awareness. It was not all that difficult for my partners and I to steal your stuff.

"So, the good thing about exercises like this is that usually nobody gets anything worse than their pride hurt and we all learn a lot. People, we have to make the best of what we are given. The jobs we will be tasked with have a very low probability of escaping injury or death. That's why we do this training. To give you the best shot of making it out unhurt as we can.

"So kudos to the SAS this time and the booze is on them," Rick said pointing at his group. "I and my group after all completed our objective. Have a good time tonight people. My troop, on the bus in front of the mess at 04:00."

It was a long and sombre six hour bus trip. Rick, Bill and Julia slept for the whole trip. The other ten, kept going over what they could have done differently. Once in a while asking another a question, but mostly just sitting and thinking. There had been other mock battles over the years where the result had been close, but never in doubt. This one was the first time in memory that the Regiment had lost. It hadn't been a loss. It was a wipe out.

Unfortunately for them, it was a Saturday and they pulled into the barracks yard just after 10:00. All five thousand of the weekend warriors had just finished the weekly regimental run and were about to disperse when the bus pulled up. The whole command group was present and lined up in front of the Regimental flag. Nicolas, as commander in the centre, flanked in order of descending rank, by all of the senior officers. Rick had no choice but to parade his troopers and line up in front of the whole Regiment.

The ten lined up behind Bill, Julia and Patricia. Rick moved forward, called them to attention and had them salute.

"Warrant Richard Bekenbaum and commando one reporting sir!" Rick said. "All present and accounted for, sir!"

Nicolas, followed by the two Colonels and the Master Warrant, kept them at attention and at the salute as he slowly trooped the line. Stopping and looking each trooper up and down and then looking each trooper in the eye. He stopped longest in front of Rick, then marched back to his line of commanders and lazily returned the salute.

"Report!" was all he said.

"Sir! The commando failed to accomplish its objectives and suffered ninety percent casualties. Sir! This Warrant regrets that he did not express his instructions on the mission clearly enough, which resulted in the mission's failure. Sir!"

It was so quiet on the parade ground you could hear a pin drop.

Nicolas let them stew for a full minute under his stern glare.

"The instructor cadre is fined one and half months pay. The commando is fined one months pay. The whole lot of you are confined to barracks unless on duty for the remainder of the training cycle.

"Dismissed, get off my parade ground!"

"That went better than I thought," Bill said. "I was expecting to get busted back to private and kicked off the team."

"Nobody else wants the job Bill," Rick said. "We're stuck with it."

"Don't worry about the pay, Pat," Rick said. "The three of us will make good on it for you. We can afford it and the General knows it. As far as being confined to base? We are not going to be here much anyway. But he makes it look good. Everyone gets punished for failing and the honour of the Regiment is upheld. He also knows the commando was over confident and cocky and would disregard what we taught them. That was the other point to the exercise. We'll see if they learned anything on the next one."

The next one proved to be three days later. Once again, they were issued full combat loads and supplies for a week and loaded onto helicopters in the dark of the morning. This time they were flown to Penhold and loaded onto a Hercules cargo plane with American markings on it. Stage two of the training was about to begin.

After two hours of flying they landed at an air force base and the aircraft taxied to a remote corner of the airfield and the commando was off loaded. They were ushered into a nearby hanger and allowed to use the washrooms and grab some refreshments before being lead to an area that was set up to brief them. A large map was set up on the wall with an area blocked off in red on it. The man giving the briefing was in desert pattern camouflage with naval insignia on it.

"A terrorist group has set up operations in this area and is actively conducting retribution raids throughout the area. Your mission is to eliminate this group. They number approximately one hundred and at this time we have been unable to locate their base of operations. If you locate the base, you are to radio in its location and standby to guide air assets and laser target it for the aircraft. Three of us will be accompanying you as referees and will in no way influence your decisions or tactics. Every effort will be made to resupply you while you are in the field, but you may find that due to extenuating circumstances, you will left to your own resources at times. All of you will be issued with copies of this map. Pickup your parachutes as you leave. Flight time is just under an hour and it will be a Halo drop. Good luck."

"Where does your GPS put us lieutenant?" Rick said after they had all grouped together after the drop.

"Right here Warrant," the lieutenant said, marking their position on the map.

"We're what, a couple of miles from that river we saw from the air?" Rick said.

"Looks like it," the lieutenant said. "I recommend we move to the river and do what we can to dull out these green uniforms."

"Ok. Sounds good. We need to get off this drop zone and fast. I don't know if these guys spotted us or not or if they do or do not have motorized transportation."

"I think we should assume both sir," a corporal said "The bad guys could be anywhere. We should get down to the river, get our bearings and make some kind of a plan. Those guys could be on top of any mountain or behind any pile of rocks out here."

"Ok, there is not much of what we are used to as cover," another corporal said. "But there are still a lot of terrain features we can use to our advantage just the same. We need to conserve our batteries, so I think after the river we should find a high point and look around. I think we can see for a long ways around here. We can use that to our advantage."

"Is that the plan then?" Rick asked. Everyone concurred and they set off for the river.

"Anything moving out there?" Bill said, as he plunked himself down beside Patricia and brought his binoculars to his eyes.

"Nope," she said. "Just the odd dust devil. We're going to have to call in for resupply soon. We're down to one Meal Ready to Eat each."

"We got a couple of rabbits in the snares and a rattler," Bill said. "We're good for a couple of days yet. We mix them in with half the MREs and we'll have a half decent meal."

"With all the track we spotted in that draw, I figured sure we'd have some sightings by now," Patricia said. "It's been three bloody weeks now."

"Yo, Sarge," a trooper further down the line said. "Looks like movement. Far north side of the draw."

Both Bill and Pat swung their glasses in that direction and scanned the area.

"Yup," Bill said. "Still to far away to see how many. Yash, get Anderson up here with his spotting scope and wake up sleeping beauty there and let him know what's up."

Yash edged back down the reverse slope to where the rest of the commando was dosing or repairing gear and first tapped the bottom of the snoozing Rick's foot with his toe to wake him up and pointed up at Bill and Pat then walked over to Anderson, who grabbed his high powered spotting scope and came up the hill. Anderson was the backup sniper and his main job was to spot for the regular sniper. He quickly set up the tripod and focused in on the spot where the movement had been detected.

"Twenty three. Walking along as if on a stroll. Three with red arm bands, definitely referees. One M60 and one radio. Radio guy is skylarking with his buds up front. No point man or flankers. Captain and two Lueys walking together chatting it up with the referees. Easy pickings," Anderson said.

"Ok," Rick said. "You and George set up here. I'll turn my radio on now. Let me know if they change direction from what we figured they would do. Bill, Pat, get the gang ready to move out to ambush positions and make sure everything works once we get there. Not before. We need to conserve the batteries for the laser equipment and the radios. The way they are moving we have a couple of hours yet."

In a half hour, the commando had set up an L shaped ambush. One minimi and three troopers across the front of the path, the other seven spaced along one side of it, using the large rocks and whatever scrub brush they could find as cover. The weeks' worth of dirt and dust added to the river mud they had put on their forest green camouflage uniforms the first day, made them blend in almost perfectly with their surroundings. Now they turned on the radios and laser targeting systems and tested them out. The C7's were loaded with blanks that would sound like real rifle fire, but when the triggers were pulled, a laser mounted on each weapon would activate and send a beam to the target. That laser would trigger a receiver on the targets uniform that would render their weapon inactive and send a loud shrill sound to let the wearer know they were out of action.

After the tests were complete. Each trooper settled down, making sure they had a clear field of fire and after a short time of no movement, the birds and animals in the area resumed their normal activities.

After an hour with no word from the snipers, Rick knew the enemy patrol was following the track and shortly after that an alert ground squirrel gave its warning chirps. This was soon followed by a number of birds giving theirs and a deer stomped the ground with her fore hoof and whistled before she and her sisters trotted down and across the track away from the approaching troopers. Rick smelt the drifting cigarette smoke before he heard them and he heard them five minutes before they came into view. He flipped the safeties off the C7 and the grenade launcher mounted underneath it and heard his commandos doing the same all along the line.

The approaching troopers were talking and someone had just cracked a joke, because there was a lot of laughter. The whole gaggle was grouped together, M16s slung on shoulders. The M60 man had his weapon slung across the back of his neck and there was not even a belt loaded into it. At the front, the point man and three others with the radio man were together and in the middle, so were the officers. They passed within five yards of Rick's position. So close, he could make out from the flashes on their shoulders that they were from a regular US Marine battalion.

Rick was at the tail end of the ambush and he waited until the last group of marines were two yards ahead of him, before he sighted half way down the ragged line and fired the grenade from the launcher. The rest of the commando let loose with a series of single shots and lasers emitters were screeching immediately. Within thirty seconds, before the enemy had time to pull the rifles from their shoulders it was all over. Then Rick broke the silence and stood.

"Ok folks it's all over but the crying," Rick said. "Snipers, any tail end Charlie's we missed?"

"Negative," Anderson said. "We're on our way down now."

"Well Mr. Referee," Rick said. "Are all these fools dead?"

"Um..Yes it would appear so," the referee said. "Where the hell did you guys come from?"

"Bill, secure their radio. You Jarr heads, drop your packs, weapons and weapon harnesses," Rick said. "You're all dead and you won't be needing that stuff anymore. Empty all your pockets and pull the insides out so we know they are empty.

"Commando, we want all the batteries, spare ammo, GPS units and maps you can find. Take all their rations but one each man. Everybody grabs an M16. Let's go people, I want to be out of here in half an hour tops."

"You can't do that!" the Marine Captain said. "That's US Government property."

"You're dead captain," Rick said. "You got no say in this. I have programmed a spot for you to head to on your GPS unit and wiped the memory of anything else. Tomorrow afternoon, I will radio in the coordinates to the head referees and they will come pick you up. Now if you will excuse me, my people and I have to plan an attack on your main base. Have a good day captain. Ok, people, let's go! Rest period is over."

"God damnit Captain!" a sergeant burst out as they were leaving. "I told you this would happen! I'm sure as hell not taking the hit for this one. Major, you heard him order me to stop pestering him?"

"It's all in my report Sergeant, it's all in my report," the head referee said. Then he looked at his fellow referees and they all laughed. "Now that Captain, is really funny, unlike your lame jokes."

The Major and the other referees were from the 81st airborne.

"Sempherfi Captain," the Major said.

"Hoorah," his team mates said, laughing louder.

After jogging down the track for about a kilometre, Rick called a halt and the commando members sank to the ground and started dividing up the spoils. Rick called up the information from the GPS unit he had liberated from one of the Marine Lieutenants and found where the enemy base was located.

"Looks like we are about ten Klicks from the base," Rick said. "Copy the coordinates to the units we swiped and ours, then shut ours down. Swap out all the batteries on our equipment and turn them off. We'll use their radios, that way we disappear again and they look to be coming home. We should be in a location to observe their base just before sundown. Then we can make a plan and call in the airstrike."

"Two days to extraction?" one of his commando officers said.

"I don't know," Rick said. "I'm getting a little tired of being dirty, eating crappy MREs and sleeping on rocks, aren't you? I think we can make extraction by 02:00 and get back to base for a shower and breakfast."

"Sounds like a plan," the officer said.

The base was located in a bowl and there was little in the way of security. The machine gun positions were only manned by a single marine and there were only four of them. The rest of the Marines were playing football, baseball or lounging around.

"Do we agree on the count?" Rick said.

"Ya, if they adhere to a standard company, the only ones missing are the ones we whacked," Patricia said.

Julia started to chuckle and took the earphones off one ear.

"They want to know why we are not coming in," Julia said.

"Tell them we saw some suspicious track that we want to check out," Rick said.

"Ya Echo Bravo, Captain said he wants to check out some tracks. Looks like some deer track to me, but what do I know?" Julia said.

"Ya Roger that. I think I got a cold or something."

Two hours later, the commando was set up. The Marines were headed to their platoon tents as the sun was going down and the commando had the laser designators out and had a clear field of sight for them. The snipers were targeted on the machine gun posts and the rest of the commando would let off grenades and shoot at anything that moved once the ball got rolling. After five minutes of causing general mayhem, they would stop and head for the extraction point, abandoning all of the captured equipment except for the ammunition and rations.

"Charlie Tango, Charlie Tango, this is Tango India, over." Julia said on their own radio.

"Roger Charlie Tango, we have traffic. One company sized encampment with eighty, I repeat eighty, hostiles. We have five laser targets over."

"Roger Charlie Tango. Tango India confirms, two fast movers in thirty mikes over."

"Roger Charlie Tango. Tango India on standby out."

"Air force is sending a couple of F16s our way Gadget," Julia said. "It'll be about half an hour."

"Ok gang," Rick said into his headset. "Half an hour until show time."

"Zoomies three minutes out Gadget," Julia said.

"OK boys and girls, light 'em up and let's get ready to rock and roll!" Rick said. He took the safeties off his weapons and sighted the grenade launcher for the middle of the camp.

Three minutes later, five practice bombs popped their parachutes with flares and screamers attached over the three occupied platoon tents, the command tent and the communications tent. Rick pulled the trigger on his grenade launcher and then placed his C7 on the ground to his right side and picked up the captured M16 and let go a five second burst on full auto spraying the whole encampment. The rest of the commando followed suit, with the two machine guns the commando had, belching out also in full automatic. The enemy's four M60 positions opened up belatedly, also in full auto, but randomly spraying, not having any fixed targets to fire at. These positions, went silent one by one as the snipers took them out. To all the noise and mayhem, two F16s came roaring down the centre of the camp, at about fifty feet of altitude, with their Gatling guns going full out.

"Tango India, Tango India, break break!" Rick said into his headset after he had fired four clips worth of captured ammo through his M16 and dropped it picking up his C7 and starting to jog away from the ambush. He fired the green flare grenade he had put in his grenade launcher up over the centre of the camp to make sure the commando knew to break off and head for the extraction point.

"*Tango India Six, this is Red Fox Three over,*" Rick heard over his ear piece.

"*Red Fox Three, gotcha go,*" Rick said as he ran from the camp.

"*Thanks for the invite to the party,*" Red Fox Three said. "*You guys sure know how to have a good time.*"

"*Any time Red Fox Three any time,*" Rick said.

"*Red Fox Three and flight, RTB. Have a good night.*"

The two F16s once again roared over the camp at low altitude and then rotated to vertical, lighting up their after burners as they zoomed out of sight, blue flames from the after burners lighting up the night sky. For good measure, they fired off a round of anti-missile flares, further adding to the light, noise and mayhem.

As Rick jogged to the extraction point he was joined singly and in pairs by the rest of the commando and once they were all together he called a halt. Breathing heavily, the commando ridded themselves of all the captured equipment they had but the rations and got their breath back.

"*Charley Tango, Charley Tango, Tango India six,*" Rick said.

"*Roger Charley Tango, mission accomplished. Request pickup at extraction point four, in five hours over.*"

"*Roger Charley Tango, extraction point four in five hours. Will confirm when at extraction point. Tango India Six out.*"

"All electronics off, batteries out and let's head out children. I hear a hot shower, bacon and eggs calling my name," Rick said.

"Sir, the commander wants to see you ASAP," the helicopters crew chief said to Rick as the base came into sight.

"Ah shit!" Rick said. "Just what I needed. Any idea what about?"

"No sir," the crew chief said. "I do know that a Canadian Hercules landed about three hours ago and the guys that got off looked like they was all serious and such."

"Ah crap! So much for a couple of days off," Rick said.

"Mr. Doom and Gloom," Bill said. "Maybe they brought us some nice juicy Alberta Beef steaks."

"And maybe I'm a blushing virgin on her first date," Patricia said.

"You Canadians, always doom and gloom," Bill said. "What do you mean you're not a virgin? My grandmother and mother will be appalled. My future bride not a virgin."

"In your dreams black boy," Patricia said. "Future bride my ass. All you want is to get in my pants."

"Mmm, mmm and such a sweet ass it is too," Rick said. "Fills out those pants right nice, don't you think Billy Boy?"

"You two better watch it," Julia said. "I might have to file a report on your behaviour."

"Ya right," Bill said. "Sticking up for each other again. Can't even give a compliment to a girl anymore."

"Why should Miss Prissy get all the compliments," Julia said. "Just because she's tall and skinny and cute. Maybe some of us get jealous now and then."

"I didn't know I was your type," Bill said.

"You're not" Julia said. "You're too fat for me. But a girl likes to be noticed once in a while you know."

"To fat!" Bill said. "Do I look fat to you Gadget? I'll have you know this is all solid, mean lean fighting machine. But hey, she does have a nice butt Rick don't you think? A little bit on the small side though."

"How the hell would he know," Patricia said. "I think the only butt he ever noticed was Sandy's and that didn't last but one date."

"Now children," Rick said. "Play nice or daddy will have to spank you."

"Really?" Pat said. "You promise. This naughty girl should be spanked."

The helicopter landing and shutting down got Rick off the hook and he exited the machine amidst heavy laughter from his team mates and the crew chief shaking his head and smiling.

"Jesus," he said to the pilot. "Did you catch all that?"

"Ya, we'd be in deep shit making comments like that," the pilot said. "Canadians. Different kettle of fish those guys."

"Holy shit do you stink Gadget," Harold said. "You could have at least left some of the smell in the bush."

"Ya, ya. They said ASAP, so ASAP I am here," Rick said. "What's up?"

"We have a situation back home," Harold said. "You and the gang are going active as of now. Have a shower and change uniforms. The aircrew will pack your gear up while you get some hot food, which is waiting for you. I'll brief you on the way. We are wheels up in two hours so you better hustle."

As promised, the aircraft was off the ground two hours later. The commando was showered, fed and in fresh green cammo uniforms. Harold waved his arm in a circle over his head and tapped his right ear. The commando turned on their communicators and each member gave a thumbs up as they came on line.

"The day after you left for your latest training exercise, a group of heavily armed Natives took control of the headquarters of a ranch north of Williams Lake. The reason they gave was that the ranch was located on lands that some native group says was never granted under any treaty. They are demanding the return of the land and reparations. Attempts to negotiate by civilian and RCMP negotiators have been rebuked. The BC provincial government has asked the Feds for help and DND asked us to supply the troops. The General has contacted the Assembly of First Nations, who of course are wringing out all of the PR they can out of the situation. All of the Alberta and Prairie First Nations have disavowed the group as had all but the group that is sponsoring the action of the BC First Nations. The group sponsoring it is a very radical group that has absolutely no ties to the land in question. A treaty from the original First Nations band that had historical rights to the land had been signed and honoured from the late eighteen hundreds, so the band sponsoring it has no claim. The band in question says they do not recognize the treaty and that as a sovereign nation they will negotiate with no one but the head of state.

"As recognized agents of the Dominion of Canada, you are authorized to use whatever means are necessary to repel this take over. Reconnaissance shows that there are one hundred armed people in the encampment. The Ranch owners, their family and ranch hands are being held hostage. As are a number of paying customers of the fishing lodge, foreign and domestic.

"Yesterday an ultimatum was given that starting in three days, a hostage a day will be killed unless all demands are complied with and that demand would increase daily after that. You are to proceed to the ranch and take whatever steps you feel are necessary to end the illegal take over. At this point, we have a Coyote and two LAVs waiting, all fully armed. Sandy has two Eagles overhead and two Adlers on standby. Warrant Bekenbaum is in full command."

All eyes were on Rick as he sat, head down rubbing his eyes at first then putting a hand under his chin.

"Right, we go in loaded for bear," Rick said. "No pissing around. These guys surrender or we take them out. Tell Sandy I want to know where all the bad guys are and what fire power they have. If we need zoomies, I will let them know. I think we will hit them hard and fast and be in to close for air support, but have them on standby just in case. I want a full layout of the ranch buildings waiting for me when we land and tell the Mounties to get out of our way when we get there."

Then he turned off his radio, leaned his head back and went to sleep.

The Hercules landed on a gravel strip reserved for fire fighting duty and taxied back to the middle of the strip, where two of the regiments Pavlov helicopters were waiting. All the commandos took with them were their weapons, ammunition and weapons harnesses. They had removed all identification badges and pulled balaclavas down so that only the eyes were visible as they left the aircraft. The print and video media that was on site only saw the Canadian markings on the Hercules, the helicopters had no markings at all. Any photos or videos showed only fourteen heavily armed people with Balaclavas covering their faces and not even a rank badge in evidence. The pilots and crews of the helicopters had their dark shields of the helmets down so only the lower jaw was showing and similarly had no badges or patches denoting who or what they were. As soon as all the commando were loaded, the helicopters fired up and took off in a cloud of dust, door gunners scanning the area the whole time. It was a relatively short hop to the staging area outside the ranch yard. The heilos landed, keeping engines running and were airborne again heading back to refuel and be ready for support if the commando should ask for it.

Rick motioned for Bill to follow him and while the rest of the commando moved to the two LAVs and the Coyote, he and Bill walked over to what appeared to be the command post. Two Atco office trailers had been put together and four Mounties were standing guard, two per entrance. Another four Mounties were keeping the media at bay about a hundred yards from the trailer behind traffic barriers. All the major Canadian broadcasters were there as well as a CNN crew, cameras busy filming the commando as they exited the helicopters and moved to the armoured vehicles. Several high ranking RCMP officers came out of the trailers and met the two commandos outside.

"Warrant Smith and Warrant Wesson sir," Rick said, he and Bill saluting the RCMP Inspector.

"Welcome to our sorry excuse for a party," the inspector said. "We have members surrounding the ranch yard and the Serious Incident Teams are in place to keep things in hand. How would you like to proceed?"

"I would like to wrap this up before night fall," Rick said. "That gives us what, until about 23:00 up here? Keep your people in place and they can gather up or eliminate any of the enemy that escape the assault. Otherwise, ask them to keep out of the way. Once we get going, anyone armed and not a member of the commando will be shot."

"What do you mean assault?" a man in civilian dress asked. "Are you not going to try and negotiate with them?"

"I will accept their unconditional surrender, nothing less," Rick said. "I am not here to negotiate, I am here to put an end to this. Inspector, gentlemen, we have a job to do, if you will excuse me."

Rick and Bill saluted once again and began walking toward the armoured vehicles when the media began clamouring for attention. He looked at Bill who shrugged his shoulders and they both moved to where the media was stationed.

Rick just stood there looking at them, his C7 on his shoulder and hand grenades and spare ammo clips attached to his weapons harness. He said nothing until they all stopped yelling questions at him.

"I will answer no questions," Rick said. "We are with the Canadian Army and we have been tasked with putting an end to this unfortunate situation. The situation is highly volatile and dangerous. No one will be allowed to join us or enter the combat zone. Have a good day."

"Are you kidding me?" the CNN reporter said as they were walking away. "Fourteen troopers and three armoured vehicles and he's going to put an end to this? Christ, the Montana State Police has more armoured vehicles than he has. There is no way they are going to do anything with the amount of troops he has. This is going to be a disaster."

"Hey Sandy," Rick said climbing into the Coyote. He pulled the balaclava up getting some fresh air on his face. "What have you got for me? Put it threw the net."

"We've got three in the big barn loft covering the front. An RPG and heavy machine gun. The same on the other side and in the centre second story window of the house. All three are effectively covering the whole yard. The other ninety or so combatants are armed with surplus AKs and a few AR15s. I don't think they have much, if any training. They mostly use their numbers to intimidate."

"Ok, left LAV takes out the big barn, right LAV the right and the Coyote the house. Dismounts spread out and take out targets at will.

Bill and I will make an attempt to get them to surrender, but when it happens, I want it over in a hurry, no messing around, just like we have been doing in training. These people have been having it their own way for so long they will not be expecting us to do anything. Patch my comms to the media until the shit hits the fan and then cut it off. Questions?

"Ok then let's go.

"Sandy, stop about a hundred yards from the house, LAVs flank the Coyote twenty yards to the side. Dismounts, five yards in front of the vehicles. When I give the signal, weapons free. Anything that has a weapon is fair game."

The vehicles came to a stop and the dismounted troopers took their positions. Bill and Rick walked slowly toward the ranch house, weapons with a round in the breach, but on safe and hung on shoulders. About fifty yards from the house they stopped and stood with their arms behind their backs and waited.

Soon enough, the enemy came out and grouped together making a show of their weapons and making war hoops. All had their faces covered by bandannas. To Rick, who had been in much more dangerous places, it was kind of a joke. Two men broke from the crowd and strutted up to them, brandishing their weapons as they came, coming to a stop almost nose to nose, chests pushed out and eyes defiant.

"Who the hell are you?" one of them asked. "We will not change our demands and I refuse to negotiate with people who cover their faces."

"I am Warrant Smith and this is Warrant Wesson of the Canadian Army and I am authorized to accept your surrender."

"Surrender? You will comply with our demands or we will begin executing hostages. The Sovereign First Nations are tired of negotiating. We are at war here."

"According to international law, when one sovereign nation invades and takes position of another sovereign nations territory, it is an act of war. Therefore you are at war with the Dominion of Canada and I am here to defend my country. If you surrender now, you will be treated as prisoners of war under the Geneva Convention. If you do not surrender, I will be forced to open fire and kill you."

"Hey Smith, these guys have a lovely shade of blue in their eyes and awfully pale skin. I didn't know Natives had blond hair and blue eyes," Bill said.

"I am an adopted member of the Mohawk First Nations," the man said defiantly.

"I am sure the Mohawk Nation will be thrilled to find that they are in a state of war with the Dominion of Canada, The Commonwealth of Nations and NATO. Just to put you in the loop, the First Nations of BC, Alberta and the Prairie and Atlantic Regions have disavowed you and your actions and the Assembly of First Nations is meeting right now with the purpose of doing the same. Now once again, I ask you to surrender."

"Oh big man," the enemy spokesman said. "You and your fourteen people against me and my one hundred. Piss off."

"As you like," Rick said, sliding the rifle off his shoulder and slapping the barrel hard against the mans temple, dropping him like a stone. Bill did the same with his man and both commandos dropped to one knee.

Rick sighted at the middle of the stunned group in the open and fired a grenade from the launcher, then flipped his C7 to fire three shot bursts and opened up on the rest still standing. All three armoured vehicles fired three high explosive rounds from their 20mm cannons, waited a few seconds then turned the turrets to add the coaxial machine guns to the fire from the dismounted troopers who were firing at anything moving with a weapon in the yard. Within minutes, it was over. Those that were not wounded or dead, had thrown their weapons away, gone to their knees and held their hands above their heads. Of the original one hundred combatants, there were less than twenty unhurt.

"Sandy, tell the Mounties to come in and collect the prisoners and have the EMTs come in to treat the wounded. Situation is under control. Commando, keep your perimeter until the Mounties take over. Sandy have the Hurc and the transport crews for the vehicles ready for us at the strip. I want to pull out of here ASAP."

"Sweet Jesus," the CNN man said. "What a blood bath."

"I guess you've never been to Kosovo," a veteran Global reporter said. "This kind of thing happens every day over there. What did you expect? Trained combat soldiers against jumped up hoodlums. Those idiots should have surrendered when they had the chance."

"Who the hell were those guys? Navy Seals? Force Recon, Delta Force?" the CNN man said.

"I doubt it. They were Canadians," the Global man said. "And before you ask. We have different rules here. If the government doesn't want us to know who they are, we will never find out."

"Job well done gang," Rick said after they were once again airborne. "I'm telling the boss we're taking a month off when we get back home. And if he don't like it, to flippen bad!"

"Pop, that was a little bit much don't you think, sending us in?" Rick said. "The Mounties could have handled it or a couple of platoons of Pixlies."

"No, the PM wanted to make a statement," Paul said. "There has been a little to much of this kind of thing happening. As well, he wanted to put the Quebec Nationalists on notice that this is what they could expect if they declared independence and war against us. No, the Mounties would not have been the answer, nor would have a normal army group. It had to be us or someone like us to make a statement. Oh and you and Bill called it right. Those two you clobbered were members of an anarchist terrorist cell out of Germany. In fact, over a third of the combatants turned out to be that. The Mohawks are disavowing all knowledge of them."

"Well, even though my people have been blooded, it really was no contest," Rick said. "I also think it's time we had some time off. We have been at it for over six months now without a break."

"They are waiting outside?" Paul said. "Come on then I have a few words to say."

"Officer on Deck!" someone said as the two Bekenbaums walked out of the office and the whole commando came to attention.

"At ease," Paul said. "I just wanted to say job well done people. The PM and cabinet are pleased, the General is pleased and so am I. Your Warrant has told me that if I don't give you a month off, you will mutiny and I agree. So after dismissal, I don't want to see any of you around here for a month.

"Now, intelligence has been telling us for some time that a Muslim extremist organization is planning something big for some time later in the year. We don't know what exactly, but they are well funded and organized, so it will be something big. If it happens to occur in America itself, I am afraid the Americans will not take kindly to it and we will be at war people. Canada will honour its NATO and North American treaties, so this regiment will be in the thick of it. We want four more commando units like you as soon as possible and you people will make up the core of those commando units. So get some rest and come back here ready to work and work hard."

"Dismissed! Rick, your mother and I would like you for dinner tonight please."

"Ya, no problem pop," Rick said. "Let me get a shower and some normal cloths and I will be right over. I don't know how much company I will be though, I've been up since daybreak."

"Yo, Carol!" Rick yelled as the group disbursed. Carol was the defiant blond girl from the graduation ceremony the year earlier. As she came up Rick came to attention and saluted.

"It has been a pleasure mam," he said. Carol was a lieutenant. "With the lieutenants permission mam, I have recommended the lieutenant be given command of her own commando. Well done mam."

"What?" Carol said. Rick had not even acknowledged that she existed before.

"Credit where credit is do kid," Rick said. "Julia and Bill said they are impressed too and if the exalted lieutenant feels like slumming, they are buying at Macie's tonight. Unfortunately, the Master Warrant and the Colonel feel it necessary that I have dinner with them tonight, or I would join you. Parents can be such pains some times. I'd serve with you anytime anywhere Carol. I just wanted you to know that. See ya."

Carol watched him walk away, for all the world, just like any other young man, albeit a soldier, just come home from extended duty. It suddenly hit her. What everyone had told her. She was just as good as they were.

Lest We Forget

Captain Nicola Goddard, Royal Canadian Horse Artillery
May 17, 2006 Panjway District Afghanistan
While serving as a forward observation officer for the Princess Patricia's Canadian Light Infantry, Captain Goddard's LAVIII was hit by two RPGs in the opening moments of a large Taliban ambush.

Master Corporal Kristal Giesbacht, Medical Branch
June 26, 2010, Southern Kandahar Afghanistan
Master Corporal Giesbacht's vehicle was hit by an IED while responding to a call for assistance.

Corporal Karine Blaise, 2nd Battalion, Royal 22 Regiment
April 13, 2009, Shai Wali Kot District, Afghanistan
Corporals Blaise's Vehicle was hit by an IED while on patrol.

Jacqueline Kirk, Shirley Case, Civilian Aide Workers
August 13, 2008, Afghanistan
The Aide workers two vehicle convoy was ambushed and the workers shot by a Taliban Ambush.

Michelle Lang, Civilian Reporter attached to Princess Patricia's Canadian Light Infantry
December 30, 2009, Kandahar, Afghanistan
The LAV that Ms. Lang was traveling with, hit a large IED while returning from a patrol.

Four other troopers were killed, another female reporter and four troopers wounded.

Also BY R.P. Wollbaum

Bears and Eagles Series
Bears and Eagles
Eagles Claw
Eagles Talon
As Eagles Swarm
Bears Maul
Wind Riders Series
Oaken
Cals Quest
Part One